The Brothers' Keepers

A Modern Literary Novel

by

John H. Paddison
& Charles D. Orvik

The authors wish to express their gratitude to all of the people that have made our work possible . . . the friends and relations who contributed to the completion of this novel. Additionally, we want to emphasize that the characters in this book are entirely fictional and are the creation of the authors' collaborative imagination. All people and events, except those of historic record, were created for the purpose of fiction.

Additionally, we would like to dedicate this book to our wives, Jeanne and Bonnie, without whose help and encouragement our work would never have reached fruition.

**"...Your children are not your children.
They are the sons and daughters of Life's
longing for itself.
...You are the bows from which your children
as living arrows are sent forth . . . ."**

from *The Prophet,* by Kahlil Gibran

Contents:

Chapter One—
The Brothers

Those Lambson brothers have always been very much of a puzzlement to me. The world the five boys existed in always was and continues to be somewhat of a different sort of milieu . . . an enigma . . . a contradiction . . . a difficult set of circumstances to understand. Yet a good deal can be learned from their story . . . about people and society . . . about human responsibility . . . about tenacity. For their existence seemed as inscrutable as the huge cottonwood tree that stood timeless in the barren farmyard in which they played . . . the one with roots like talons that dug deeply into the North Dakota prairie, just a few miles outside the town of Farmington.

Late one listless summer afternoon in June of 1939 a weather-beaten, gray-black front tire, pulled off an old Oliver tractor and discarded in a nearby vacant field, hung down invitingly from one of the middle limbs of that cottonwood tree. Sunlight flickered through the branches as the midday breezes disturbed the dead stillness of the dilapidated buildings and surrounding beaten-down croplands that years earlier had been the prosperous Sheppard farmstead. The warm, light winds moved the homemade tire swing back and forth listlessly, as though it was being put into motion by unknown, mystical powers . . . those same phantom forces that so often stirred up swirling dust devils from nowhere, or that waved gently across vast, brown fields of wheat, or that shimmered the old cottonwood's gray-green leaves.

Decades earlier ol' Elvin Sheppard had planted the cottonwood tree precisely in the middle of his and Edna's homestead, right atop the small hill that rose slightly up and away from the house. He originally built the farm house so that in the spacious front yard, about fifteen yards from the front porch, stood the cottonwood tree. When it matured, he claimed, it would provide shade for the entire residence. Elvin named and claimed the cottonwood as his "grandchild tree"—the one that his future grandchildren could use for their many childhood activities . . . the family tree that would allow them to childishly rejoice in its largeness and sturdiness. But his dream never came to pass. Since then two smaller, lesser poplar trees had grown weakly in the shadow of the cottonwood, back over by the rutted remains of Edna's small, once fertile vegetable garden. Beyond the vaguely defined yard lay the outhouse and the slightly leaning, almost rust red barn and empty tool shed, and further out from that, the vast, fallow fields that once had been so productive. As the years passed, the timeless, solid tree matured steadily and had now become a joyous gathering place, a playground, if you will, for the young Lambson brothers — the wayward, unkempt sons of Cora and Iver Lambson.

Nearly a year had gone by since Uncle Red purchased the abandoned farmstead and moved the boys and their mother into the house, and several months since their wandering, absentee father had been home for a brief visit. During that time much of the thin, brittle bark of the massive tree had been stripped away by the children, who when they had nothing else to do etched and hacked and whittled on the trunk, using meat cleavers and butcher knives with broken black handles, which they had snuck out of their mother's kitchen. Myriad rusting spikes had been driven into the tree and numerous boards and wooden steps had been nailed to the trunk and outstretched branches. Sap oozed and dried from the wounds, but the tree lived on . . . surviving and even thriving. The central tree trunk, with its huge canopy of thick limbs and shimmering leaves, and its location atop the small rise, about thirty-five or forty feet from the house, never failed to provide a cool canopy of shade to the entire yard.

But the real story of the Lambson children probably best begins with the creation of that tree swing. Dewey, at eight, symbolized constancy, and more importantly authority to his younger brothers, especially Duane, aged seven. And he wielded that authority mercilessly. Earlier on that summer day, Dewey bet Duane that he, Duane, could not climb the tree and fasten the rope from which to suspend the moldering old tractor tire that they had found and labored to roll back to the yard. Actually, Dewey goaded Duane into trying the feat, telling him that if he didn't, he would hold him down and put diapers on him. To reinforce the challenge, he pushed his younger brother's shoulder sharply several times. "You're a little shit if ya don't!" Dewey said for emphasis. To both Duane and Dewey's surprise, Duane skillfully accomplished the task; he scurried up between the branches, climbing as though he had been born in that tree. In the process of testing the knot that was cinched up around the high limb, Duane looked down scornfully at his older brother. However, while shinnying back to earth from the dizzying height, Duane had slipped and fallen, crashing down through the twigs and leaves. One of the lower tree limbs broke his fall, but the youngster still landed on his shoulder and fore- arm with a thud in the soft dirt.

"Son-of-a-bitch!" Duane wailed after he hit the earth and rolled over, clutching his injured arm. A few moments passed and then he sat up and moaned softly.

"Jesus Christ, that was neat!" Dewey, the mentor and tormentor, exclaimed in praise as he ran up excitedly to as- sess the damage.

The two smaller brothers, Lloyd and Leeland, stood their distance, waiting to see what was happening, care- fully measuring their reactions, wary, ready to flee if nec- essary. Watching and calculating, half excited and half frightened. Tears began to streak down and mix with the dirt on Duane's face, but he forced his teeth together and vowed not to cry in front of his brother. Duane's cheek and upper lip had knocked against one of the rigid branches on the way down and his nose began to bleed as well; soon a steady stream of thick red drops fell on his narrow chest and onto the bib of his overalls. But because the boy's trousers had not been washed for several weeks, the drops became invisible when they blended in with the embedded dirt. He just brushed away at them with his shaking hand and pinched his nose tightly.

"Shoot almighty, did ya bust your nose too?" Dewey hunched over him, arms on knees, acting more in curiosity than in help and consolation. "Ma's gonna wring our necks for sure when she gets home! Whadya have to be climbin' the durn tree for, anyway?"

After the bleeding had subsided somewhat, Duane grad- ually pulled his small frame together and stood up to assess the damage. He swayed slightly and then slowly swiped the back of his hand across his face, leaving a thin trace line of blood laced with snot trailing from his first knuckle to just above his thin wrist. The action made the blood flow again a bit more steadily and the several drops that dribbled from his nostril landed insignificantly on the ground, mixing darkly with the dirt. He held his head back for a few minutes more and when the blood stopped completely and his arm quit hurting so badly, he finally spoke to his older brother, who was years ahead of him in worldly experience and knowledge. His voice was edged with a tone of accomplishment and satisfaction: "Okay, rope's up! Where's that dang tire?"

While the two older boys rigged the harness for the tire swing, Lloyd and Leeland still watched in fascination from the periphery, not daring to get too close. They seemed born to follow rather than lead. Though few years separated all of the youngsters, the two youngest were far apart from their older siblings in terms of experience and were thus never quick to pick up on, and then participate in, what was going on around them. Lloyd was the next youngest at five years and some months, and then came Leeland at three. All of the brothers had deep-brown eyes and shocks of brown hair and skinny frames; all of them were dressed the same, too: shoeless, with one size of bibbed overall that seemed to universally fit them all. Leeland was the only one whose pants legs were rolled up in thick knots to keep them from dragging beneath his feet. What set him apart from the others boys that day was the pronounced limp he had acquired when he stepped down on a shard of glass the previous day. Dewey, who had applied first aid following the accident, said his brother walked like a peg-legged pirate and this had somewhat consoled the wailing child. Now a bulky dressing of gray and brown-blood-spotted gauze bound Leeland's dirty right foot and as he followed his brothers the unraveling cord of bandage trailed behind him in the dirt.

When the Oliver Tractor tire was secured, Dewey and Duane began pushing and spinning each other around. Only after becoming reasonably assured that all was right with the world did Lloyd and Leeland join in the fun. The four brothers played together, enjoying greatly their new swing until well into the warm semi-darkness of dusk, when they went happy and exhausted into the dark house. That was one of the all-too-frequent occasions when their mother Cora had not bothered to purchase lamp oil before she took off, so in the waning half-light they made themselves mustard sandwiches, using the last few scraps of bread and scraping out every bit of yellow from the empty jar; their hunger somewhat satisfied, they went tiredly upstairs to bed where they slept deeply the sleep of the innocent.

The next morning came gradually, with sunlight seeping up over the eastern horizon, out beyond the hill and the centering tree. The dampness and the slight chill of the evening were slowly pushed away by the growing warmth of the new dawning; along with the maturing morning came the growing promise that the day would be just as hot and rainless as those of the past month. The early morning breeze caused by the rising heat of daybreak again began to move the tire swing slightly, swaying it gently back and forth, as though some wandering, forlorn spirit of a past, or a present, or a future child lingered there.

Upstairs in the weathered, grayish-white house, the wind blew in gently through the broken window that looked out onto the yard and the cottonwood. The breeze traced across Dewey's young body; he only shivered slightly and then pulled the cover up around his chin as he turned away from his brothers and assumed a fetal position. A bit later, though, the sun shone in through the window and hit him warmly, brightly in the face, and he awoke and stretched fully, lazily...peaceful and secure for just the briefest of moments. Beside him, on the bare mattress, his three brothers slept soundlessly, front to back, burrowed and huddled together, molded into each other, beneath the flowered, dingy, urine-smelling patchwork quilt. Immediately he knew that Leeland had wet the bed again, thus jerking him back into the reality of the morning. Dewey's brief moment of peacefulness quickly dissipated and he checked his own underwear to see if it was damp as well; it was, so he knew that Lloyd had probably peed himself also. But as he slipped his overalls on, the hunger in his young belly quickly began to take his attention away from his brothers and from the anxiety and loneliness welling up within him.

Silently, slowly, he descended the steep staircase, which only creaked lightly under his slight weight. He stopped at the door to his mother's room and put his ear to the cool wooden surface. After standing breathless for several moments, he furtively turned the worn, white doorknob and pushed the door open slightly, not wanting to make any noise in case his mother Cora had come home in the middle of the night and was not alone. Cautiously he stuck his head into the mother's lilac-scented room, which was also laced with her essence. He longed desperately to see her there. But her bed, still unmade from her presence the day before yesterday, lay empty. He entered the still, semi-dark chamber carefully, almost reverently, for he and his brothers were seldom allowed in there. A lingering sense of her pervaded the room and he breathed her in deeply. Slowly he ran his hand across the softness of the faded comforter that still carried the light impression of her slender body. Picking up her rumpled night dress, tossed haphazardly across the covers, he rubbed the silky softness along his cheek and mouth for a moment or two. Holding the gown up to his nose, he smelled the funky, melancholy odor that evoked his mother love. After several moments he replaced the gown, arranging the piece of clothing so that it looked undisturbed. Her bedroom was nearly as barren as his and his brothers', except for the pretty mahogany vanity and dresser pushed tightly up against the outer wall. Several scrape marks had been etched into the faded, light-blue, flowered wallpaper, caused when Cora and one of her various visitors, on more than one occasion, had wrestled the heavy dresser in front of the door to bar the curious children from the room. Dewey had once sorely hurt his skinny shoulder when he persistently pushed against the door and the immoveable piece of furniture, straining to get to the strange noises and his mother's woeful voice coming from behind the door. Now rubbing the remembered soreness of the injury, he again moved on through the quiet.

On top of the dresser, sitting by itself in a large gilded frame, sat his parents' wedding picture. His mother's visage smiled down only slightly at him; his father's likeness, which glared down sternly at him, pictured a man he barely recognized or remembered. In the cool silence Dewey walked over to the large oval mirror mounted on the vanity. On the narrow shelf below the mirror sat several perfume bottles and a lavender scented powder puff resting in a red bath powder container. He lifted the fluffy applicator up and sniffed at the lavender smell before carefully replacing it. Looking up, he did not even recognize his own strange image in the looking glass; he put his thin hand up to the reflection and left several prints in the fine dusting of face powder that lightly covered the mirror's surface.

Several competing emotions swirled through Dewey's young mind and he struggled to understand them. He was not really disappointed that she was not there. She had, after all, told him curtly before leaving, "I'm goin' out with a friend," which he instinctively knew meant a man friend. But still he would have been relieved, maybe happy to see her beautiful form filling the bed, even if there was someone else lying next to her. Oftentimes Cora would bring uncles home for her sons to meet and these fellows would stay around for a day or two. Sometimes there would be soldiers, who would tell the boys "army stories," or skinny salesmen, with sour smelling breath, who would lean forward to tell the boys about pirates and far off lands. The week before, one of the uncles had taken all four boys to the Dakota Theater to see *The Sea Hawk*, where they had marveled at Errol Flynn at his sword-fighting best. He had even bought them Mr. Deelish Popcorn and Burch's Sarsaparillas. Dewey decided that probably he was the one that she'd gone to be with . . . . She'd said she loved him because he had such a "way with her children" and would "make a good father."

The silent emptiness of the tomblike bedroom mirrored Dewey's own silent emptiness. A quick shudder of fear raced down his narrow spine; he felt as though some unseen presence was closely watching him, so he crept out and quietly shut the door. The child left his mother's room, emerging as vulnerable and forsaken as the day he had dropped from the depths of her womb.

But Dewey, who was gradually acquiring a protective shrewdness, knew all too well the significance of her non-presence, on a more practical, pragmatic level. The morning was only Saturday and his mother would probably not be home until late Sunday evening or Monday, if then. Although loneliness and responsibility lay heavily upon him, the almost overwhelming hunger he began to feel drew him sharply back to reality. The burden of his brothers' well-being fell upon him. In the kitchen, from the warm icebox, he took the last of the milk in the glass bottle; it only had just begun to spoil, so he was able to still drink it. Because the warm liquid tasted like buttermilk, he was able to keep it down and it did somewhat relieve the rumbling in his belly. Carefully he put the empty bottle back on the wire grating shelf in the bare icebox, and only felt a little guilty that he had saved none of the milk for his younger brothers.

With his young, slender body bent a bit under the lingering burden of guilt and aloneness and hunger, he walked out onto the front porch and into the yard. His stomach began to really hurt as he remembered his mother's parting words. "You're in charge, Dewey!" She had grabbed his skinny arm tightly as she jerked him away from the others; her sharp nails pinched into his skin as he tried to pull away in fear. "You better be sure that nothin' happens while I'm gone, ya hear? If there're any problems, I'll lay inta ya good." She gave his arm one final, sharp shake and then vanished quickly.

Close to the front door stoop, numerous pieces of jagged window glass littered the ground and he poked at the shards with his bare toe. The upstairs bedroom window had been broken out two days earlier during a game of "pirates' raid," just shortly after Cora left. About an hour after their mother's stern warning about being good and staying out of trouble, the four brothers had retreated to the upstairs, rejoicing in their freedom. The mattress on the floor had been the ship and Duane had been an enemy pirate trying to board. Dewey had torn out a two-foot section of wallboard and thrown it at Duane to repel the boarding, but Duane had ducked and the piece of plaster went skidding across the bare floor. In both frustration and excitement, Duane hurled a partially full chamber pot cannonball at his older brother. Dewey had ducked quickly and the ceramic container crashed through the window, knocking out most of the pane of glass. Though the glass was carried outward into the front yard, a good many of the shards landed in the front entryway, beyond the porch, creating a hazardous pathway. To make sure that the other children didn't cut their feet, Dewey and Duane went down later and laid bricks and boards over the glass. The dangerous threshold even tied in nicely with the "pirate" motif of their play and games and later became the "plank." The plank worked out quite well until stupid Leeland's foot slipped off one of the boards and a sliver of glass sliced his heel open. Leeland began simultaneously bleeding and screaming until Dewey finally found an old roll of gauze and wrapped his brother's foot tightly. Dewey still remembered his brother whimpering for hours; he was tired of taking care of his troublesome brothers.

After carefully negotiating the pirates' plank covering the glass, he stuck his hands in his deep pockets, walked to the outhouse, and relieved himself. The building smelled even worse than the upstairs bedroom and he was glad to get back out into the fresh air of the yard.   The dew-wet tufts of prairie grass that grew on the periphery of the yard, all the way back past the collapsing barn and the broken down split rail fence, felt nice on his bare toes and heels as he walked back toward the house. The heavy shade from the tree prevented anything from growing beneath it and the gray dirt for ten yards around the thick trunk had been ground down by small bare feet into a soft powder. The tree had constantly been a daytime gathering place for the brothers and several ruts had been worn around the base, ruts filled with the fine dirt. Dewey went to the hanging tire and sat in the swing, moving back and forth idly, dragging his large toe in the cool earth and listlessly making lazy swirl marks on the loose ground. His thoughts fell to food for the day. The leftovers his mother had gathered together for the boys were already gone and now nothing remained for the four rapidly growing youngsters, with raging appetites, to eat. Bread would be the easiest thing to make, he decided.

A bit later in the morning, when his brothers had all risen and drifted hungrily down to the kitchen, Dewey revealed his plan to Duane, whose eyes were still sleepily half closed. Partially to get his attention and partially out of anger or meanness, Dewey slugged yawning Duane hard on the ball of his injured shoulder, driving his knuckles into the boney part.

"Ouch! What the heck ya do that for?"

"Listen ta me, ya nitwit!" Dewey's fist hurt from the punch, but the psychological relief from delivering the sharp blow to his brother had been immediate and so he slugged him again even harder for emphasis. "We gotta get somethin' ta eat 'cause the ol' lady probably won't be home until tomorrow night. I seen her make bread once and that's what we're gonna do."

Either because of the false confidence in Dewey's voice, or because in their early morning hunger they would agree to just about anything, all three boys nodded enthusiastic agreement to their brother's plan. Dewey and Duane jointly began the baking project, working together as true brothers, while Lloyd and Leeland looked on hungrily, sitting back out of the way on the dirty linoleum floor in the kitchen. Based upon his recollection of how his mother had done it, Dewey led the experiment. He could find no lard or salt or baking powder in the barren cabinets, so he decided that these items were not really necessary. With Duane's help he took a large mixing pan from beneath the sink and put in some water from the kitchen pump and several cakes of yeast from the nearly empty top cupboards. When the water and yeast were ready, they merely added flour by the handful until the mixture became a sticky blob. Then they carefully lit the fire in the stove and began kneading the dough; in unison the brothers set upon the white mass and when the four sets of dirty hands were done, the dough had become quite gray. All of the boys began laughing and poking at the puffing up and lowering of the sticky blob, delighting in their newfound game. Dewey made the final decision that the dough was right for baking, so he and Duane loaded the loaf into a large baking pan, shoved the heavy pan gently onto the grate in the kitchen oven, and closed the doors. After getting the kindling well lit, Dewey put a heavy load of wood into the stove and then placed a stick through the oven door handles to keep any heat from escaping. With the preparations complete, the four went off to play out in the yard, joyful in the prospect that they would soon have fresh bread in their empty stomachs.

Some minutes later a loud blast from the kitchen quite suddenly interrupted the youngsters' play. A few moments of uncertainty passed before Dewey yelled out excitedly "She's ready!" The brothers ran back inside the house, Dewey first, and they stopped abruptly at the door leading into the kitchen. "Gol dang!" said Duane in amazement and joy.

The expanding bread had blown the door of the oven open and gooey blobs, the remnants of the doughy concoction, hung suspended from the cabinets and the sink and various places around the kitchen, dangling like brownish icicles. The boys reveled at the sight only for a few moments and began immediately to eat without question. When at long last their hunger had been satisfied, they just looked at each other and then gravitated back outside to resume their play. The force of the bread explosion had been so strong that the oven door hung off of one of its hinges. But the four brothers would have plenty to eat for the remainder of their mother's absence; now whenever they were hungry all they had to do was go in the kitchen, merely peal a piece of bread off of the wall or one of the cabinets or off the floor, and they would have food. Life again turned good for them, primarily because of Dewey's innovative, fearless spirit.

With their basic needs taken care of, the boys could continue their pursuit of exploring the world around them. The game of pirates continued. The cottonwood became the sweeping, fully sailed ship. Dewey and Duane created more and more details to embellish the pretend atmosphere and then decided to venture off to the junkyard that lay a few miles down the road, on the other side of the Indian's place. Leeland and Lloyd wanted to come along and even cried violently in fear of being left alone when Dewey and Duane emphatically said "No!" and walked off toward the highway. The two youngsters carefully tagged along behind anyway, trailing their older brothers at a safe distance, until Dewey and Duane turned around and began throwing stones at them. But the two did not move, except to dodge a rock or two, and stood there silently in the middle of the dirt roadway. Becoming angrier at their disobedience, Dewey decided to lock the two young brothers in the upstairs closet to keep them from following; their tiny, hysterical cries were no longer audible when Dewey and Duane reached Highway 2 and turned toward the junkyard.

On the way they checked out the bums' camp in the grove of box elder and ash and elm trees beside the Great Northern railroad tracks that paralleled the road, but the camp contained no food to be scavenged. Continuing their odyssey in the warm sun, sometimes walking with their arms on each other's shoulders, kicking at small stones, they headed due north to Art Jenkins' Truck, Tractor, and Auto Junkyard. Once there, they ambled slowly through the several rows of vehicles rotting in the afternoon sun, excitedly looking for plunder. They were able to salvage a small, dead automobile battery and then a trumpet horn from the wrecked hulk of a '36 Packard Town Car and a large, shiny hubcap from a '33 Cord 810 with which to steer their pirate ship. With a good deal of difficulty, the boys hauled the booty home. They piled the battery and horn onto the hubcap, struggling greatly to carry the goods between them along the road. Arriving back at the farmyard, they set the treasure at the foot of the cottonwood.

Dewey took command and immediately began shouting orders. "Duane! Go get them damned prisoners! We'll make 'em walk the plank!" Using a palm-sized rock, he roughly nailed the shiny Cord hubcap to the tree and was soon carefully steering the imaginary cottonwood pirate ship, skillfully guiding it through troubled waters.

Duane obediently went upstairs to release the captives, but when he got up there the two brothers had cried themselves to sleep. He roughly pushed at their shoulders with his dirty bare foot until they woke up and then he ordered them downstairs. When the two younger brothers finally emerged from the house, bleary-eyed, blinking at the bright afternoon sun, Dewey immediately commanded that they again be taken captive. Duane obediently tied them to the cottonwood tree, using a section of rotting cotton rope from the sagging clothesline in the rear of the house.

As captain of the ship, Dewey kept barking out orders through the trumpet horn. Meanwhile, because he was such a good climber, Duane had secured the battery to the last remaining length of clothesline rope and began climbing the tree. When he had reached a branch half way up, he looped the cord over the limb and let the end fall to the ground. Together he and Dewey hoisted the battery up to about seven feet off the ground and secured the line. "This is the anchor for the ship!" he yelled out proudly to Dewey, who had returned to the helm. "Good work, Duane!" Dewey hollered back.

Dewey converted the trumpet horn to a telescope and began surveying the far off horizons. The late afternoon wind began to pick up, once more rustling the leaves in the tree, making them appear to be the billowing sails of the ship. "Throw me the telescope! I think I see something!" shouted Duane, but Dewey just ignored his brother and kept steering the ship off towards the horizon. An argument quickly erupted between Dewey and Duane and when Dewey climbed up into the tree to confront his brother, a heated swordfight soon ensued between the two. Using butcher knives that had earlier been brought out from the kitchen, the two hacked away at each other, the sharp metal making clashing sounds as steel blade struck against steel blade, leaving heavy nicks on the sharp edges. In all of the excitement, Lloyd and Leeland had worked themselves free from their bonds and gleefully danced around beneath their swashbuckling brothers fighting in the branches above. The brothers' flailing swords cut swaths in the branches and scraps of leaves and twigs fell to the ground. All of the movement in the tree, though, began to gradually loosen the rotted rope they had wrapped around the battery anchor; when the binding finally let go, the suspended battery fell and, before hitting the ground, landed a glancing blow to the forehead of Leeland's uplifted face, splitting open the surface skin.

Little Leeland didn't let out a cry or make a sound—just fell backwards flat on the ground. His small knees didn't even buckle and so his head made a muffled thud when it landed on the soft dirt beneath the tree. His eyelids were opened slightly, but his eyes were somewhat rolled back in their sockets. Dewey could only helplessly watch the accident, mouth agape, paralyzed for several seconds before his instincts and past experiences forced his actions. He scampered down out of the tree and skidded up on his knees to where his brother lay semiconscious.

"Shit, oh shit! Please don't be dead, Lee! Please don't be dead!" Dewey cradled Leeland's head in his hands, rocking back and forth, moaning and beginning to cry. "God, don't make him be dead!"

Duane was still up in the tree, looking down, transfixed by the sight of his brother's bleeding head. "Get sumpthin' to stop the bleeding!" Dewey yelled up at him. Duane climbed down out of the tree, ran into the house, and grabbed the towel lying on the front room floor. Red splotches of Leeland's dried foot blood already covered most of the cloth, but there was still enough clean space to hold over his new wound.

After several minutes Leeland regained consciousness and smiled up listlessly at his brothers' concerned faces. Though the bleeding had mostly subsided, the skin on both sides of the gash lay flayed open. Dewey, in his young wisdom, instantly made the decision to take his younger brother to town for medical attention. "Come on!" he commanded Duane. The two older boys lifted up and cradled Leeland between them and began walking unsteadily out toward Highway 2, with frightened Lloyd trailing behind at a distance. When they reached the roadway, it was not too long until Orville "Buck" Lund came by, stopped, and with only a few questions loaded the four up on the back of his flatbed pickup. Lund put the accelerator to the floor and sped into Farmington, where he pulled the truck up with a slight skid in front of Doctor Christianson's office/house. Before the truck had come to a full stop in the driveway, Lund bounced from the cab, scooped up Leeland in his big, farmer-tanned arms and carried the youngster towards the doctor's office, with the three other brothers following behind closely.

18

"Doc! Doc! You in there?" Orville yelled out excitedly as he took the front porch steps two at a time.

Doc Christianson knew the boys quite well, at least their fractures and contusions, so he reassured Orville that the children would be all right, commended him several times for his act of caring kindness, and sent him on his way. After stitching up Leeland's oozing wound and making sure that he only had a mild concussion, and then cleaning out and dressing the two-day-old gash on the child's foot as well, the doctor got all of the boys a few pieces of hard peppermint candy and commenced to phone the sheriff.

"Ben, I got them Lambson boys in here again. Yeah. Yeah. All of 'em. I stitched up little Leeland . . . the youngest one. . . . Yeah. Busted head, but I think that he'll be all right. Okay, but you need ta come over here. I don't know where their mother is and I don't know what ta do with 'em."

About twenty minutes passed before Sheriff Bennett Wilt came over to the doctor's office and almost immediately began to interrogate the brothers. Dewey, being the eldest, was the unofficial spokesperson.

"Where's your ma?

"Dunno."

"When'd she leave?"

"Dunno. Coupla days ago . . . . Thursday, I think. Maybe Friday. Dunno."

"I think she's workin'," volunteered Duane and Dewey just gave him a deadly Dewey stare.

"I checked down at the Ideal Bar on the way over and she ain't there. No one's seen her. Red wasn't there neither, so maybe they're off somewhere together," Sheriff Wilt said to no one in particular. The sheriff looked again at the boys, stern and intent, as though he was trying to sort out and categorize all of the incoming facts and information so that he could make the correct decision. Then he stood directly in front of Duane, hands on his thick hips, and looked severely down at the boy. "When's she gonna be home?"

"Dunno," said Duane softly and he looked at the clean, brown-and-green-specked white linoleum beneath his dirty, bare feet.

Sheriff Wilt backed off and turned to the doctor. "Ain't she pregnant? Seems like every time Iver comes home, she gets knocked up. Then he runs off again. Never sends her any money, from what I hear." He spoke directly to the doctor, as though the children were invisible. "But she always takes him back. Every dang time."

"Yeah, I saw her a while back. She came in for a checkup . . . said she thought she might be in a motherly way. Wanted somethin' for the sickness. She must be six months along by now."

"You'd think she'd be a bit more careful. Some folks say it's Red's."

"I don't know. Could be." The doctor surveyed the four children reflectively. "Could be anybody's, far as that goes.

"What's the boy's condition?" Sheriff Wilt asked, pointing his sagging, dimpled chin towards Leeland.

"He's okay, I think. Just addled his brains a bit. I sewed him up and bandaged his foot, but like I said, I think he should stay here overnight. I'll keep him here and the wife'll give him a bath and get him cleaned up. Maybe find him some clean clothes. She's got some left over from Edward. But you'll need to find someplace for the others." Then the doctor turned to the sheriff, a deep seriousness in his voice.

"And, Ben, you *really gotta* do something this time before one of 'em gets killed. This is the third time this year I've sewn one or the other of 'em up. Ya' know I don't mind . . . it's my job. But I don't get any money for it either."

"Yeah, these Lambson kids are some pretty rough monkeys. I'll keep the other three with me and pick this 'ere one up in the mornin'. Tomorrow I'll drive out after church and sees if the mother is ta home. Maybe talk some sense inta her. I've gotten several complaints from other folks as well."

Sheriff Wilt sighed heavily under the pressures and responsibility of his job, then turned and took Dewey, Duane, and Lloyd home with him. "Come on, you kids," he said as he took Duane and Lloyd by the hand; Dewey followed sullenly behind.

There was no place else to take them, except to the jailhouse, and Sara, his wife, would certainly not have that. When they arrived at the sheriff's home, the three brothers ran excitedly around the house and only settled down when Sara fed them dinner. Both she and Ben looked on, slackjawed, at the amount of food the boys ate and ate and ate. Dinner was followed by thick slices of apple pie with cheese on top; afterwards, the children helped clean up and then pestered Sara and Ben long into the night with questions about the sheriff's badge and gun and why the two had no children. The couple tried to clean up the boys to make them presentable at church the next day: Sara washed their filthy clothes and Sheriff Wilt stood guard while the three youngsters washed themselves almost raw and reveled and frolicked in the murky, tepid bathwater. Sara rubbed the soft towels across their scrubbed-red bodies and tussled lovingly the damp tufts of clean hair on their heads, telling them all the while that they were handsome little men.

The boys slept well and Lloyd didn't even wet his bed. In the morning Sara dug out several sets of shirts, trousers, socks and shoes she had packed far back in the closet after the death of her own two young children from influenza. When the three were all dressed, with their hair slicked back on their heads, she sat them down at the kitchen table. Joyfully she prepared a large breakfast of blueberry pancakes, pork sausage, and eggs, all the time humming softly and fussing pleasantly over the youngsters. The Lambson brothers again ate like they had not seen food for days; in fact, Sara and Sheriff Wilt could hardly get the boys away from the table in time for them all to make it to the 10 a.m. service at the Zion Lutheran Community Church. The group purposely sat in the rear of the church to avoid attention; however, more than one member of the congregation craned his or her head to catch a glimpse of the brothers. Most of the parishioners had heard about the unruly, ill-behaved Lambson youngsters, so a good deal of curious gawking took place amidst the congregation before the start of the service.

At the beginning of the worship time, fascinated by the seriousness of the ceremony and the solemn singing of the first hymn, the boys behaved fairly well, considering they had no history of being around other people for extended periods of time. Their socialization processes had been limited. Cora had registered Dewey and Duane in Farmington Public School #2, but they hadn't attended any of the classes for well over six months. Though Dewey and Duane were a year apart, they were placed in the same classroom, two grades below where they should have been. Dewey was quickly labeled a "bully" because on the first day of school Edith Welty said he stunk and Dewey punched the young girl hard in the stomach, out by the sandbox, knocking the wind right out of her. From that point on his teacher, Miss Jane Ellen Marmen, considered him a disciplinary problem and thus frequently isolated him from the class by placing him for long periods of time in the hall outside of the classroom. "You two Lambson kids are dumber than a couple of rocks!" she once said, her severely pursed lips barely moving, as she grabbed Dewey's narrow shoulders and slammed him into a wooden chair in the hallway. Miss Marmen, who also taught Sunday school at the Methodist Church, disliked the two boys intensely and smiled smugly whenever a choir of children would surround them in the schoolyard, chanting a delightful chorus of "One, two, three, four, five, six, seven, all good children go to heaven. When they get there they will say, 'Lambsons, Lambsons, where are they!'" Then one day when the two brothers were walking the long dirt road home from the schoolhouse, several older students caught up with Duane, who had fallen behind, and began to taunt him. When Dewey ran back to defend Duane, both of the brothers were pretty well beaten up; at that point they decided *NEVER* to return to the school.

As the service progressed, the three became infatuated with the lighting of the candles. They stared intently as the symbolic altar candles were lit one after the other, and the flickering flames reflected in the intense stare of their sparkling, curious eyes. The three held their mouths open in unison for several moments until Lloyd mumbled to his brothers, "Is there gonna be a fire?"

And before too long, as a result of their lack of formal training and because of the excitement generated by their participation in an actual religious activity, their curiosity overwhelmed them and their inquisitiveness continued unabated throughout the remainder of the service. Sitting between Ben and Sara, the boys knelt and then stood up in the pews to get a better view, squirming restlessly as they watched the drama being played out before them.

"Why's that guy hangin' on them pieces 'a wooden fence posts?"

"Lookee, he's bleedin' from his guts!"

"Is he dead? Who kilt 'em? How come?"

"Why's he almost nekked?"

"How come that window got different colored glass?"

"Who's the guy in that piture on the wall? Why're all the kids and sheeps around 'im?"

"How come he's kneelin' by 'em?"

"What's that big hook he's holdin'? Is he gonna hit 'em?"

Despite being hushed and double hushed, their questions and childish observations did not cease for the next thirty-seven minutes. Sara and Ben's faces became bright red as more and more of the congregation turned and looked at them with condescending glances.

"What's in the plates that them guys is passin' around?"

"I hope it's sumthin' ta eat!"

"Wow! It's money."

"Can I take some when it comes ta me?"

"Whatta we doin' now? Prayin'? What's prayin'?"

"Do we gotta bow our heads, too?"

"Who we prayin' to?"

"Can I talk if I jus' whisper?"

"Gimme that Bible book! You can't read!"

"Can so! Gimme it back!"

"Now see what ya done! Ya tore the pages!"

Sometimes the volume of their questions and insights about the Christian epoch almost overcame the words of the liturgist, as well as the profound sermon of the minister. But the good Reverend Halstad prevailed by delivering his words on Christian responsibility more forcefully and certainly with much more eloquence and rigor. The message, after all, needed to be heard. In his heart, however, Reverend Halstad gave silent thanks during the closing hymn that the services that day did not include communion worship.

After church, Sara guided the children home and fed them a lunch of thick shepherd's pie while Sheriff Wilt stayed behind to talk to the minister. Reverend Halstad backed away a bit when he saw the sheriff approaching; however, with a bit of cajoling, the minister reluctantly agreed to accompany Sheriff Wilt to return the boys home. The two public servants earnestly discussed the possibility of talking at length to Cora, perhaps making her own up to her own Christian and civic responsibilities and take better care of her children.

Immediately following lunch, and after handing them each a paper sack containing their freshly washed trousers and food enough to last them for a few days, Sara embraced the boys warmly and gently, then tenderly stroked their faces. She also had packed some clothes and provisions for Leeland, which she entrusted to Duane. As they were walking away, a smiling Duane turned and waved and called out "Bye, mom!" Then Lloyd and Dewey began the chant and they all repeated the chorus of "Bye, Mom! Bye, Mom! Bye, Mom" until Sara began weeping quietly in happiness.

The sheriff, the reverend, and the three brothers packed themselves into the sheriff's car and traveled the short distance over to pick up Leeland, who sported a large gauze bandage down the center of his forehead and two huge black eyes. Dewey, Duane, and Lloyd excitedly welcomed him by pounding him on his back and exploring his darkened eyes and swollen scalp and heavily wrapped heel. The six drove on out to the Lambson house in the early afternoon; the boys, filled with food and energy, bounced excitedly on the backseat, yelling and shouting joyfully, asking rapid, unceasing questions of the reverend and the sheriff. When they pulled up into the yard, the boys jumped from the car and disappeared into the barn, plundering the supplies Sara Wilt had provided for them. The sheriff and the reverend inspected the house, shook their heads sadly in unison at the smell and at the sparse conditions, and then went back outside to wait. While the two authority figures from the town sat relaxed in the police car, sometimes talking about civic affairs and sometimes dozing lightly, with their legs stretched out through the open doors of the vehicle, the Lambson children scampered around the front yard and through the house. Later in the afternoon, with the reddening sun dipping down towards dusk, the reverend and the sheriff called the boys together. Well fed and happy . . . safe and secure for the moment . . . the youngsters returned to the two authority figures with no hesitation.

"The Reverend and me are going to have to go back to town, so you boys stay right here until your momma comes home," the sheriff told them sternly, looking at each with a firm gaze. "When she gets here, you tell her what you done. You tell her, too, that the reverend here and me will be back out here tomorrow mornin' to talk to her. Got that?! Let's go, Reverend."

Before the two officials left, Reverend Halstad gathered the boys around him, under the long shadow of the cottonwood tree, and ordered them to bow their heads. He placed his hands on Dewey and Duane's shoulders and gathered them close. He lowered his own head as well and spoke slowly, deliberately, in a deep and resonant tone: "Heavenly Father, I ask that You look down upon Your flock and bless us all. I ask, dear Father, that through Your divine will You intercede and change the ways of these misguided lambs . . . return them to Your fold, oh Lord. In Jesus' name, amen."

Excited that the reverend would pray with and for them, the brothers crowded around him, clutching onto his pants legs as he made his way back to the car. Brushing away their small, clinging hands, he sat down in the front seat, pushed the children back, and slammed the heavy door. The brothers waved and waved as the sheriff's car left the farmyard, then they ran after it until it became enveloped in a swirling ball of dust, chasing it along the dry dirt road until it turned onto Highway 2 towards town and disappeared.

Later that night, after the boys had gone to bed, Cora came home and went immediately to bed without even going up to look in on her children. The next day the brothers excitedly related to their mother the full details of their adventure, but she said nothing . . . did not scold them or beat them or anything. She merely shook her aching head heavily, wished that she had never been born, and left again that same evening to see a friend.

Meanwhile, Sheriff Wilt became involved in another investigation and Reverend Halstad was called away to pray for a dying parishioner, one who had tithed regularly. So the two Farmington public servants never did come out to see Cora that day, or the next, or the next, for that matter. Nobody from the town, it seems, chose to take responsibility for the plight of the Lambson children.

Chapter Two—The Lambson Family

To this very day, what remains so strangely perplexing about the Lambson children and their woeful circumstances is that there had forever, or ostensibly so, been a sense of community in Farmington, North Dakota, the town in which they were born and spent their forlorn childhood. From the town's very beginning, people apparently possessed an inherent spirit of taking care of each other. Always there appeared to be a sense of continuity . . . a seemingly deep seated awareness of the continuous, flowing cycle of renewal . . . of life. That is to say, a pervasive belief that one person's destiny was bound tightly to the destiny of others . . . to the fate of the community. That is what makes the boys' story so difficult to understand: how could those youngsters become so denied, so disowned, so disavowed by the community to which, one would suppose, they inherently became an integral part of at the very instant of their births?

From Farmington's very inception, the family appeared always to be a sacred entity, integral to the life or death of the town . . . of society itself. With the passage of time, these minimal social units grew and coalesced, bonding closely with other families and in so doing weaving the very fabric and tapestry of the community.

The spirit of family became evidenced early on in the photographs that collected on mantels and settee tables, and that hung on the pastoral, wallpapered walls of homes in the town and the surrounding farms . . . the black-and-white, sometimes faded, sometimes glossy pictures that brought life and memories, permanence and stability to the people within. As almost a motif, the household pictures of the early town families often showed bonneted and shawled women standing beside their bearded, stern-faced men whose thick eyebrows always furrowed in on themselves; various numbers of children stood docilely beside or knelt or sat in front of their two parents. Yet even the earliest tintypes of Farmington citizens portrayed a contradictory, ever-present sense of self and other . . . or perhaps an arrogant distain for weakness. These pictorial slices of life, of history, captured the images of crowds of inhabitants, all bundled up against the elements, standing atop snowdrifts that sealed the narrow street between the facing rows of wooden buildings . . . smugly proud of their role in the growth of the new town . . . haughty with the sense of their own tenacious spirit. Some showed couples that were Farmington's founders: heavy-bearded, serious, unsmiling men and narrow, hardened, desperate looking women, staring suspiciously back at the camera. Other images, some taken as early as the spring of 1892, pictured those same or similar residents trudging through the mud-stuck streets, steadfastly bent into their tasks. Invariably the visages conveyed a rugged sort of pride . . . of unsmiling happiness . . . of uncompromising fortitude . . . of raw individualism. The unrelenting physical work and the anguish of sickness and death were always mirrored in the photos. The lined and sometimes blurry faces of the people continually put forth a hardened demeanor . . . a constant appearance of rigid gratification and self-satisfaction in the midst of hardship. One aging, faded black-and-white picture, its yellow edges cracking and turning upward, taken in August of 1889, captured the adults of the Swede Gunderson family at harvest time, standing in a field of hard wheat shock, resting momentarily beside their horse-drawn grain binders, looking tired and solemn-faced at the photographer . . . just daring the elements to once again storm and destroy the newly reaped crops. Through all manner of pestilences—the sudden, terrible blizzards that froze cattle dead in their tracks; the turbulent, murky brown floodwaters of spring; the desiccating winds and crop-flattening hailstorms of summer; the wheat blight and the gray funneled tornados and yearly crop failures and train wrecks and social upheavals and diphtheria and measles and influenza—through all of these trials the people of Farmington somehow prevailed.

The photographs spoke volumes about the concept of family in the small town. When the men were beaten to the ground by their circumstances, the women always stood nearby to raise the men's vision back to the present and more importantly to the future that was to be passed on to their sons and daughters. In return, their children were obedient, even subservient, which contributed to the overall bonding processes of the society. The family was held to be sacred, so much so that the approval or disapproval of the general populace seemed to continually coerce people into doing the right thing—that is to say, making the members of the community severely aware of their familial as well as their social responsibilities. The people's determination to build strong families, and thus leave a strong heritage for the future, seems to have served as the driving force in the evolution of the town and the people who populated it.

Moreover, though the townspeople invariably appeared to become fused together by adversity, the paradox of self-actualization versus preservation of the society would persist for generations to come, hidden perhaps under a cloak of social propriety. Over time, the conflicting ideals of primacy of the fittest and of society being responsible for even the weakest of its members continued to permeate the very social fabric of Farmington, incessantly shrouded by the self righteousness engendered by success and prosperity and by the cultural myths that the town's people created in order to delude themselves over generations. And certainly these myths had their origins in both a need for conformity to cultural norms and a harsh skepticism and suspicion of anything different, or aberrant, or outside of the defined community.

This dichotomous heritage provided the background and foundation . . . the template, if you will . . . for the Lambson family: Cora (Jenson) and Iver Lambson, and the five children created from their union. Indeed, their very existence as a family unit certainly serves to confront the pervasive familial myths that the people of Farmington immersed and cloaked themselves in. As well, the story of the Lambson children undermines the homogeneity of that rural culture by bringing to light the unspoken, unanalyzed indifference the society bore towards them and the emotional paralysis that their existence evoked.

* * *

The story of Cora and Iver Lambson's marriage really begins with the birth of Cora Jensen in the year 1910. She was born in Harveyville, on the border between Taft and

Neilson County, about thirty miles east of Farmington. The last of five children born to Alyce and Harley Jensen, Cora came from good Irish and Danish descendents. Her parents, however, passed on when she was only a small child: her mother died of lockjaw when Cora was just nine months old and a little over two years later her father died in a tragic farm machinery accident when he was mauled by a belt-driven harvester. Afterwards, she was raised by a paternal aunt, Marian Wills, whose husband, George Wills, farmed a fifty-acre spread five miles southeast of Harveyville. George and Marian Wills had five children of their own, so Cora's four siblings were distributed around various farms in the Harveyville area. Cora never knew her real brothers and sisters very well. In addition, because she came as an extra mouth to feed, and a female one at that, George Wills resented her presence from the very start. Sensing their father's feelings, Cora's adopted siblings somewhat ostracized her, causing her a good deal of loneliness during her formative years. Only Mother Wills showed her any special attention, so Cora became quite close to the surrogate mother.

Cora grew up fairly intelligent, but was always quiet and lacked confidence. She was of average height, but thin, and thus she was never very outstanding. She kept her brown hair short and bobbed, which rather accentuated her pale complexion. Though Cora was extremely slender and her shoulders were narrow, her hips, as Mother Wills pointed out once, were naturally wide for the delivery of many children. This reproductive ability came as a joy to Marian, who adhered strictly to the tenets of the Catholic Church. Marian loved Cora as though the girl was her own daughter, even though the young girl oftentimes became rebellious and insolent in her adolescent years, especially to George Wills, who on more than one occasion had to beat the girl into obedience. And just as with all their other children, Marian and George raised the girl in strict and rigid accordance to Catholic catechistic teaching.

After completing high school, Cora spent several months at Moorhead Secretarial School before dropping out and returning home, where she waited for something to happen in her life. Without any solid direction, she just seemed to drift from opportunity to opportunity. During the next six months she worked at various odd jobs. Then one day she saw an advertisement in the *Harveyville Weekly Dispatch* for a cook in the town of Farmington, over in neighboring Nielson County. Certainly in her years with Mother Wills, one skill Cora had acquired was cooking, so she eagerly sent out a neatly written letter to the post office box and was hired for the position. The job involved preparing meals for the farmhands on Nels Lambson's spread, all during planting and harvest time. She did have to move away from the Wills' home to live on the Lambson farm, but she enjoyed the change. Cora settled in quietly at the Lambson's, residing in a small room immediately off the kitchen, and everyone commented on her ability to prepare delicious food, especially her bread and biscuits. In response to compliments, she smiled a slight smile, nodded briefly, and looked down at her hands as she wiped them on her white apron. And during that new and somewhat happy time of sweating in the hot kitchen, hovering over the black stove and oven during long harvest hours, she fell in love with strong Iver Lambson, especially his broad, crooked smile, despite the fact that she was a year older than him.

Iver, the son of Nels and Inga Lambson, had grown up on the one-hundred-and-seventy acre spread, which had been in the family since 1899. The farm was located about six miles from the old Sheppard homestead, on the other side of town. Iver had only an 8th grade education; as his father's minion, his work had always been that of farmhand. More than once his young, closely sheared head had felt the sharp knock of a hoe handle when he did not move fast enough for his father's liking; his old mother would often gather the weeping boy in her skinny arms and console him gently with old Scandinavian folk tales. He was the youngest of the four children sired by Nels Lambson, and the only boy. Nels was as stern and unforgiving—mean, most folks said—as he was tall and lean. Because of his undisguised disappointment with the gender of his first three children, Nels put all of his dreams on Iver, and invariably expected a good deal from the boy. Inga went barren after her fourth birth, so Iver was the father's last chance to leave his name, and thus part of himself, as his legacy to the world.

Nels farmed because he was born into it, but breaking horses remained his real passion in life. Most people in the area said that, though his methods of horse training were not humane, sometimes even brutal, Nels proved time and again to be the best horseman in the county. The man did, after all, seem to know the name of every horse in the area. Being as tall as most of the horses he worked with, he could almost look them squarely in the eye and stare them down. During the breaking process, he lashed himself tightly to the saddle of the bucking horse until the animal gave in to his dominion. If and when that didn't work, Nels tied a rope around the front ankles of the animal and pulled its legs out from under it when it did not behave. Once when he stood eye-to-eye with a chestnut brown mare, the animal suddenly reared its head, snorted violently, and bit off the upper half of Nels' left ear. The irate, swearing horseman chased the mare around the corral with a whip, flailing violently at the animal, all the while holding his dirty kerchief to the bleeding side of his head.

Though Iver stood in fear and awe of his father, he managed to elude Nels' efforts to break him as if he were one of those horses. As a child he had a boyish grin that Nels detested, but that somewhat innocent smile eventually evolved into a self-confident, almost-haughty smirk . . . a look that came to characterize and define Iver, providing him with an aloofness that girls found both intriguing and alluring. All during the boy's growing up years, to make up for her husband's rigid indifference, Iver's mother fawned over him, and his older sisters—Adell, Clara, and Edith—continually indulged their "baby brother," always telling him what a "handsome boy" and "good looking young man" he was becoming. As he reached maturity, because of his tall and comely appearance, Iver forever delighted the local ladies; he especially liked to impress them with how much he could drink and still appear sober. Indeed, those that knew the Lambson family said that Iver's only weaknesses were drinking . . . that and stepping out with so many of the local girls. Rumors about Iver's prowess spread amongst the young men of the town, who no doubt embellished his ability to handle not only women but his liquor as well. And certainly Iver did nothing to dissuade the building of his manly reputation.

But Cora probably wouldn't have cared, even if she had known about Iver's youthful reputation and his womanizing ways—she was smitten by him: his strong, field-tanned frame; his dark-blue eyes and confident half smile; his strong jaw and narrowing chin; his dark brown, wavy hair, combed straight back from his forehead, accentuating his prominent widow's peak. While she prepared the noon meal, she would keep looking out the back screen door of the Lambson kitchen, waiting anxiously to see his tall, lean, slow-moving figure emerging from the fields. Stepping up onto the wood platform of the wash area adjoining the house, stomping the dust from their boots, the farmhands would begin jostling each other as they washed the field dirt from their faces and necks and hands and arms. Seth Miller would sometimes playfully push Iver's broad shoulders and asked him in an overly sweet voice if he was anxious to see his "honey."

Always, when the men entered the kitchen and were all seated, Cora would serve Iver first, much to the ongoing kidding of the others at the table. "Hey, Iver, she gonna save any for the rest of us?" Larry Peters once laughed as he roughly elbowed Iver in the ribs and looked clownishly around the table. "What cha suppose he's getting' for dessert?" Milt Sawyer asked as he winked at Larry and settled himself into a white wooden chair, scraping it up to the large wooden table. All the men laughed lightly; Cora's face reddened, but she smiled slightly and looked at the men out of the corner of her eye. The table was crowded with platters of hot meat, steaming bowls of vegetables and potatoes, smaller containers of gravy and pickles and jellies, and plates of home cooked pies and bread, along with cool glasses of lemonade.

The gentle, manly chiding subsided into the silent grunts of midday hunger eating. Cora fluttered proud and wife-like at the rear of the kitchen, trying to anticipate the needs of the men, especially Iver.

The summer matured, with its sweltering days and its warm evenings of longing. Iver began to become more fully aware of shy Cora and he too became smitten, but in a different way. She was quite nice looking, even though she always appeared rather plain and somewhat coy. He started to more closely notice her slight, sweating body moving expertly around the kitchen, dishing up the noon meal to the other hands. As he admired her hips moving beneath her light, pale white cotton dress, a strong yearning stirred within him. The two gradually became lovers and their passions grew. Iver's full, six-foot frame dwarfed her; when they walked together down the streets of Farmington, her head only came up to his broad shoulders. She seemed to yield to him totally, which could have been explained very easily. In her hometown, Cora was known to be a somewhat weak person who could be easily influenced—from infancy through her teen years, she was always a follower. This tendency, ever present in her youth, became especially exacerbated after a few drinks of alcohol, which is probably why Iver was able, after several bottles of beer, to talk her into lying with him in the short, sweet grass one warm, romantic evening in mid-July, out by Skunk Lake, shortly before the beginning of the harvest season, when the loons called out to each other from far off banks.

"Come on, ya know I love ya."

"No, Iver! Stop! Stopit! No! Somebody'll see us!"

"No one's out here!"

"No, I can't . . . . I'm a Cathol . . . ."

"You know what I want!"

"Yur hurtin' me! Stopit, Iver!"

Cora tried to resist him at first, but with one large hand he held her skinny wrists hard on the ground, above her head, as he kissed wetly at her face and neck. The dizzying smell of sweat and beer and Iver's aftershave made her breathing quick and shallow. When she felt his sweaty cheek pressed against hers, she realized the inevitability of the moment, relaxed, finally yielded softly to his dominance, and stopped her sobbing. Even though the lingering moments hurt her severely, she realized through her pain that much good would come from relinquishing herself to him. They were now, in effect, husband and wife. Later, with long, slender pale fingers trembling from the ache deep inside her, she stroked his wet, dark hair and his long face, which he held just a few inches above hers.

"See, it's okay. Nobody saw us," he chided her in his deep, brusque voice.

"Yeah, you're right," she whispered to her lover in the fragrant darkness. "I love you more than anything."

"Yeah, me too," he answered curtly and rose up off of her.

Cora knew that evening solidified their relationship and proved their love, and she doted over Iver even more. Every evening for the next week they hurried off to their favorite spot by the lake to reaffirm their blossoming affection for each other. Iver was not as rough and forceful as on the first night, so their lovemaking grew more tender and pleasurable.

Iver, however, being still young, began to realize that he cared for his freedom much more than he did for Cora. He longed to spend less time with his new love and more time in town with his friends, doing the things he did before he became involved with her. Probably that is why, in late September, when he found out that she was with child and it surely was his, he became extremely nervous and wanted to run away to Montana, perhaps to break horses like his father, maybe at a ranch in Miles City that he had heard was hiring cowboys . . . maybe use the one valuable skill his father had taught him. He certainly did not consider himself anywhere near ready for marriage, and certainly not to a homely dame like Cora. Inga only shook her head slowly, sadly, when Iver sought his mother's counsel; she knew the trouble that lay before her young, handsome son and could only gently stroke his smooth face in consolation. Iver's sisters were much more sympathetic when he told them; all agreed that Cora intentionally set out to trap poor Iver into marriage. "That's the oldest trick in the book," asserted Clara. "She isn't anything but a little tramp," agreed Adell. The two sisters could speak with a voice of authority because they were both being courted by two prominent gentlemen themselves, one being Hal Bigley, a farmer from Langdon, and the other being Eddie Cropper, who owned Cropper's Independent Grocery Store. Edith was away at Midwestern Teachers College in Fargo, but she would have also certainly agreed with her two younger sisters concerning Cora's character and motives.

Iver's father, though, did not share his wife's or his daughters' sympathies. Nels became incensed when he found out about his son's reckless, less-than-honorable behavior. The first person that he blamed was Inga; responsibility for the son's lack of morals most assuredly rested on her and the way she continually coddled the boy . . . always filling his head with fairy tales and other such nonsense. In anger he slammed his fist onto the dining room table, making Inga's pigeon-like frame jump. As the wife and mother began to weep softly into her apron, Nels summoned his "worthless" son in from the fields.

"I'll be Goddammed if you'll be sweet-talkin' your way outta this one, boy!" he screamed at Iver, when the young man finally appeared before him; Iver avoided his father's fierce eyes by looking down at the floor. "Is that kid in her belly yours or ain't it?"

His sisters and mother, seeking to avoid the confrontation, had already meekly retired to their rooms for the afternoon, so without any allies, the young man cowered under his father's assault.

"Yeah, I suppose so."

"Then make it right before she starts showin'!" the father commanded as he clenched and unclenched his large fists, ready to lay into the boy at the first sign of resistance.

Without looking up from his dusty work boots, Iver turned and left the room, defeated. He knew that he now had but one choice.

"I'll not have you ruinin' my good name!" Nels screamed at his departing son.

Later that evening, in the long diatribe that began and ended the family dinner, Nels angrily emphasized to his son that running off to Montana was not an option; Iver would do the honorable thing and marry Cora, or Nels would damn-sure make him regret the day he was born. Nels *WOULD NOT* have his Farmington neighbors talking about him and his kin. Nels knew firsthand the feeling of shame, of walking into Stan's Cafe or the Farmington Mercantile and sensing the smirks and snickers and the stares from the corners of his "friends'" eyes. All too well he knew of the consequences of unsubstantiated gossip, whispered behind cupped hands, and how those innuendos spread like a wildfire throughout the community. The rumors and semi-lies could so quickly become like knives that would shred one's reputation, one's community standing, one's relationships, indeed, one's livelihood in a matter of just a few days.

Almost immediately following the prolonged, some-times violent confrontation between Nels and his son, the young man grudgingly proposed to Cora. He met with her in the warmth of the next evening; the two young people stood together yet apart on the slightly sagging front porch, which creaked with their every awkward move, neither knowing what to say, where to begin.

"My ol' man's mad'r than hell 'cause yur in a motherly way. Says I gotta make it right." Iver started rather unceremoniously, his set jaw and pronounced temple protruding from the darkened skin of his young face as he stared out far beyond the empty fields. "If it's mine, I expect we're gonna have to get married."

"Yes, oh, yes, Iver, honey, it's yours! I ain't never been with no one else! Ever!" responded Cora, overwhelmed with relief and happiness. "I'll make you happy, just you watch! Thank you, Iver! I love ya!" Cora, in her excitement, clasped her hands joyfully before her face, but Iver just stared off towards the distant horizon and then a few minutes later shuffled on down the road towards town, where he stayed until the next afternoon.

Iver's proposal greatly relieved Cora's well-founded fears about her future. The religious Mr. and Mrs. Wills had already told Cora that they would have nothing to do with her and her illegitimate child if no marriage took place. So even though the engagement and courtship were quite abbreviated and not the most romantic, Cora remained more than willing to join her life with Iver's. Soon after the proposal and acceptance, Reverend Halstad married Cora Jensen and Iver Lambson on October 29th, 1930, at Zion Lutheran Community Church, before a large congregation of people from both Farmington and Harveyville.

Their wedding photograph was a snapshot of not only their nuptials, but the picture served as almost a philosophical commentary on their lives and their future. The black and white photo showed the two posed seriously, standing in front of the church altar. Iver stood rigid. He wore a gray suit with wide lapels and a fancy white handkerchief protruded neatly from his left pocket. Cora stood to Iver's right, holding a bouquet of probably red roses, and his imposing form seemed to tower over her. Even though Cora was probably over three months along, she loosely filled the white wedding dress; a full-length white lace veil flowed all the way to the floor. Nels paid a large amount of money for the beautiful dress and veil; "People *WILL NOT* speak ill of me or my family," he had said emphatically. But people did talk. Cora's pregnancy was no secret to the townspeople. In fact some of the wiser folks said that Iver and Cora were far too selfish to ever build a life together, much less one which involved children. Indeed, the slight, tightly withheld smiles on both of the newlyweds' faces in the photo could almost be confused with looks of trepidation or apprehension . . . or even distrust. The connection between them was only tenuous at best and was certainly not tempered by overpowering love. In fact, on the very evening of the wedding, the two experienced their first real fight; Iver had already gotten somewhat drunk following the ceremony and after arguing violently with Cora for a few hours he left his father's house and went downtown to the Palace Bar where he drank well into the early morning.

* * *

Soon after the marriage of Iver and Cora, the severe economic circumstances of the early 1930s bore down on the small agricultural community with increasing severity. Prolonged droughts, brown clouds of dust, swarms of ravenous grasshoppers, depressed markets, and the meager farmland yields of the late 1920s spilled over persistently into the early 1930s. Not only did insufficient rainfall result in withered crops, but the desiccating winds turned the hardened topsoil of the fields into fine, powdery dirt and sand that filled drainage ditches and drifted up along fence lines and across the graveled roadways. Choking billows of grit continually filled the air, coating and penetrating everything. As rainfall decreased with each passing year in the early part of the decade, scorching heat and dry thunderstorms and unrelenting dust clouds continued to suck out the little subsoil moisture that remained in the cracked ground. After the spring plantings, when the nourishing rains normally appeared and didn't, the only thing that emerged from the gray and copper-colored storm clouds were funnel-shaped tornados that arbitrarily flattened barns and houses and swept away valuable livestock and farm implements, further sustaining people's miseries. Headless durham or rusted soybeans or mustard thistle seemed to be the only things that sprouted forth from the fields. Driven by the dryness, swarms of dun-colored, bug-eyed locusts devoured almost every plant and crop in the town, if not a large portion of Neilson County and indeed the state of North Dakota. Before going out to harvest what little crops there were, the farmhands bound up the ankles of their coveralls and the wrists and necks of their shirts, and pulled up red or blue bandanas over their mouths for protection against the hordes of insects, which snapped and jumped relentlessly before them as the workers ambled along the desolately dry earth. And what the hoppers didn't get, the gophers did, with the rabbits getting any meager leftovers.

The idleness and stagnation that resulted from the drought and depression of the 1930s not only settled upon much of the nation, but also had an equally terrible effect on the Midwest, on North Dakota, and on Farmington alike; wave upon wave of pestilence and economic downturn evoked almost a sense of hopelessness in the people of the town. Some called the times "the dry years," while others more succinctly dubbed the era "the dirty thirties"—everyone seemed to have a name for those desperate times.

Under these declining conditions Iver and Cora started out their life together and tried to maintain as best as possible. At first they lived in one of the small houses that Nels had built on his farm for the transitory harvest farmhands. However, Nels, long frustrated with his own failed crops and hard times, continually interfered with his son and daughter-in-law's life, constantly telling them what they should and should not do. Inga had little to say to her new daughter-in-law; in fact, she had very little to say to anyone. She seemed to withdraw into herself as a defense against her husband and the outside world. Clara and Adell were as obvious as ever in their adoration of Iver, but to Cora they only gave dirty looks and mean stares. The declining economic conditions had forestalled the sisters' marriage plans, so Cora became the focus of the two's matronly frustrations.

The birth of Cora and Iver's first child, Dewey, in late April of 1931, exacerbated the couple's economic powerlessness, but nothing the young couple did could change their circumstances. To divorce would bring scorn upon them and their families, as well as leave them more economically destitute than they already were.

The severe depression that had settled over the country, the state, the county, and the town left many people, including Iver, with little or no work. Too proud to become a panhandler, and lacking the confidence to successfully become a peddler, he oftentimes found himself with nothing to do but to spend the long, non-productive afternoons at the Farmington Mercantile, his dirty boots propped on the slatted cracker barrels of apples or brown and white eggs that the manager Elmer Hollingsworth sold or bartered. Iver felt listlessly comfortable nestled in amongst the open wooden crates that sat atop the long, rough lumber tables. The splintery boxes, which smelled strongly of pine, held sugar and coffee, smoked hams and salty bacon, dried fruit, cans of Dutch Maiden baking soda, and boxes of oatmeal and Cream 'O Wheat. Several crocks of yellow-white butter and boxes of fresh produce set in front of the tables, and nails, hardware, used tools, dry goods, notions, and cut glassware randomly filled the shelves behind. Iver would make small talk with the browsing customers, or if so inclined would slowly, aimlessly wander down the dusty sidewalks, stopping occasionally to hail a fellow down-and-outer whose dull-black, weather-beaten Ford pickup stood parked diagonally on the main street, his two-tone, tan-and-white left arm hanging out the window, his cracked fingers holding a smoking, nearly gone Chesterfield cigarette. Iver would lean against the doorjamb and put his foot up on the dusty running board. The discussion would always be uncomplicated conversation about nothing . . . everything . . . cursing the weather and the "gol darn" Republicans and generally their lots in life. If he could mooch a bit of change from Edith or filch a dollar of county relief money out of Cora's purse, Iver would spend his evenings idling downtown at the Palace, drinking down the long hours while Cora stayed at home, pregnant once again and resigned to the task of caring for Dewey. Sometimes she would join him, but not often, a fact which certainly contributed to the stagnation of their relationship, at least in Iver's view.

In the latter half of 1932, after the April birth of Duane, Iver and Cora's second child, the effects of various forms of public relief began to trickle down to the "grassroots level" of Neilson County and Farmington in the form of federal relief programs. Under the auspices of the United States Congress, the Neilson County Commissioners appointed a committee of local citizens to set up relief projects and implement emergency projects mandated and funded by the federal government. The committee saw to it that food surpluses were distributed to the hungry and poor, which certainly included Cora and Iver. Additionally, Mr. Hyram Welty, the Neilson County Social Services Officer and one of the original members from the County Welfare Board, found odd jobs for Iver. In 1933, Hyram also located a small house for them and the young family finally separated itself from the oppressive dominance of Nels. The house, located on one of the side streets on the north side of the town, was very poorly built and cold in the winter. But times were tough for everyone and no one complained. Though small and simply furnished, the house provided the couple with their first real "home." Finally away from the relentless criticism and scorn of Nels and his daughters, Cora kept the place neat and homey and comfortable and the couple appeared, at least initially, to be getting along reasonably well.

All throughout these desperate drought years Iver worked on WPA projects. In the later part of 1933, the Works Progress Administration took the place of the Federal Emergency Relief Act of the previous year and finally provided work for the many men languishing in the area. For $35 a month, Iver kept busy working on local roads, digging water bypass canals, and constructing outdoor toilets for public facilities. Iver seemed reasonably satisfied; as long as he worked and sweated in the outdoors he appeared somewhat happy. However, even though Dewey's birth had been somewhat joyous for the couple, when Duane arrived, the money that sustained the family became even scarcer. Iver's demeanor changed as well in those years; he seldom spoke with Cora and found more reasons to stay away from the cold house every evening, especially after she tersely informed him that she was pregnant with their third child, on the day of their third anniversary–October 29th, 1933. Iver reacted with little excitement when Cora told him the news and he withdrew more into himself down at the Palace.

But then Iver's circumstances improved drastically. During the exceptionally dry growing year of 1934, when nothing was productive except the multitudes of ground squirrels, gophers, and rabbits that overran the dry fields, the people in Farmington, as well as other surrounding communities, could not meet their debts; farm foreclosures were rampant and numerous businesses closed down. An abundance of auction announcements filled the pages of the *Farmington Review*, advertising rusting hay mowers and reapers and manure spreaders and tractors and grain conveyors that stood silently immersed in the high weeds of the doomed farmyards. Though the State of North Dakota had imposed a farm foreclosure moratorium in early 1933, the legislation failed to save a good number of farmsteads. Many families were still left destitute by the declining crop yield and the plummeting farm product prices. Driven by the desperate times, a number of the townspeople, especially the younger fellows, moved off to the bigger cities, along the west coast, where the ship building industry had begun hiring quite a number of people.

Nels Lambson became one of these exiles when he found he could not sustain his farming or his horse training endeavors. Not only could he no longer raise viable crops, the resulting loss of pasture hay required him to wholesale all of his livestock, which the packing house representatives purchased at ridiculously low prices. Moreover, the loss of livestock meant that there were no horses to be broken . . . most were being sold to out-of-state buyers. And this final blow proved to be almost too much for Nels. In frustration, almost in tears, he left his beloved farm and family to go to work at the Henry J. Kaiser Shipbuilding yards, south of Portland, Oregon, where several people he knew had already been put to work because of their farm machinery experience. He himself had been broken by the very circumstances that had given him his unbridled spirit.

Nels' departure gave Iver the chance he needed to finally make his break. One spring evening, after meeting and drinking long with some Montana horse buyers at the Palace, Iver came home and announced to Cora that he had decided to travel to Miles City to break horses for three dollars a head. The two fellows had hired him already and he would be making over a hundred dollars a month. Cora, weighty and almost ready to deliver the third Lambson child, had little argument with which to dissuade her husband; she just sat down heavily at the kitchen table, knees apart, mouth half opened in bewilderment, and stared at Iver while he explained in detail his wild plans to her. In his excitement, Iver gestured often, emphatically, in order to elaborate the main points of his argument. Cora saw the desperation in his dark face and fierce blue eyes and could only relent.

"It'll be great, Cora, honey! I'll only be gone for six months and then I'll be home for winter." For a few moments he put his face close to Cora's, almost pleading with her. "Makin' them WPA shitters is killing me. I'm suffocating." Cora sighed slightly and he knew he had her. "Besides, we'll have plenty of money when I get back."

Cora was overwhelmed and essentially beaten; the next morning, when the two Montana horse ranchers came by in their black Ford pickup to get Iver, she stood large with child on the front porch, loosely holding the hands of her other two young children. The three began weakly waving goodbye, none fully understanding what would happen next. Without looking back, Iver threw his duffle sack into the bed of the truck, jumped joyfully into the cab, and the three sped off down Dakota Street and on out of town.

* * *

In the middle of a late-June dry thunderstorm, when billows of sterile, dark gray clouds yielded only sparse sprinkles of rain, when fingers of dry lightening streaked vertically across the sky and thunder buffeted the town, and when townspeople almost in unison looked to the southwestern sky, scanning it for funnel clouds, Lloyd was born. Because none of the Lambson women gave any indication of wanting to help, Marian Wills came over from Harveyville to assist Cora for a month. She did what she could for her poor step-daughter and her children, but she was quickly overwhelmed with hopelessness and guilt as she became more and more involved in the Lambson's circumstances. For the most part, however, the situation remained well beyond her comprehension and she could not wait to leave the despair.

During Mother Wills' stay there, Cora wrote a long letter to her husband, telling him of her love and longing for him, and even enclosed in the envelope a small black-and-white photo of his new son, whom she had unilaterally named Lloyd, after one of her own brothers that she had never known. But several months went by before she got a return letter, which contained no money . . . only a brief, superficial note in which Iver described his day-to-day life on the ranch in the eastern part of Montana. He wrote as if addressing a casual friend and the tone of his words most assuredly indicated that more might be separating them than the distance of mere miles.

Iver did return the following fall of 1935 to see his newest son Lloyd, who was already almost a year-and-a-half old. He was happy to see his children, but they retreated from him as though he was a frightening newcomer; all during his visit, they kept a good deal of space between themselves and their tall stranger of a father. He and Cora thoroughly enjoyed seeing and being with each other, probably more so than at any other time of their relationship. The happy couple had a good time drinking down at the Palace Bar every night and one might say they got along better than they ever had in their marriage. Money seemed to be plentiful and Iver even bought new shoes for all of the children, and a new dress for Cora, from his earnings. Then after a few brief months, and just before the first hard storm of winter, Iver left as suddenly as he had come. Cora missed her husband badly and cursed her children for being born. If it wasn't for them, she could have gone back to Montana with her virile, loving husband. Several times she thought about just dumping the kids off at the Wills' farm and following Iver out west. However, these plans were abandoned when, ironically, a short time following Iver's departure, Cora found out that she was pregnant with her fourth child.

Happily, yet with much apprehension, she wrote to Iver in Montana to share the news with him. His response again took several weeks to arrive and when the long awaited return letter finally did appear, she tore it open hesitantly; her lips moved as she read, sounding out the words silently as her eyes passed along the message. After she finished reading, her hand, still holding the letter tightly, dropped down to her side in sadness and disappointment . . . even trepidation. Iver's terse note did not quite mirror his wife's expectations. He essentially blamed Cora for the pregnancy and castigated her for her lack of foresight. How, he asked pointedly, could she expect them to ever have enough money to do anything but subsist if she kept continually having kids? With the use of many exclamation marks, he asked if she knew how hard it was for him to work and to go without in order to save money for the family. He also added that because work had slowed at the horse ranch, he did not know how much money he would be able to send her in the future. He closed by telling her that she would have to somehow get by herself, as best she could.

During the time he had been gone, Iver sent Cora small amounts of money at irregular intervals. Sometimes twenty dollars, sometimes thirty. One Christmas he had sent a crisp fifty-dollar bill. With this money, along with the public subsistence from Neilson County and the small monetary gifts from Mother Wills, Cora could barely maintain the family, especially after the birth of Leeland in May of 1936. But when Iver became stingier with his earnings, supporting herself and her four children became almost impossible. In fact, her husband did not come home in 1936 or 1937, even though their fourth son had never seen his father. Even worse, he stopped sending money to her all together. Cora eventually found that she could no longer take life as it came. Desperate, she decided to take her destiny into her own hands and find a job.

Cora was fortunate in this sense because a financial recovery had begun in the late 1930s, an economic rebirth that drew a number of new entrepreneurs to Farmington. In late 1937 the Ideal Restaurant re-opened under the proprietorship of Jim (Red) Elgin. Red had seen the restaurant advertised in the *Minneapolis Tribune* and needing to leave the Twin Cities in a hurry he gathered all of the cash that he could, traveled by train to Farmington, and bought the business from the Farmers Commercial Bank. Norman Phillips, the portly bank manager, welcomed the new investment and the opportunity to get the restaurant off of the default ledger.

However, because Red could be considered somewhat of a "foreigner," most of the townspeople seemed at first to be resistant to him. Rumor had it that Red had made quite a bit of money on slightly shady business dealings in Minneapolis in 1934 and 1935 and that he had moved west to avoid either the law or perhaps the anger and revenge of cheated clients. Someone else started the rumor that he had been heavily involved in bootlegging and then other various crime-related activities in Minneapolis before his near arrest drove him westward. Though the accusation never proved to be more than speculation, many in the town chose to affirm it.

But he brought new investment capital to a struggling town, so few people pursued finding out the truth. Red reopened the Ideal Café in its old location, which was in the Halverson Building on the east side of town. Sandwiched between the New Farmington Hotel and Louie Anderson's Barbershop, the location of the Ideal made the establishment easily accessible to all who might want a decent meal. Red remained ever ambitious and enthusiastic . . . a visionary, some would say of him when they saw him on the street . . . for he recognized the true potential of the town. A short and stocky man, with tufts of red hair emerging from below his slightly tilted Panama hat, which he often used as a fan, he ambled resolutely down to the Ideal every day, greeting people pleasantly as he went. The wide straw brim of his hat, and the long-sleeved white linen shirts he wore, protected his pallid and freckled skin from the sun.

When Cora read Red's help-wanted advertisement in the *Farmington Review,* she walked right down to the Ideal, her hand wrapped around the paper, and told him of her desperate situation and how she needed work. Red liked Cora immediately and gave her a job waitressing and cooking at his new restaurant, starting the very next day. Cora's small house lay just a few blocks from the Ideal—certainly a short walking distance—and that was one of the reasons she applied for and accepted the job. Because she needed to work many hours throughout the week, she had to leave her older children alone with the new baby. But that arrangement never really bothered her much. Given the hard nature of the world, she reasoned that she needed to force her sons to grow up quickly and face life's uncertainties as little men.

With what Red paid her, and what she got from the county, Cora managed to get by. Because of her cooking skills, Red started her out in the kitchen. She made the soup-of-the-day and lemon meringue pies and with the palms of her narrow, white hands pressed raw hamburger into flat patties and then tenderly placed the patties between sheets of wax paper for cooking during the day. Red even admired the way she kept the dining area spotless. Late in the evening, when all of the customers had eaten and left, she diligently washed the white and green checkerboard linoleum flooring with a gray and stringy mop until the floors shone. Red would sometimes watch intently her hips and arms sway with the

swabbing motions. During the day, when she wasn't cooking and sweating at the hot grille, she would be out taking
orders from the townspeople who, sitting at the several
wooden tables that looked out the dusty window onto the
main street, sipped the hot coffee from the cups that they
held close to their lips with both hands. Red, because he
liked Cora so much, allowed her to keep the meager tips that
were left by the few customers. She relied mainly on these
tips for anything extra that she wanted. Some evenings, after
closing, the two would sit together in the quiet darkness of
the restaurant and drink sloe gin, laughing at the townspeople and the events of the day.

Red put much effort into restoring the eatery, but in
the end the Ideal could not compete with Stan's Café just
down the street, which served the best fried chicken, mashed
potatoes, corn, green beans, ice cream and pie for seventy-
five cents on Sunday afternoons. When business slowed to
almost nothing, Red wisely decided to convert the fledgling
café to the Ideal Bar and Grill, with on- and off-sale liquor—
an idea he brought with him from St. Paul. The Old Palace
Bar and Laddie's Tavern stood as his only competitors, but
neither served food and as such proved to be no competition for Red's innovative business. In fact, of the several
restaurants and bars in Farmington, the Ideal proved quite
successful in meeting both the appetites *and* the thirsts of
the locals, for the bar and grille provided a place where the
townspeople could gather and talk and eat, and where they
could imbibe as well.

He hired another waitress and made Cora a bargirl, so her
tips became much better. The customers, who were mostly
male, very much enjoyed Cora because she would not only

serve them, she would drink and laugh lustily right along with them. Often she would even stay and talk with them long after closing time. Red would lower the lights and lock the door so as not to raise the suspicions of Sheriff Wilt, and then continue to sell booze to his "better" customers. Many nights, after working very hard, Cora would stagger home at three or four o'clock in the morning and sleep most of the next day. Cora's new position often required her to be gone in the evenings and on the weekends, thus forcing her to leave her children alone for even longer stretches of time. This was all right, she reasoned. Her children needed to learn very early to be conscientious and to take care of themselves and each other.

The economic recovery of the area was still only in its infant stages and Red's business seemed to always be operating on a week-to-week basis. At least that is what he told Cora when she inquired about a raise in her pay. However, Red did suggest that he reward Cora for her conscientious dedication to the Ideal in a different way. For her diligence he gave her a discount on the rent of a house he had acquired . . . the old Sheppard homestead that he had recently bought on a contract for deed and refurbished as a rental property. So one warm day in the middle of June of 1938, with the help of several loyal customers of the Ideal, Red moved Cora and her family into the house. The boys and their mother were ecstatic with the spaciousness of their new quarters. And because of the distance now involved in Cora getting to and returning from work, Red would often pick her up and bring her back home.

Cora's relationship to Red immediately became suspect and thus the topic of a good deal of hushed speculation by the people of Farmington. Cora was still young and pretty in her plain sort of way. In contrast, Red was older and much of his wavy, reddish hair, which at one time had a part down the center, had receded to the sides and back of his head. To compensate for his hair loss he grew a large handlebar mustache, which made his plump face seem even rounder. Because of his large paunch and the squatness of his body, he needed to wear suspenders to hold up his pants. In the wintertime he would constantly wear button-up sweaters, of which the lowest two buttons could never be fastened. And he always seemed to look different from the other citizens of Farmington. Even though Red was a fairly successful and capable businessman, he never really did overcome the sense of being an outsider. In fact, though they willingly consumed a good deal of his food and drink, many of the upstanding townspeople never really trusted Red. They always thought the worst of him and often suspected he might be up to something but couldn't really ever prove it. And because they could not affirm anything, and because he maintained the aura of the flamboyant businessman, the local gossips just tolerated him, biding their time until his actions should betray him and they could pounce.

Cora's boys, however, were more accepting of him. Red ever remained rather like a grandfather figure to the boys. He would, after all, bring them candy when he came to visit. Sitting up amongst the limbs of the huge cottonwood that gave them great pleasure, they would eat the sweets leisurely in the front yard . . . slowly unwrapping the delicacies, savoring the delicious taste quietly while Red went in to talk with their mother for an hour or two. The boys were always pleased to see his Buick coming up the road. As seemingly ingenuous as Red's intentions were, though, the closeness of Cora and Red's relationship provoked a good deal of conjecture around the small town.

Of greater consequence, though, was the fact that Cora and Red's friendship caused Iver a great deal of concern when he returned home unexpectedly from Montana in late October of 1938. Iver arrived in Farmington just a few hours in front of an unusually wicked snowstorm and happily admitted that the quaint farm house provided a warm and cozy shelter. The reason he gave to his stunned wife for his abrupt return was that he wanted to celebrate their eighth anniversary. After settling in he found the home to be a great windfall and he even thought about moving back to his family once again . . . giving up the cowboy life in Montana that he so loved. Though initially skeptical, Cora quickly expressed her approval of that plan. And Iver was much taken by how his children had grown during his absence. However, he spent little time with them. When Cora left the house and children to go to work, he would follow along beside her as she walked out to Highway 2 to wait for Red's Buick. He would do little jig steps and other funny things to try to make her laugh, which she did. In fact, he wound up spending most of his time down at the Ideal, trying to rekindle his romance with Cora. But there and then he realized how close the relationship between Red and Cora had become . . . how interdependent they were on each other. Added to this was the fact that Red had so frequently in the past visited Cora when she was not working . . . bringing by treats or provisions, or finding things around the house that needed to be fixed. The conflict between the three adults became full blown one evening in mid-November, when Iver, exceedingly drunk, caught Red and Cora talking closely in the back room of the Ideal. Accusing them of adultery, he punched Red deliberately in the face and stood over him for several minutes, daring him to be a man and get up and fight. All Red could do was raise himself up on his right elbow, cup his bleeding nose, and decline the challenge. Still engulfed in rage, Iver trudged back home, packed his few belongings, and set out once again for Montana, just in front of the year's second big snowfall.

Red's nose had been broken and so stayed swollen between his equally black eyes for several days. The local gossip became thick after the incident, so he distanced himself from Cora. Eventually Red folded under the surreptitious, yet relentless censure by the townspeople; the following July he sold the Ideal Bar and Grill to Bill Bailey, a businessman from Jamestown, and drove his Buick back to the Minneapolis/ St. Paul area where he eventually died of a heart attack, someone later reported.

Cora especially missed Red's support and generosity when her and Iver's fifth child, Darrell, was born in early August of 1939. Speculation around Farmington became rampant when Doc Christianson reported that the infant had carrot-red hair and a pale complexion. The revelation caused quite a stir with the men of the town and became the subject of many coarse jokes and crude comments. Then in September she sent her husband a long, sorrowful letter, telling him about the difficult birth of his fifth son Darrell and how unmanageable the four other children had become, detailing for him the dire straits of the family, pleading with him for help and financial support of any sort that he could manage.

But a month later her letter came back to her, returned as "undeliverable." Seems that Iver had become discontent with the horse trading profession and, like his father before him, had gone off to the West Coast to seek employment in the booming shipbuilding industry. But wanting to avoid the possibility of perhaps having to face Nels again, Iver wisely went further north to the Bremerton Shipyards in Seattle.

Chapter Three— Lost Ways

Strange how one cannot describe, and thus understand, any particular collection of people without first considering their means and methods of nourishing and protecting themselves, and that being done, how the group cares for and about those on the periphery. This same principle holds true when one attempts to comprehend the Lambson boys' perpetual state of privation and neglect.

Harsh circumstances very often prove to be binding forces. At least that seemed to be the prevailing philosophy of the rugged peoples that inhabited the plains states—a locale that would frequently and quite easily prove desolate and inhospitable. And time and again, the severe and unforgiving environment of the region tended to drive the people of the Dakota flatlands together . . . perhaps making them ever aware of the tenuousness of their very existence and providing them with a keen sense of their own need for each other. Along with food and sustenance, the need for reliable shelter and warm, dry, safe surroundings seemed always to be common, primary requisites for the folks existing there. Especially in the frigid depths of winter, lack of any of these essential elements quite frequently meant almost certain death.

The persistent quest for these basic necessities became particularly acute for the folks of Farmington because winters seemed to come ever earlier and with ever more intensity. For the many decades of the town's history and collective memory, August and September and sometimes even October provided the warmth of the day and the gentle evening that infused people's very souls, making them happy to be alive, even in the most difficult of times. But the end of the drought of the early and mid-1930's somehow also meant the end of the long Indian Summers, those serene times that often occurred even before the end of the town's harvest celebrations. Starting with the years of 1935 and 1936, winters bore down with increasing ferocity on the residents of Farmington without even giving autumn a chance to broadcast its beauty. In late September, chill strong winds from the north would bear down on the town, a harbinger of the bitter cold that was to come too soon, and once in a while there would even be a premature, early-October ice storm that would catch the townsfolk totally unprepared.

Through innate survival instincts, or perhaps intuition or communal conditioning, the wives of the town would be the first to sense the need to start preparing for the inevitability of winter. Almost collectively they would begin dragging out and repairing heavy winter clothes and commence canning the fruits and vegetables that were to sustain the families until the spring time. Mason jars lined the wooden shelves in all the mildew-smelling cellars and basements of the town and the outlying farms. The children would put away the carefree joys of summer and take more seriously the chores and jobs assigned to them. Condemned to school, they slowly made the daily back and forth trek to the large brick schoolhouse located on the western outskirts of town. Farmers, even before the crop yields had been fully calculated, would hasten to get the winter wheat crop planted before the first hard freeze turned the ground to concrete. Yielding to some primeval force, almost in unison, farmers would begin to shut down their farms to the approaching frigid temperatures and barren months of winter. The townspeople could almost visualize the huge drifts of snow that would inevitably cover the land . . . could almost feel the sub-arctic air of Alberta Clippers freezing their eyelashes and whiskers and nose hairs and upper ear tips, smarting their eyes until they watered with frozen tears. Thinking about the cold future would send a shudder down one's shoulders, arms, and body and stir phantom needles of pain in once frostbitten fingers and toes. The goal of each winter was to persevere . . . that is, remain healthy and well fed inside one's own established order . . . only leaving those warm, safe confines to "bundle up" and trudge out to the barn through the frozen tundra in order to milk the cows and tend to the livestock. If a blizzard suddenly came about, turning the outside world an infinite solid snow-white, one always had the lifeline of cord rope running from the barn to the house . . . a trusted umbilical cord that assured a safe return to the warm womb of the home. Such were the pursuits that preoccupied the people of Farmington, year after year, during late fall and winter and even into spring.

For the Lambson brothers, the precious essentials of food and warmth and shelter also became a primary fixation during that foreboding time of year; those crucial elements were vital for the survival of these youngsters, as well, only always with a much greater degree of urgency. Whenever fall started to bring with it the first hint of the approaching frigid cold, fire and food and security grew scarcer in the

Lambson home; the search for these essentials thus became a dominating part of their troubled existence. Indeed, the boys seemed to be acutely aware of the need for all three elements because, with the birth of Darrell in August of 1939, their numbers had grown to five.

Their obsession became particularly pronounced in the autumn of 1941, when their mother left them for an extended period of time. One late afternoon in mid-October, on a gray and chilly pre-winter kind of day, Cora came home and told the boys that she planned to be gone for a while, probably only for a week or two. She had met Harold Wilcox, a skinny, well-dressed, cocky-confident implement salesman from Bismarck, and was going to interview for a secretary's job with his company—The Mobility Tractor Company—in the capital city. Cheerfully she explained to them, as she hastily looked around for her travel case, that if she got the job, which fast-talking Harold said was almost certain, they could all move to Bismarck where they would have a new father and a nice, big home.

The boys were older then: Dewey was ten-and-a-half, Duane was nine, Lloyd was seven, Leeland was five, and Darrell was two. They certainly should be able to look out for each other and take care of themselves, their mother told them. "You boys be good, now, you hear? Don't spoil this for me . . . . It's my one big opportunity." She moved hurriedly around the house, trying to determine quickly what she needed to take with her. She entered the bedroom and pulled a tattered brown suitcase from under the bed. The boys all followed closely behind her, not fully comprehending what was going on. Dewey, however, clearly understood and quickly began to grow more apprehensive. "Dewey is in charge, so you all mind him and do what he says," were her hurried instructions. The young boy, with the mantle of responsibility again thrust upon him, felt a large, apricot-sized pit of fear and anxiety lodge once more in his stomach.

Their mother had already been drinking a little when she came home; her drummer/sponsor—Hal, she called him affectionately—had parked in his dark green Chevy roadster just beyond the yard. She staggered several times as she packed; in her haste she spent no time in folding the clothes . . . just threw them into her suitcase. Outside Hal blew the Chevy's sharp horn several times rapidly, and then revved the engine loudly, in order to prod her along. "Don't any of ya dare go outside, ya hear! Stay right in here! I don't want Hal to see ya!" she warned them.

After a few moments, Duane stepped forward and put his hand on his mother's hip. "Don't go, Ma." A high, almost imploring pitch accompanied his voice, a tone that none of his brothers recognized, and this rather frightened them.

"Yeah, don't go, Ma. Don't leave us no more," Lloyd and Leeland chimed in, moving closer to her and starting to snivel. Dewey hung back by Darrell, though, half anticipating his mother's reaction.

Almost instantaneously she whirled around toward them, bending forward at the waist and pointing a severely rigid finger of warning directly into their faces: "You don't give me no sass! You jus' do what I say!" She remained silent for a few moments, and then added emphatically, "An remember, if you get inta any trouble, the big Indian fella that lives down the road will come and scalp your little butts. Cut yur ears off, too, he will!"

The brothers had only seen the large, somber Indian drive by, way off in the distance, in his old '27 Ford Tin Lizzy, hunched over the steering wheel, heading back from town to his shanty home a mile further on past their house. They would frighten each other late at night, conjuring up stories of how the Indian would sneak into the house and cut their throats. Sometimes, when they were all alone in the late afternoon, the brothers would hide from his imagined, ugly, threatening visage. When they had buried themselves in the itchy piles of moldering straw strewn about the empty barn, Dewey would make low, guttural noises to further scare the heck out of them. Cora often used the "big Indian" threat effectively to intimidate her young sons, or whenever she needed their cooperation or respect; and because of the boys' vivid imagination, the potency of that warning never diminished. Given their mother's pleas, and her ominous admonition regarding their neighbor, the boys silently agreed to mind her, behave themselves, and obey Dewey. "Yessum," they acquiesced in small voices, their chins touching their chests so as to hide any watery eyes from her.

The five all followed silently, woefully, behind her as she moved briskly from room to room. "If you run outta food before I get back, go into town and tell the sheriff that he needs ta call yur grandma and grandpa Wills over in Harveyville. Tell them they have ta come down and get ya and take care of ya 'til I get home. If he won't do it, hitchhike on over to their place. Grandma Marian won't turn you away." As an afterthought she added, "But don't you DARE go near Grandma Lambson or any of them others. They don't want you near 'em and neither do I!"

Dewey figured out that they could only survive for a few days before they would have to go to their grandparents' home, but that didn't concern him. They were very adept at foraging. But the sense of emptiness he felt was what bothered him the most . . . what made him the saddest and the angriest. At that moment he hated his mother more than he ever had; however, he knew he could not let his face or his actions reveal his feelings to his siblings. Allowing them to be fearful would certainly not help his situation, he reasoned silently. In order for them all to survive, he needed their subservience and cooperation. They all needed to be tough.

Cora finally scraped some cosmetics into the stuffed brown case, cinched the metal hasps in place, looked around the room once more, and then called all of her children to her. She kissed each one tenderly, affectionately, and told them individually how much she loved them; having done her motherly duties, she happily exited the cold house, ecstatic about all of the possibilities and the potentials . . . the excitement and thrills . . . of the new life she was embarking upon. Slamming the screen door with its corner of wire mesh flapping, Cora almost skipped like a young girl to the waiting car, smiling and waving childishly at Harold. Looking furtively out of the front window, kneeling closely together, peering out head-to-head, their eyes all just above the bottom sill, the brothers watched the young man roughly embrace their mother as she bounced into the front seat. After the two shared a drink from a thin, brown flask, the gentleman friend put his arm around her and stepped down hard on the accelerator; the Chevy fishtailed down the road, throwing gravel and a plume of dust from the rear wheels as it headed toward far off Bismarck. Though Cora did not even look back to see them, the boys began to wave weakly from inside the house until she and her new friend and the car had disappeared down the narrow ribbon of dirt road that connected the farm to the highway and the world. As it turned out, their mother would not return for nearly a month.

In the first several days that she was gone, the boys ate well. In fact, they consumed every speck of food in the kitchen. And in their glutted and happy state, they decided they were actually having too much fun to go to their grandparents' house. They were, after all, survivors.

The lingering months of autumn had already started to bear the first harsh hints of the terrible winter cold that would soon arrive. Each day the sun rose and melted away the thin layer of white frost that had formed overnight on the shingled roof of the farmhouse. Because the mornings started off so very cold, whoever got up first would stir up the ashes and heavily stoke the fire in the large, blackened pot-bellied stove in the front room. Luckily Cora had ordered in, and even paid cash for, a load of wood and coal. Because of such a surplus of fuels, the boys constantly fed the fire, keeping the house stuffy warm, even with the front door almost continuously left open throughout the day. Always glowing almost cherry red hot, the stove seemed to symbolize their collective obsession with fire; indeed, their daily activities constantly took place in close proximity to that round, ever-reliable source of heat and security.

The days without their mother, and without any other human contact, were long and the youngsters became creative in the ways they found to amuse themselves. They had never attended school for any extended period of time and as a result their collective quest for knowledge, as well as their spirit of discovery, often operated at an extremely high level. And given their young curiosities, they needed much to occupy themselves. At first they were able to pretend they were driving cars and trucks by using empty cardboard matchboxes and tubular oatmeal containers and aspirin tins on the kitchen and living room floor. This led to the creation of a sprawling imaginary town in the two rooms. To recreate roads for their pretend city, the boys hauled in the powdery dirt from beneath the cottonwood tree in the front yard and carefully poured it into streets that led between the cardboard houses they had built. In their curiosity, they would hold twigs to the side of the stove, watching the ends smolder and burst into small flames, and then blow them out and do it all over again for hours. Sometimes they would pretend that the matchbox cars were in accidents and would light them on fire. Or they would torch the cardboard houses, pretending there were people trapped inside before stomping out the black cinder ashes.

But soon even that became boring and the brothers began to stare at each other. "I dare you to touch the stove!" Dewey finally said to Lloyd one afternoon.

Without questioning the challenge, Lloyd slowly walked up, licked the tip of his index finger, and then placed it against the red, shimmering surface. Almost immediately he let out a yelping scream, jerked his hand away, and held the injury between his knees.

"Gawd-damn," Lloyd screamed loudly as he stuck the wounded finger into his mouth up to the first knuckle. "That sumbitch's hot!"

Dewey began laughing at his brother's stupid bravery. "Whata idiot," he said, doubling up in laugher.

Almost immediately Lloyd was upon him, his arms and tightly fisted hands flailing, the blows falling ineffectively on Dewey's balled-up, laughing body. "Oh, stop! Stop! Yur killing me!" Dewey said, all of the while laughing harder, pushing and kicking Lloyd away.

Finally, when he had had enough, he put his foot into Lloyd's stomach and kicked him hard, propelling him almost half way across the room. Lloyd flew backwards out of control and in the process the back of his arm glanced across the hot stove. In that instant he screamed loudly, mostly out of surprise, but when he landed he grasped the three-inch by two-inch area of bright amber, seared flesh. Rolling on to his side, he assumed the fetal position and began moaning and crying softly, then commenced bawling more loudly, with real tears tracing down his dirty cheeks.

"See what happens when you mess around!" Dewey scolded his brother. Immediately he went to the kitchen sink, found a dirty rag, wetted it by pumping the creaking pump handle, and then applied it to Lloyd's wound. "Stop yur whinin' . . . . You'll be all right!"

The four brothers gathered around the wounded one; after a brief caucus and after everyone had somewhat given input, Dewey decided that the injury was not serious enough to warrant a trip into town to the doctor's office, which would certainly end their freedom. Instead, he wisely thought about how to redirect their collective energies into other activities.

As they sat around the kitchen, silently reflecting on what to do next, Dewey watched his siblings. The brothers seemed to get along well and work toward their common good. All of the boys had similar facial and physical features, except Darrell, who had sky-blue eyes, soft amber, almost reddish hair, and a dead front tooth that had turned brown. His freckled complexion set him off even more from his brothers. More than once Dewey had sat on Darrell's chest out in the front yard, almost to the point where the child would gasp frantically for breath. Taking handfuls of loose dirt, Dewey rubbed them vigorously into the screaming boy's scalp and his freckled face. Dewey claimed he was going to make the youngest brother a true Lambson, one way or another. "I'll get the 'Red' outcha, one way or t'other!" he would scream at his youngest brother, as though the child possessed some infectious evil. When Dewey finally released him, Darrell would get up panting and sniveling uncontrollably; Dewey, feeling immense guilt, would go over and put his arms around the young child to comfort him. For the most part Darrell only stood back passively and watched his older brothers, usually with an empty baby bottle hanging from his mouth, a perpetual pacifier keeping him quiet. Sometimes in the evenings, when the brothers were sitting around the stove, Darrell would hesitantly come over and sit in the oldest brother's lap, smiling up at him. On such occasions Dewey would once again be reminded of, and thus overwhelmed by, his familial responsibilities.

A short time after the burned arm incident, Dewey was struck with a new way for them to entertain themselves. "You guys remember the movie we seen a while ago?" He was referring to *Kit Carson*, the movie shown at the Dakota Theater the previous week. They had hitchhiked into town and then snuck into the show. So as not to be seen by the usher, the five waifs, hunching over, crept down along the darkened side aisle to the front row. By keeping little

Darrell between them, Dewey hoped to silence him immediately if he made any baby noises; however, Darrell seldom made any attempts at verbal communication. Jaws collectively agape, the brothers watched up in amazement as Kit Carson led a brave band of frontiersman in a wagon train across the western states towards California. Marauding Indians attacked the wagons, riding their horses in furious circles, setting the white canvas of the wagons afire with flaming arrows. But before the brothers had seen the entire presentation, just after the shooting and burning had begun in earnest, the usher caught them. Several wagons were aflame on the wide screen and the frontiersmen were on the losing end of the battle as the attendant roughly ushered the boys from the theater, pushing and prodding them along whenever they hesitated. Jerked abruptly from the fantasy they had been delighting in, shoved rudely out into the alley behind the theater, immersed back in the bright afternoon sunlight, their eyes blinking, the boys were once again plunged back into their own reality. Dewey immediately decided their unjust treatment certainly called for immediate revenge, so they crept around to the side of the building; he took several ladyfinger firecrackers from his pocket, carefully placed them in a slightly opened window, and lit them. As the fuses sparked and sizzled, the brothers took off running and gathered momentum as they came around the rear of the building and down the alleyway. The Red Devil Blockbuster fireworks, being old and thus more powerful than the boys expected, blew out several windows in the theater and stopped the showing of the film. Luckily the back streets were nearly deserted and no one saw their escape, so they laughed heartily as they headed towards home.

The thrill of that prior afternoon at the movies, with the vision of ol' Kit Carson standing bravely before the flames, still burned in Dewey's memory. "Let's play cowboys and Indians," he announced and the others joined him excitedly. Lloyd almost all but forgot the injury to his arm.

Outside the air had become deathly cold and a harsh, bitter wind blew billowing black clouds in from the north. Without putting on their heavy coats, they moved quickly to cut branches for rifles, and limbs for bows and arrows, from the ancient cottonwood tree and the poplar trees beside it. The boys ran back inside the house, with the tongues of their broken down, unlaced, ill-fitting shoes flapping. As they warmed themselves by the stove, they chose up sides for the coming battle: Dewey and Lloyd became the cowboys and Duane and Leeland became the "dirty redskins." Darrell just stood back by the kitchen door and watched, the empty baby bottle hanging from his mouth, the nipple gripped tightly between his baby teeth. The cowboys turned the ragged brown davenport around for their fort, which they defended mightily against the fearsome, relentless attacks. Tying string to the ends of their green branch bows, Duane and Leeland were able to launch numerous shafts at the defenders. The fort proved to be impervious to the assault, so Duane decided to reach a new degree of realism. He tied dry mop strings to the tips of his and Leeland's arrows and then lit them on the stove before launching them. Most fell harmlessly to the floor and went out. However, one particularly well-aimed shaft flew past Lloyd's head and landed in the dingy chiffon curtains, which ignited instantly. Sparks and wispy ashes rained down on the two defenders inside the fort until they finally jumped up, pulled the curtains down from the rod, and stomped them out. Other than a few elongated black burn marks on the dirty white wall, and a few blackened burn marks on the davenport, little damage had been done to the house. It was not like the time that the four had set an entire couch on fire. There had been so much damage then that Red had to redo the whole living room. Cora had become enraged and beat them all with a splintered one-by-two that finally broke on Leeland's small backside.

But their collective memories did not go back that far and while Dewey and Lloyd were trying to control the fire, Duane and Leeland successfully stormed the fort and took their brothers as prisoners. Duane stood on the back edge of the battered couch, pointing his bow and arrow straight at Dewey's heart.

"I give! I give!" shouted Dewey and almost immediately, given his position of authority, he crossed over to the enemy's side. "Okay . . . now we're gonna get even!" he yelled and he threw Lloyd down and sat on his stomach. Impulsively planning as he went, in his young mind he began to rewrite the bit of history that he had learned in the movie.

"Woooo weeee! Now Lloyd's a dirty redskin and we're the cavalry. Let's burn him at the stake!" Dewey began shouting orders. "Duane! Getta chair from the kitchen and some rope from outside! Leeland! Get some hay outta the barn!" Energized by their brother's excitement, the two scampered to their assignments.

Lloyd, sensing some impending danger, struggled heartily, but with no success. Dewey got off of Lloyd, grabbed his thin wrist, and dragged him to the middle of the living room. Darrell apprehensively retreated into the kitchen and peeked at the action from around the doorframe.

Lloyd strained to pull his wrist from Dewey's grasp, but his brother's grip became vice-like in the exhilaration of the moment. Lloyd whined a bit apprehensively when the boys returned from their assigned tasks, but he knew that resisting his brother would be useless. Dewey wrestled struggling Lloyd into the chipped, dirty white kitchen chair and forced his hands behind the slats. "Tie him up, Duane!" Duane tied his brother's hands tightly to the chair back and then looped the binding around his squirming brother several more times. With Lloyd secured, he then began to help Dewey and Leeland spread the armload of dry hay in a rough circle around the chair. Lloyd tried to remain calm, knowing that his brothers would certainly do nothing to hurt him. However, his level of anxiety rose severely as his siblings spread the fodder around gleefully. He really began to panic when Dewey lit a twig on the stove and deftly touched the small, struggling flame into the straw at several strategic places. The three cavalry brothers circled the growing flames and shouted and laughed loudly; Lloyd began to rock the chair in all directions and scream even louder than the others as the fire produced puffs of gray smoke that rose and filled the ceiling.

"Jesus Christ! Oh, Jesus Christ! Put it out! Put it out! It's startin' to burn! Help! Maaaaaa!" Lloyd pleaded helplessly while his brother continued laughing hysterically.

Finally, when the small fire was just about out of control and his clothes had just begun to smolder and were close to igniting, Lloyd rose up, the smoke-darkened chair still lashed to his hunched back, and ran from the room, coughing and crying, snot dripping from his nostrils, smoke and tears stinging his tightly shut eyes. The brothers continued laughing and then began stomping on the straw with their

broken down shoes until the last few flames were extin-
guished. When calm again prevailed, Lloyd hesitantly
returned to the room, still bent over with the chair clinging
to his back. Dewey got a butcher knife from the kitchen
sink and cut him loose. To avoid again being the focal
point of any follow-up roughhouse, Lloyd felt it best to join
nervously in the laughter.

So as not to incur their mother's wrath, when and if she
came home, the boys opened up all of the windows in the
downstairs and let the captured smoke escape. Using the old
and yellowed straw broom from the kitchen, the four swept
up all of the ashes and half-burned straw and threw it out the
window into the front yard where hopefully the wind would
carry the evidence away. To cover the large burn mark in
the wooden floor, the boys took the throw rug from in front
of their mother's bed and placed it carefully over the large
black scar. It barely covered the mark, but they all agreed
their mother would probably never notice it.

The afternoon's excitement proved to be a bonding
activity for the five brothers and they truly felt closer to
each other that evening, probably more so than ever before.
Lloyd felt that his older brother had finally accepted him.
After the air had cleared, they closed all of the windows and
let the house warm up comfortably again. Dewey used what
was left of the navy beans to make up a thick soup stew and
they divided the remainder of the cornbread into five large,
equal blocks. They gobbled up all of the dinner, down to the
very last few scraps, and though the house smelled strongly
of smoke they felt safe and secure in each other's presence.
Dewey even authorized the use of the last little bit of butter,
to be spread on the throbbing red burn welt on Lloyd's arm.

Because of his baptism of fire, Lloyd held somewhat of an exalted position in the circle of brothers that evening. The exhausting activities of the day and the full evening meal let the boys sleep deeply; they slept heavy and dreamless . . . contented under their dirty quilt, warming each other with their naked bodies as the cold wind from the north bore down on the house.

The next morning the brothers slept long and late, huddled together. While the others dreamt on, Dewey, who was usually the first to rise, had already gotten up and stoked the potbellied stove. With great care he had stirred the ashes. He brought the hot coals to life by blowing hard on them. When the embers turned bright red, he covered them with small and then medium-sized kindling from the wood box just inside the kitchen door. He broke a few of the larger pieces across his knee, carefully opened the hot grate door, and tossed them in. The fire began crackling softly and warmth slowly filled the cold house. Dewey shook the grate at the bottom of the stove and sparks and gray ash fell to the hearth below. Sullenly he mixed the last of the oatmeal with water in a large pan and then warmed it on the top of the stove. As the water came to a boil, the cereal thickened; when the breakfast was almost done, Dewey retrieved some hidden brown sugar from behind the cupboard wall, mixed it in, and then set the large pot in the middle of the floor. When his responsibilities were met, he woke his siblings.

"Wake up, you guys! Come on! Get up!" He indiscriminately shook the bare white shoulders that began protruding from under the covers.

The four younger brothers all sleepily resisted his prodding, so he threw back the thick blanket and nudged them with the worn down toe of his shoe. A few minutes later, when the brothers all dressed and shuffled down to the chilly kitchen, the oatmeal had cooled enough to eat. They shared the final feast by scooping out the gooey meal with their curled, dirty paws. The oatmeal stuck to their hands and they contentedly licked the breakfast from their fingers. When they finished they sat replete in the four corners of the kitchen. The smell of smoke from the previous day still permeated the air in the house.

"Well," Dewey announced, "We gotta go over to gramma and grampa's. There ain't anything to eat here in the kitchen and I already checked the cellar. Ain't nothin' left down there neither."

Duane boldly responded. "Shoot, I don't wanna go there. Gramma and grampa are too old. Maybe we can find somethin' down at the bums' camp." Lloyd and Leeland agreed eagerly with their brother.

"Yeah, and I don't want Grampa George hittin' me again with that damn hoe handle," added Dewey reflectively. "Sometimes he's a mean ol' bastard!"

Anything would be better than the long trip to Harveyville and the boring time with the two old people . . . especially unkind old Grandfather Wills. Why should he and his brothers be blamed for their mother's misdeeds, Dewey wondered. And so, with a final, approving "Okay! We'll stay!" he made the command decision to remain and attempt to forage for the food they needed to survive.

The band of five brothers set off, their relationship closer than ever before, to survey the bums' camp about three miles to the west. Taking turns carrying Darrell on their backs piggyback style, they turned left on Highway 2, heading west. Slowly, with muffled laughter, they snuck carefully past the old Indian's shack, stopping only to tempt fate by hurling a few stones at it. One rock hit the front door and when the tall, heavy red man staggered out onto the leaning front porch, they hunkered down in the dry drainage ditch, giggling childishly into their cupped hands until he scuffled back inside. A half-mile past the Indian's house, just before the Great Northern railroad tracks, on the Jenkins' farm, stretched a vast field containing rows of wrecked automobiles. Art Jenkins had turned a good deal of his acreage into a vehicle junkyard. While farming had been so poor, Art had become a part-time and then full time mechanic, using the junked-out cars and trucks and tractors and farm implements as a ready warehouse of used parts for his repair shop.

They skirted Art's hut-like, corrugated metal shop and his small farmhouse and his barking collie dogs, walking far out in the empty fields to the north until they came to the rows of partially plundered vehicles. A fence—really, just a tangled barrier of barbed wire and rusty corrugated sheet metal—set off the confines of the Jenkins' wrecking yard. The makeshift fence had been nailed to thick, pilfered railroad ties that had been set at close intervals into the ground. This barrier isolated the outside world from the mounds of rotting, decomposing Ford trucks and Chevy coups and ravaged Lincoln touring cars and Farmall tractors. Within the junkyard, the dented and bent and sometimes twisted hulks and pillaged, skeletal remains lay randomly stacked against and upon each other.

Dewey went over to the fence and forcefully pried open a separation between two of the corrugated tin sheets so that his brothers could squeeze past. The thin edge of the metal began cutting into his young fingers, leaving thin, crimson, almost bleeding welts across his hands as he stared stoically into the graveyard-like stillness; then beginning to wince in pain, he hurried his slow brothers through the tiny entrance and finally released the metal with a sharp slam. His brothers in turn pushed out the metal opening for him as he crawled in. Once inside, they all sauntered freely down the rows of wrecks, some of which still contained crusted, deep red blood stains on the windshields and dashboards.

"Dare ya to touch it!" Duane yelled out to Dewey.

Dewey just nonchalantly walked over to a large crimson spot on one of the metal dashboards, brushed his hand across the dry flakes, and rubbed the redness between his thumb and forefingers, inspecting it closely. The brothers gathered closer.

Suddenly Dewey stuck his hand in Duane face. "Want some?!!" he yelled and then laughed.

Duane recoiled back instinctively and pushed the hand from in front of his face. "Cut it out, Dewey!"

Awed and frightened, even inspired by Dewey's bravery, the boys fanned out to closely search the vehicles and the surrounding grounds for useful objects and toys. Upholstery stuffing and crankshaft bearings and con-rods and blackish oil patches adorned the ground; panel screws and shards of windshield glass and bent chrome rims and peeling grommets, along with weathered-gray sparkplug boots, were pressed into the dark dirt pathways, which wove like empty veins through the rows of wrecked automobiles and trucks.

At the far end of the yard they finally reunited. After placing all of their acquired booty in a communal mound, they then gleefully piled into a '36 Lincoln-Zephyr, its once sharply pointed front end twisted and buckled upward and back by a collision three years ago at the junction of Highway 2 and Country Road 37. Instantly the Lambson brothers became racecar drivers, bouncing wildly, roughly in the seats as the auto rumbled down the road of their collective imaginations. The automotive noises they made sounded very real and added to the excitement. Even Darrell smiled from behind his bottle as his small feet kicked at the springs and stuffing poking up from the back seat cushion.

But in the wild excitement of turning the steering wheel sharply, Dewey's left wrist passed over an exposed shard of glass in the driver's window frame, causing a thin cut that in a few moments began to bleed with a good deal of purpose. As the brothers gradually ceased their play, Dewey first licked at the blood and then he grabbed an old rag that lay on the floorboard and bound up the wound. At first he just opened the dirty bandage and stared at the still seeping blood. Then, always willing to find meaning in any situation, Dewey looked over around at his brothers.

"Hey, you guys! Who wants to be *REAL* blood brothers?" he said excitedly after a moment. "Ya know, like the injun and the cowboy in the movie we saw. We'll do it the way they did!"

The brothers were all silent, not really wishing to participate in the proposed ceremony, so Dewey grabbed on to Duane's thin left hand and wrist, choosing Duane only because he sat right next to him in the passenger seat. Holding the arm tightly, squeezing and twisting it to overpower his brother's weak resistance, Dewey quickly passed his brother's wrist over the piece of window glass that had cut his own, moving it so swiftly and deftly that Duane felt hardly any pain. As the blood began to flow, Dewey completely unwrapped his own wrist and held it against Duane's. Both boys felt an extreme burning sensation as the two bloods mixed and the other three brothers could only look on in silent amazement, awed by the inscrutable symbolism of the moment.

"Okay, now we're blood brothers, see!" His dark, mesmerizing eyes stared hard into Duane's frightened animal look, and his face revealed no hint of pain . . . only intensity. His eyes narrowed, drawing his brows almost together. "If anything happens to me, now you gotta take care of 'em, see." He jerked his head in the direction of the three quiet youngsters in the backseat and Duane could only nod slowly in acquiescence. "Got that?!" Duane nodded once more in affirmation. After a few moments the pressure of the bonding stopped the flow of blood and Dewey released his brother's wrist, actually almost throwing Duane's hand and arm back at him. The solemnity and violence of the almost sacred ritual seemed to hold all five brothers transfixed for several moments.

Before long, however, the intensity of the ceremony, as well as their earlier bursts of energy, had burned off their meager breakfast, so the boys gradually returned to reality as Lloyd and Darrell's stomachs growled loudly several times, almost in unison. Dewey, once again assuming his role as patriarch, made the decision to return at a later time for their piled-up spoils.

"Let's hide this stuff so nobody gets it," he commanded. "We'll get 'er later, on our way back home."

Much of the plunder, especially the heavy Packard differential gear and pinion that Leeland had found, could be

used for inside toys and devices during the upcoming winter, when the frigid cold and accumulating mounds of snow
would make them virtual prisoners in the farmhouse. Without question the boys all placed the various greasy parts into
the rumble seat of a nearby Model T Ford and then carefully
shut the creaking access door.

Leaving the junkyard, the youngsters continue on their
quest for food. The railroad tracks stood within the boys'
view and beyond the tracks lay their objective: a thick
shelterbelt of trees that hid the bums' camp. The area had
become somewhat of a haven for Dewey. Sometimes he
would sneak off by himself to go there, especially in the
dog days of summer, when he would walk listlessly along
the tracks, glad to be alone. In the far off distance, where
the iron rails came together into infinity, the shimmering
heat warped the horizon, and he would wince and squint his
eyes, holding his hand to his forehead to ward off the glare.
Often he would just yield to the fast moving trains, standing off to the side of the rocky railroad bed, waving to the
train engineers leaning out the locomotive windows: they
invariably wore gray hats and faded red bandanas and gray
striped bib overalls, their arms and heavy-gloved hands resting on the drab window railings. He wondered where the
trains and their pilots had been . . . where they were going
in their great escape from the town of Farmington. But at
other times, watching the trains, Dewey stood spellbound . . .
enthralled by the train's gathering force. Having just left
the depot, gaining speed, the black locomotives lumbered
past, tailed by a long line of hoppers or flatbeds or boxcars.
Sometimes in the late afternoon heat, he would position himself resolutely in the dead middle of the railroad tracks, arms

defiantly folded, waiting to see how long he could stare down the roaring, blurred mass hurtling towards him, the glaring white headlight watching him hypnotically as it bore down upon his slight body. When he finally did jump, just as the train was less than ten yards from him, he would stand shaking beside the rail bed, barely three feet from the train, gaping up, fascinated by the seemingly endless string of brown cars, overwhelmed by the force of the swirling wind driving past him, pushing him back. The ground would shudder beneath his feet as he screamed into the terrific din, just for the hell of it; the intense, rushing motion seemed to almost suck the voice from his throat and the air from his lungs. When the rust-red caboose at last swished by, he would chase after it, throwing the hard, gray stones from the rail bed at it, running hard until it was too far away to matter. Finally, when he stopped shaking, he would walk slowly on down to the bums' encampment or else saunter on home. He guessed he was too small for the engineers to see, so they never applied the emergency brakes. Either that or they recognized him from previous attempts and didn't really care to make the effort.

Because Dewey was so familiar with the area, he took the lead. He set a good pace and the line of five began to become strung out. In their fatigue and hunger, they stopped to play in the loose gravel of the railroad bed, throwing rocks and skipping along the evenly spaced, oily ties. "Come on, you guys!" Dewey yelled out, but not very assertively. Duane found a heavy iron rail spike and when he caught up with Dewey, Dewey quickly confiscated it. He weighed it in his right hand and placed it into the frayed rear pocket of his coveralls. Duane, growing tired and hungry, didn't even argue about the right of possession with his older brother.

The boys gravitated towards a long windbreak of willow and sycamore trees that paralleled the railroad tracks. Then cutting through the thick stand of trees they walked lazily into and through a mixed grove of barren ash and elm and box elder trees, all growing near the slimy, murky waters of a slough that was as pea-green as silage. The barren gray limbs, some still holding on tightly to small patches of yellow and brown foliage, interwove to form almost a canopy in some spots. There had been little rain during the late summer and early fall, and the dry branches and twigs and the auburn, curling leaves crunched and snapped beneath their careful steps as they entered the thick underbrush. The boys ventured out into the muddy, dark edge of the slough and their feet made loud sucking sounds when they struggled to pull them from the thick muck. In the denseness of the thicket the only other sound was the chirping blackbirds as small flocks retreated from the surrounding brush. Two reddish pheasants shot up suddenly ten yards in front of the boys, the flapping of their wings making the sound of a snorting horse, momentarily stopping the startled youngsters in their steps. As Dewey proceeded on cautiously, skimmers darted across the brackish surface of the bog; the first hard freeze had not killed off all of the insect life and even a few mosquitoes rose from the mire. Soon the boys' shoes became solid, heavy blocks of clay earth. Lifting high and laboriously the blackish clods of earth clinging to their feet, they made their way into the empty campsite.

During the warmer months of the year, transients who rode the empty boxcars across the railways of the Midwest would oftentimes inhabit the camp, which lay hidden deep inside the grove; camouflaged by the thick, twisting underbrush, the encampment stood as a natural refuge from the elements and the railway cops and the local sheriff. Dewey, and sometimes Duane, often went to visit the hobos, who were always hospitable, offering the youngsters hot, rich stew and sharp, black coffee in fire blackened tin cans. But the camp now sat empty; the bums had already headed south for the winter, probably quite recently. Only a few wisps of smoke rose from the gray ashes in the fire pit of roundish, gray-black rocks. Disheartened, the boys walked around the camp, poking and probing for any food that had been left. But the area had been picked bare and their scavenging yielded nothing.

"If it wasn't so cold, we could catch some frogs. Poke a stick through 'em and roast 'em." observed Duane. "Just like we done before."

"Yeah! Stick 'em in their fat yellow bellies and fry 'em alive in na fire! Let their guts drip out!" said Lloyd excitedly.

While Dewey deeply pondered where and how to get any measure of food, and inwardly debated their next course of action, Duane and Leeland and Lloyd began piling crumpled sheets of yellow newspaper on a few smoldering ashes that they had stirred up with crooked, blackened willow branches. Impressed by the initiative of his older brothers, Darrell stood and watched intently. Soon the fire grew to be knee high, crackling pleasantly. Then all of the boys, infatuated, began to pile scraps of leaves and trash on the flames until the campfire raged higher. The nice warmth from the flames provided defense against the cold breeze blowing in from the north, so they kept piling branches and small logs on the growing flames in order to dry their shoes and warm their feet. The increasing heat dried their socks and shoes quickly; using sticks, they scrapped the caked mud off their curled shoes. The fire leapt up to almost above their heads; they excitedly added more fuel and took turns spitting into the blaze, then urinating on it, laughing happily at the hissing steam.

As the fire ritual and the shoe-drying process drew to a close, Dewey talked the situation over with Duane. The wind had begun increasing steadily, cold and harsh. The night would surely be freezing and, without food, would be an exceptionally hard one for the boys. Together Dewey and Duane made the decision to go back home and, if nothing edible turned up along the way, to continue on to their grandparents' home. When the fire finally died down into a mound of smoking glowing embers, and the gusts of wind began blowing smoke and ashes into their faces, all of the fun was gone. Dewey began herding the brothers out of the thicket and on in the direction of their house. He encouraged them with the notion that perhaps Mrs. Jenkins might have something cooling in her kitchen window for the noon meal . . . maybe a pie or a whole chicken. With the image planted in their minds, the brothers moved out smartly; Duane even volunteered to sneak up and steal whatever might be there.

However, before they had traveled less than a mile and a half, Darrell, who rode piggyback on Dewey, turned back around. "Lookie!" he said and pointed a tiny finger in the direction of the bums' camp. A huge, brown and black smoke plumb rose up ominously from where they had just come; the cloud quickly grew, carried by the strengthening winds, moving rapidly beyond the coulee and the shelterbelt of trees.

"Oh, shit damn," Dewey exclaimed and immediately started to run; the other three looked back and seeing the growing conflagration began to run like hell as well.

During the sprint for home, Darrell's head bounced jerkily as he rode on Dewey's back. They took the long way home, through empty fields and down long drainage ditches, avoiding the main road and the few farm houses of their neighbors. Dewey looked back and the cloud of smoke had grown bigger and blacker, so he and the others ran ever faster. When Leeland or Lloyd fell behind, Dewey or Duane would go back, grab the scruff of the laggard's jacket, and drag him roughly along. Fear prevented them from stopping until they all reached their own house; they retreated to the barn and burrowed into the straw, collapsing in unison, winded, fatigued, lying silently, their clothes smelling heavily of campfire smoke.

"Jesus, what are we gonna do if the fire burns down the damn Indian's house! He'll come here and murder us fur sure," whimpered Lloyd.

Dewey told him gruffly to shut up and they all huddled together and kept still well into the late afternoon. While Darrell and Leeland and Lloyd slept fitfully for brief intervals, Dewey and Duane kept watch in case the Indian, or anyone else, for that matter, should appear. The only sound came from the wind probing the cracks in the old barn.

The false serenity of the afternoon finally broke with the sound of a car grinding down the road in first gear and pulling up onto the property. Sheriff Wilt's black police car crunched up to a stop in the front yard and the boys peered out cautiously from behind the loft door. He stepped out of the driver's side and Ed Amble, the Farmington volunteer fire chief, appeared from the passenger's side. They both stood in the front yard in consternation, hands on their hips, looking around the premises for any sign of the boys. Chief Amble still had on his rubber boots and soot darkened most of his face up to his forehead, where the fire helmet had rested.

"I know it was them damned Lambson kids," he said to Ben. "Art Jenkins said he saw 'em all headed up towards where the fire started. It's gotta be them little no accounts!"

The sheriff went into the house and looked around. "Naw, they ain't here. Their old lady ain't here either," he said as he walked out into the yard. "No tellin' where they are."

"Somebody better do somethin' about them delinquents before they burn someone's house down! Thank goodness that this time it was only a barn!" He got back into the police car and slammed the door, "Goddamned good-for-nothin' mutts! They oughtta be in jail!" Chief Amble angrily rubbed his open hand over the dirt and soot that stained his fat, red face.

"I'll come back out later and see if I can catch 'em," Sheriff Wilt said in frustration as he got back into the car; he had been through this so many times before and as always he remained powerless to do anything about the situation. He stepped down on the starter, revved up the engine several times, ground the car into gear, and drove back toward Farmington.

The boys continued to lie quite still in the barn until long after the car had left; they wanted to be certain it wasn't some sort of a cheap cop trick. After a while they finally left the barn, looked around the farmyard hesitantly, and then began walking down the dusty road towards Highway 2. Determining that Sheriff Wilt's police car was nowhere in the area, the boys gathered along the dirt shoulder of the road and crouched down in the culvert until the afternoon had ebbed. Because of the present situation, Dewey knew they could never seek the sheriff's help in getting to their grandparents' place. So shortly before dusk, they started hitchhiking eastward to Grandma and Grandpa Wills' house. Luckily, one of the first vehicles that came along and stopped was an olive-drab Army jeep with two young soldiers riding in it. The North Dakota National Guardsmen, being stationed at the Devils Lake Aerodrome as a part of the newly established Army Air Corp Observation Squadron, were traveling on assignment to the airport at Grand Forks. The driver, Pfc. Joseph Middlestrom, saw them shuffling along single file beside the roadway, Dewey bringing up the rear, walking backwards with his thumb outstretched, so he immediately stepped on the brake pedal. The jeep slid to a stop a little ways past the boys and then backed up to where they stood watching warily, tensed, ready to quickly disappear into the night, if need be.

"Where you kids headed so late in the day?" asked Middlestrom, leaning forward over the steering wheel.

"Harveyville . . ." Dewey, as spokesman, answered guardedly.

"Get in . . . we'll give ya a lift. It's a long ways over there."

So the brothers all crawled into the back of the jeep and snuggled in between the soldiers' olive drab duffle bags and field gear, relieved to be out of the chill evening wind coming in through the open sides of the jeep. Before proceeding on with their mission, the friendly troopers gave the boys water from their canteens and several C-rations, which they devoured hungrily. Pvt. Gunderson, who sat in the passenger's seat, withdrew a packet from his first aid pouch and poured powdered sulfur over the red, infected cuts on Dewey and Duane's wrists and then gently wrapped Lloyd's burned arm with a gauze bandage. "Looks like you kids was in quite a battle!" he said in a tender voice. "Boy, I'd hate to see the other guys!" After asking myriad questions about the soldiers and their jeep and their Springfield rifles and the bayonets hanging from their web belts, all of the boys fell deeply asleep, wrapped securely in the wool army blankets the caring soldiers had given to them.

Night had begun to set in full and frigid as the jeep lurched back out onto Highway 2. The brothers rode along secure and contented as the vehicle's headlights penetrated the cold darkness of the endless, empty road. As they sped off towards Grand Forks, Privates Middlestrom and Gunderson smiled with measured self-satisfaction at having stopped to help the children. Just before reaching the Will's place in Harveyville, Gunderson reached back and gently tousled sleeping Darrell's red hair. "Cute little bastids, ain't they," he observed. "I'm gonna find me a nice gal someday and get married . . . have me some kids like these."

Chapter Four—
The Wanderer

Late in October of 1941, far away from the enduring, spreading, raggedy cottonwood tree and the barren front yard of the old Sheppard spread, the people of Farmington, and certainly of North Dakota and the nation for that matter, were focused on more pressing matters than Cora Lambson and her waifish children. The world was experiencing rapid, inexorable change. German armies overwhelmed Poland in September of 1939, beginning the terrible global conflagration that would eventually grow into World War II. Germany, along with Italy, conquered most of Europe. The British, with German bombing missions attempting to pound the island country into submission and surrender, fought tenaciously for their very existence. War and rumors of war prevailed in the national discussion and local debate; civic issues of isolationism as opposed to international responsibility and involvement seemed to be paramount in the hearts and minds and spirits of the American people and in the broader public discourse.

Recognizing the weakness of the United States Armed Forces, the national leaders called for and received the first peacetime national draft, which was implemented to strengthen the existing insubstantial military. Many of the young men of the United States of America, who were between the ages of twenty-one to twenty-eight years, not wanting to miss the inevitable adventure, either registered for the draft or actually enlisted before the national draft lottery could be held. At the local level, the *Farmington Review*, published on Wednesdays and Saturdays, carried the stories of the global changes—of the mass evacuation of the British Army at Dunkirk, of the crumbling of the French Republic, of the cancer-like spread of the Nazis over the whole of Europe. More and more of the young and fearless men of the town left for military service. Because Farmington was in reality a microcosmic reflection of the real world, the bi-weekly *Review* responded to the imperatives of the nation and began to relate them to localized stories. Interspersed among the headlines and national news releases appeared articles about the brave Farmington boys, as well as those from the smaller surrounding communities, who were mobilized, or who were drafted, or who had willingly joined the military . . . those young folks heading for new and often terrible exploits in places far from the small, familiar, provincial farming communities of northeastern North Dakota. The citizens of Farmington immediately became more directly involved in the on-going civic debate about revenge and retribution. The remaining depleted male population spent a good deal of its time sitting semi-circle around the cathedral-shaped RCA Victor radio centered on the bar down at the Ideal, listening intently to the news broadcasts.

Yet these far-reaching events didn't affect Cora to any great extent; she and her children, living in their bleak, isolated farmhouse, seemed to be detached from the communities beyond their often desperate existence . . . separated from Farmington, from North Dakota, from the United States, from the affairs of the world . . . cut off from the broader commonweal. With Red gone, the house had defaulted into foreclosure; but because no one really wanted the property, the bank just ignored the fact that Cora Lambson and her five young sons were now residing there as squatters. The outside world, for the most part, seemed oblivious to the woeful woman and her ragged children and only just a very few of the local townspeople seemed to care about the desolate subsistence of the family. The Lambsons had evolved, in fact, into an anomaly to the spirit of the town . . . a blight on the community. . . certainly a discredit and contradiction to its well-established ethos of all caring for all.

After Iver's last departure and the birth of Darrell, the harshness of the family's impoverished circumstances began to show on Cora. Certainly her husband's inability or unwillingness to send any substantial financial support truly exacerbated the family's situation and the barrenness of their life added to the young woman's on-going downward spiral. The once plainly attractive and durable young lady grew extremely thin and the secondhand dresses that she wore, even though they were already too big for her, hung even more loosely from her gaunt frame. The day-to-day struggle seemed to consume most, if not all, of her energies. Fortunately for her and her children, the condition of the family depended not so much on the few odd jobs that Cora managed to hold down now and then, but rather on the scrapped-plate goodness of the community . . . not so much on the generosity of a few of the less honorable men folk, but more so on the kindness of the women folk.

Sara May Birdsong from the Zion Lutheran Community Church Ladies Aid Society and Women's Fellowship became Cora's benefactor. Because she perceived that her mission and purpose in life was to be of help to others, Sara Mae would sometimes bring burlap sacks filled with used clothes, as well as wooden apple crates of excess foodstuffs, to the Lambson household. All of the donations had been gathered and stored in the basement of the Zion Lutheran Community Church by the ladies of the LAS/WF, of which Sara Mae had been appointed the director. With her arms fully loaded, she would almost dance into the Lambson's dim household, so pleased by her own altruistic endeavors; she knew for certain that her inspired actions and inspirational demeanor would, without doubt, bring light into the family's drab existence and most assuredly gain her immediate entrance into the sweet pastures of Heaven when she passed on.

"Now you take care that you make these supplies last, Cora dear!" Sara had chortled in admonition during one of her charitable visits. She waved her white hand over the bags and boxes of commodities piled on the floor, as though she were blessing them, the flab of her upper arm wiggling with the grand motion. The five brothers danced curiously around the gifts, anxious to plunder the spoils. Cora nodded her head obligingly at Sara, mumbling in acquiescence, hoping the large, waddling woman would leave quickly. But Sara overstayed her welcome, asking a seemingly endless string of inane questions about the welfare and situation of the Lambson family.

"Any word from Iver?" she asked, and the inquiry made Cora seethe inside.

"Naw . . . ain't heard a word." The droll tone of her voice hid well her anger and she just looked down at the floor.

"Well for cryin' in the soup! What do ya suppose has become of him?" Sara Mae persisted, trying to extract any gossip she could during her brief visit . . . any tidbits of information she could share with the other WF ladies upon her return. "He needs to send ya some money, don'tcha know. Where's he workin' now?"

But Cora only answered her with silence and averted eyes. Finally she half murmured, "Dunno."

After several minutes of silence, Sara Mae rose from the depths of the old, sagging couch in the middle of the living room, grunting heavily with the effort. "Lord have mercy, look what time it is. I need to be getting back ta town. The Busy Fingers Homemakers are meeting this afternoon to do some needlework. We'll knit some warm things for you and your boys for this winter!"

When the subtle interrogation had been completed and the large community representative/benefactor had gone, Cora went immediately to the clear bottle of Night Train Express gin hidden in the very back of the cabinet, beneath the sink. Not caring that her sons were watching, or that in the urgency of the moment she had perhaps revealed her secret hiding place to them, she took a long drink from the warm, harsh liquid before returning it. Immediate relief flowed over her and shut out the world, at least for the moment.

"God-damned nosey church bitch!" She shouted out to no one specifically as she retrieved the bottle once more, took another long pull, replaced it, and slammed the cupboard door loudly. "Lookin' down her big, fat nose at me!"

With their mother's shouted curses concerning Sara Mae, and the sharp bang of the cupboard door, the five boys instantly vanished to the outdoors and up into their tree fort in the cottonwood, even though they were intensely anxious to share in the bounty. Gradually, with Dewey bravely leading the way, they gravitated back into the house and began poking into the coarse, brown sacks and rifling through the rough wood boxes, immediately gratified and pleased that their miserable lot in life had improved drastically, albeit temporarily. Quite awhile passed before Cora emerged from the kitchen to help them in the sorting of the bounty. Listing a little to her left, she almost fell over as she dropped down to her knees and began rummaging through the bags.

After such goodwill shipments arrived, Cora became an expert seamstress and cook in order to make these handouts last, especially with the ravenous, seemingly never-satisfied hunger of her five children. With so many foodstuffs in the house, she was able to prepare a number of good meals. Baking soda biscuits and creamy chipped beef gravy became the main staple of the family. Feeling in a particularly loving mood, she would use the Westfield flour to prepare delicious pies with pumpkins the boys stole from the patch three miles away. Or sometimes they would scavenge for apples from the Farmington General Store, or from a neighboring orchard, for Cora to use as pie filling. During these times, a good feeling pervaded the house. The boys always were better behaved when their stomachs were full. With their better behavior, a calm feeling came over the family, almost a sense of security that often lasted for more than a week or two.

In addition, the brothers, as they needed a change of clothes, would rummage around in the already frayed garments that Sara Mae brought in and pick through the items until they found an article most nearly their size. Cora would spend many hours mending and tailoring the shirts and trousers until the garments fit one or another of the boys. Indeed, the brothers honestly never knew until years later that clothes and socks were not made with holes already in them.

The gifts of food and clothing from the LAS were supplemented with various contributions from other, less altruistic members of the community. Different men came out to the lonesome farmhouse, often in the evenings, sometimes bringing food and candy, but mostly bottles of clear gin concealed in brown paper bags. Whenever a man came, Cora would make the children go upstairs and entertain themselves, no matter what time the visitor arrived. If the boys made too much noise, she would scream up at them through the steep staircase. When that didn't work, she would stomp up the stairs, a thick willow switch in hand, and flail at them indiscriminately until silence prevailed. Lloyd, Leeland, and Darrell would usually cry themselves to sleep after the beating; however, Dewey and Duane, who had only been doing fake crying, would sneak over to the floor vents that channeled heat from the living room upstairs and listen quietly. They would giggle into their cupped hands at the music and moans and strange noises coming up to them from the room below.

The music wafted up from an old windup Victrola that one of Cora's male friends had brought her, along with a tall stack of platter records of slow, pleasurable songs. The subtle music mesmerized the boys as they laid quietly, belly down, by the louvered heat register in the floor, chins resting on interlaced hands. Oftentimes, when the only sounds from the room below were from the soft music, the gentle tunes became their lullaby.

To Cora's credit, though, after Iver went away the last time, she had on a number of occasions somewhat tried to recommit herself to staying home and being as good of a mother as her conditions would allow . . . especially so after the birth of her fifth son Darrell. Yet as time slowly passed, she became more restive and agitated by her circumstances. Not much was needed to decimate her resolve. Disciplining her five unmanageable children proved almost beyond her abilities and she often visited the hiding place beneath the sink when she found herself trapped at home with her progeny. Part of spring, as well as most of summer and on into fall, proved to be reasonably tolerable because the children would stay outside nearly all of the daylight hours. When they did come home they were too tired from the day's curiosities and misbehaviors to disobey her. However, when they were in the house and refused to listen to her screaming commands, she would often stab at the tops of their bare feet with the stiff, yellow straw broom, or hit them across the back with its wooden handle. Dewey and Duane, maturing rapidly, were growing almost as tall as her. But even though they came up nearly to her shoulders, they, along with their three other brothers, would always scurry fearfully away from their mother whenever she evinced a particularly vindictive mood . . . when she would flail away at them with the broom or with the willow switch, shrieking obscenities at them, staggering somewhat as she chased them around the empty house. They were the reason for her being in the desperate situation she was in and she fully let them know it.

"None of you will amount to anything," she would scream at them whenever she became particularly out of control. "You're all just like your ol' man." Then, sometimes immersed in guilt, she would hug them all tightly when they finally came back into the house.

The uncontrollable nature of her children had become profoundly evident to her earlier in June, when the boys broke into one of the darkened classrooms at Farmington Consolidated Public School #3, on the outskirts of town. Coming upon the schoolyard during one of their long summer searches for something to do, and finding the confines mysteriously empty of all students and teachers, the boys quickly decided to investigate further. Tearing off the brown, peeling shutters from one of the unlocked windows on the hidden south side of the classroom building, they easily gained access to the inside silence; curiously they walked the semi-dark classroom, with its wondrous rows of double wooden oak benches and knife-scarred desks, all deeply etched with student initials and love notes; finally they came to the solitary, foreboding teacher's desk sitting sternly, resolutely at the front of the class. A beam of light shined into the darkness through the open window; minute particles of dust raised by their curious movements traced slowly through the bright light. A painting of George Washington hung at one end of the room and at the other hung a painting of Abraham Lincoln; both visages seemed to be keeping a silent, solemn paternal vigil over the sanctuary. In the semi-darkness they ravaged the drawers of the teacher's now idle desk and found an immense amount of chalk with which to "play" school. After writing illegible words and phrases on the slate blackboard, the pretend scholars pulled down all of the books from the dusty shelves behind the teacher's desk and pretended to read them, slowly turning each page. They ripped the pages out of all of the Laubach Penmanship Books and gleefully spread them all around the floor, then knocked over the cold potbellied stove that had warmed many small hands and dried numerous mittens and wool scarves over countless previous winters. Then after the boys had finished their joyful, wondrous day of "schoolin'," they left the ransacked classroom and the silent, empty school and happily returned home.

When she learned of the incident from the sheriff, Cora, under intense pressure from him and Reverend Driskoll, the new minister of the Zion Lutheran Community Church of Farmington, tried once again to do the right thing by sending Duane and Dewey to school in the fall for a good education. Lloyd, though not yet seven, was included in the educational plan as well and the overall arrangement did work for a few weeks.

But then Billy Birdsong, the pudgy eldest son of Sara Mae Birdsong, let every other student at Farmington P.S. #3 know that the clothes that the Lambson kids wore were, in actuality, his and his brother Burt's old hand-me-downs. The inevitable, relentless teasing soon began and the boys, as naïve as they were, merely laughed right along with the cruel jokes of their classmates. But this unexpected reaction infuriated Billy and all of the other children and the teasing intensified until the three brothers finally stopped laughing. Then during recess one crisp fall morning, after having had enough taunting about the sewn shut holes in his overall britches, Duane pushed his jutted chin and thin chest up against Billy's and in response Billy promptly knocked Duane to the hard ground. Suddenly all the games of tag and ante-aye-over and hide-and-seek stopped abruptly on the playground as students began to run excitedly to the confrontation. Duane shook off Billy's knuckled punch and rose up woozily; in fact, he kept getting up each time Billy knocked him down to the ground. Billy, whose fists were getting skinned and sore, became somewhat taken aback by Duane's tenacity.

"Stay down, ya little stupid!" Billy whispered breathlessly to Duane as he held him tightly in a choking headlock. "Quite fightin', ya dummy! Just say 'I give' an I'll get up off of ya!"

"My brother 'ul gitcha! You jus' wait!" Duane gasped as he slipped his mouth down and bit Billy long and hard on the left hand, just below the bottom knuckle of his thumb.

Billy winced and began choking even harder until his adversary quit biting and then he released the gasping Duane from the choke hold. Small traces of blood seeped from the red semi-circle of teeth marks on his hand. "You fight dirty, you lil' weasel," Billy screamed in pain as he lowered his thick head and came at Duane again, throwing him once more to the hard ground.

All of the excited, gleeful children had formed a tight human circle around the spectacle and even several of them urged the bloodied Duane to just stay down. But all of the admonitions were to no avail. Duane, whose nose ran with rich red blood and snot and powdery dirt, kept getting up and flailing his skinny fists at Billy Birdsong each time he escaped from his adversary's grasp.

Dewey and young Lloyd, finally seeing what was happening to their brother, raced clear from the other side of the schoolyard to join in the fray. Breaking forcefully through the line of spectators, they united with Duane and the three brothers fought as though their very survival rested on the outcome of the altercation. While Duane continued his wild, flailing frontal attack, Dewey jumped on Billy's back, grabbed two handfuls of his thick, sandy hair, and whooped out "Quit hittin' em, ya gol dang bastard." Meanwhile Lloyd eagerly kicked at Billy's kneecaps and shins until the adversary's legs collapsed. When Billy went down like a calf buffalo falling under the onslaught of chasing, purpose-driven wolves, they pummeled him with their small fists until Billy finally yelled out, "I give, dang it, I give!" When the three brothers finished working over Billy Birdsong, they turned their efforts on one of the bystanders, skinny Willie Johannson, pulling him roughly, arbitrarily from the now frightened crowd of children, who quickly scattered.

The fight ended abruptly when Harold Lundgren, the school principal, along with two of the Farmington P.S. #3 faculty, interceded to stop the mauling. Gripping the back of Dewey's neck tightly and shaking him like a rag doll, Principal Lundgren, with the help of the two struggling teachers, brought Dewey and Duane and Lloyd to the principal's office. Later that afternoon, after he had regained his composure and his face no longer flushed beet red, Principal Lundgren sternly escorted the Lambson children home and flatly told Cora that such outbursts of unruly behavior and lack of good citizenship could not be tolerated. Thereafter, to avoid any further problems, Cora would no longer be allowed to send her misfit children to the community school. She would have to teach them at home anything they needed to know, until they could learn to behave in a civilized manner. Ultimately this meant that the five boys had almost unlimited freedom to do all the exploring they needed to do in order to follow their maturation process.

Cora, most certainly, was far from being an adequate teacher for her sons. Often she would be at home with her children, but after awhile she once again began to disappear for several days in a row. At times the pressures of parenthood would weigh far too heavily on her slight frame and weak psyche and she would just have to withdraw for a time; that is to say, all too often the responsibilities of motherhood grew unbearably excessive and she would just need to leave in order to survive. Out of necessity, usually on Thursday nights, she would get cleaned up as much as she could, smear on some makeup, and walk out into the darkness, going down to the Ideal or the Palace Bar. Drinking heavily and falling in love with someone, she would go to his home, or someplace else if the person happened to be married, and stay away until late Sunday afternoon or evening. Many times when the boys woke up she would be gone and not come home, usually, for two or three days, or sometimes even longer. When she did come home, she remained sullen and non-communicative and restive. She only attained a sense of freedom while away from the lonesome house and the delinquent children. But as hard as she tried to divorce herself, both physically and emotionally, from the reality of her existence, Cora remained unable to do so.

* * *

Inevitably the ensuing events of the outside world, events over which she had no control, bore down more heavily upon the powerless, isolated woman and her offspring. Following December 7th, 1941 . . . after the bombing of Pearl Harbor, on a far off island called Hawaii that few of the townspeople knew of . . . after President Roosevelt declared war on the tyrannous Axis Empire of the Japanese and Germans and Italians . . . the character of Farmington and its people changed rapidly and irrevocably.

Federal resources were infused into the military units of the region, which were comprised of the 164th Infantry over by Langdon and the 188th Field Artillery, on down by Mayville. With the growing atmosphere of patriotism that ensued, more and more of the younger, able-bodied Farmington men volunteered or were conscripted into the service of their country. The local women and older men left behind were forced to step up and maintain the home front. Working the fields and doing the tasks normally done by their younger male counterparts, those that remained did so with resolution and no complaint. To worsen the situation, though, the folks who were tasked to "keep the home fires burning" faced numerous discomforting shortages. The human interest articles in the *Review* became surrounded by stories of the growing shortages and rationing the townspeople could expect in the coming months and probably years of war. Supplies of basic commodities became restricted, thus necessitating the strict rationing of things such as sugar, shoes, gas, tires, and coffee. Each person was issued a ration book by the United States of America Office of Price Administration and stamps were pasted into the frayed brown books each time the citizens made a purchase. No one in Farmington drove unnecessary miles or used unnecessary coffee or sugar, and the townspeople all wore their shoes until quarter sized holes were ground into the soles. Even the gradually improving financial conditions brought about by the economic demands of the war had little impact on their circumstances. The people seemed to have a bit more money, but few goods were available to buy due to the imposed shortages. Down at Stan's Café on Dakota Street, where the old Silvertone radio remained on all during the business hours, news broadcasts were interwoven with The Shadow, Tom Mix, Fibber Magee and Molly, and The Lone Ranger. Customers came and went, contributing to an ongoing and profound discussion concerning the war, as well as the injustice of wartime rationing; these were the topics that dominated the talk among the town elders who gathered every day for coffee or breakfast or lunch and some grassroots, down-to-earth ethical and philosophical debates. The conversations became particularly heated during the long winter months and the wet times of early spring, when nothing could be accomplished in the snow-covered or mud-thick fields.

But again these broader discussions concerning the human condition lay far beyond the scope of Cora's comprehension. She had little predisposition to be concerned with events outside of her own immediate needs, for the rigors and shortages experienced by the good folks of Farmington had always been much more pronounced in the Lambson household. Though the increased demand for agricultural products brought a surge of monetary growth to Farmington, Cora had been unable to do any sustained work for some time.

However, the overall effects of the war itself did tangentially help to improve her life somewhat. Whenever she felt compelled to briefly leave the farmstead and her children, venturing down to the Ideal in the evenings, seems like the men folk were much more willing to buy her drinks to take their minds off the concerns of world events. She also noticed that there were many more soldiers from the military fort over at Grafton wandering along the streets of Farmington, especially on Friday and Saturday nights. Determined to make the most of this new opportunity, she wisely made herself available during those times. And in addition, she combed her brunette hair full out, heavily rouged her somewhat sunken cheeks, and altered her loose fitting dresses so they more tightly fit her slender frame. Walking past her on the street, with their narrow waists and tight uniforms and close cut hair, the servicemen would wink at Cora and smile in a friendly way; that's how she got to know many of them.

"Shake it, but don't break it! The way that's wrapped, I'll surely take it," said Pvt. Joey Slinger one warm late-spring evening when Cora sauntered by; being newly arrived from Philly, he had heard many stories about the amorous nature of Midwestern farm girls. She needed only to look back over her shoulder and smile at him and the two were instant friends.

"Buy me a drink, soldier?" She said coyly to him and the young warrior came back and offered her his arm.

Cora's children liked the soldiers she brought home, much more than the other "fellas," probably because of the uniforms the troopers wore. The five brothers would invariably swarm over the military guests and ask myriad questions about the war and army life and firing rifles and machine guns. The soldiers were all quite generous and Cora once again became able to buy a few extras for herself and even some things for her children.

And then one day, in late spring of 1942, something quite unimaginable happened: a telegram arrived for Cora. Young

Will Hutchins, proudly clad in his gray Western Union uniform, with his impressive black hat slightly tilted back on his white, sweating forehead, rode his Road Flyer bike all the way out to the farmhouse to deliver the message. The courier's arrival, of course, unleashed a tornado of excitement from the five boys. Cora was not only astonished to received such an important document as a telegram, but more so by the fact that the message had been sent by Iver. Amid the furor, she signed for the envelope and held it before her for a long time, while Will fought the brothers for possession of his bike. Will eventually rescued his bicycle from the pack of boys and, disheveled from the scuffle, rode off shakily down the old dirt road to the main highway leading back to town. As Will wobbled off, Dewey, just for the fun of it, hurled a quarter-sized stone at the fleeing figure, which struck the delivery agent sharply on his left shoulder blade, making him again almost lose control of the bike. As the boys walked back toward their mother, they all lightly pounded Dewey on the back, congratulating him on his keen marksmanship.

Cora hesitantly tore open the telegram and narrowed her eyes as they moved along the words contained within the message. When she finished she just stood and stared at the paper incredulously, her mouth partially open, for it was almost like hearing Iver's voice coming out of the piece of yellow, crisp, letter-folded paper that she held before her: "Cora... Have joined the army. Am being reassigned to Ft. Benning, Georgia. Then going overseas. Will be home on furlough for two weeks. Plan to arrive in Farmington on June 10th. Love, Iver."

After standing quite motionless at the front door for what seemed like a very, very long while, she finally spoke to her children, who had gathered around her. "Your pa's comin' home. He'll be here in a few days." The children looked wondering into each other's faces, into each other's eyes, trying to find some clue as to the implications of their mother's comment. Dewey was the only one that gave a small glimpse of understanding, but he avoided his brothers' glances. *He* knew the significance of the message. Cora lowered the telegram to her side for several moments as ambivalence swept over her, and then she walked into the house, directly to the kitchen. The boys knew better than to follow her and scattered off into the yard, or up the cotton-wood, or off to the oblivion of the barn.

Apparently, almost immediately after the Japanese devastated the American fleet and the war began in earnest, Iver had happily quit his job as a sheet metal worker at the Bremerton Shipyards, on the Puget Sound in Washington, where he had been languishing for the previous three years. He immediately hitched a ride to Fort Lewis and enlisted in the 3rd Infantry Division. The enlistment provided him a chance to at last escape not only the daily drudgery of his metal handler/assistant welder job at the ship building factory, but also the constant litany of complaints and lamentation from not only his overworked, disgruntled fellow workers, but also his temporary live-in girlfriend. America's declaration of war against the Axis powers gave him once again the opportunity to escape his circumstances. After finishing basic training, the Army transferred him to the 41st Infantry Regiment, a unit comprised mostly of national guardsmen from Washington State.

During the next three months of his military service, Iver and the other troops of the "Fighting Forty-First" began training for war at Camp Murphy, just outside of Tacoma. Over 3,000 canvas eight-man tents had been hastily erected to house the troops and a network of paths connected the tents with the mess halls, post exchange, showers and latrines. The spring rains turned the tent city into a quagmire of sloppy, endless mud, making life even more miserable for the troopers. Lacking proper equipment, they improvised as they trained for war in the Pacific. Sticks became rifles, cans filled with dirt became hand grenades, pickup trucks were tanks, rolled up tubes of cardboard became mortars and shoulder-mounted "bazookas." During the damp and misty months of February, March, and April, the troops trained in amphibious operations on Puget Sound, using motorized wooden fishing boats as landing craft for their water-borne assault. Iver became just another one of the many tired, disillusioned doughboys that slogged ashore, stick rifle in hand, wondering what he had gotten himself into. Given the initial rigor, severe discipline, and strict conformity he experienced, Iver quickly decided that the mundane life of a lowly infantryman could never be exciting enough for him.

A bulletin went out from the 41st Regiment's Headquarters and Headquarters Company announcing a new opportunity. The United States Army's first paratrooper element, the 501st Airborne Regiment, had been formed in April of 1941, with the first jump school scheduled to start the beginning of July at Fort Benning, Georgia. A call went out for volunteers to be a part of the new type of combat infantry unit. Just as the idea of breaking horses in Miles City, Montana, had done years before, the lure of jumping from an airplane pulled at Iver and soon he had signed on for the rigorous jump school training.

When his orders were posted in May, he requested and received a two-week furlough so he could visit his family on the way to his new duty station. On June 6th he boarded an Overland Greyhound Bus in the Seattle terminal and headed east over the Snohomish Mountains, out across the wide, empty expanses of Montana and the Permian Basin Badlands, then finally the flat, endless farmlands of North Dakota. The blue and silver humpback Silversides bus seemed to stop at every small town, disgorging travelers and picking up new ones. At layovers in Boise and Helena and again in Billings and Bismarck, while changing buses, Iver continually refilled the small flask of whiskey that made the hot, stuffy, seemingly never-ending journey more bearable.

On the trip from Bismarck to Jamestown, he shared his flask with a young lady sitting in the seat next to him. Rita was her name. Rita Johnson. "What a pretty name," he told her soon after flopping down into the empty seat next to her. She and Iver became instant friends. "I'm returnin' home from the nursing school in Mandan. I hadda drop out." she confessed to her fellow traveler. "I'm movin' back ta James-town ta live with my aunt." For some odd reason, she felt drawn to him and his self-assured demeanor and confident smile. In fact, she became so taken with his dark-brown U. S. Army Class B uniform and his strong military bearing that she felt it her obligation to contribute to the war effort by inviting him home for dinner when the bus pulled into Jamestown in the late afternoon. Because he would not be able to transfer to a northbound connecting bus to Farming-ton until the next morning, he heartily accepted her gener-ous offer. After she had gathered her tan, cracked leather suitcase and he had shouldered his olive drab duffle bag, they walked to her deaf Aunt Edna's house, located only a short three blocks from the small Greyhound Depot. Rita's aunt, overjoyed to have a member of the armed forces stay for dinner, insisted that the young soldier stay the night in the spare bedroom next to Rita's. Iver and Rita sat out on the porch late into the evening, smoking Chesterfields and drinking Aunt Edna's Old Angus Scotch Whiskey. The more he drank, the more Iver embellished his military exploits and he even revealed to Rita that he would probably be promoted almost immediately from private to sergeant when he finished paratrooper training. Then, very late in the evening, Rita, swept along by an overwhelming sense of patriotism, felt it her ultimate duty to yield to Iver's advances. So, soon after midnight, the two retreated to her rose-colored, perfume-scented bedroom. The next morning she laundered, starched, and pressed his uniform, going over and over the pleats in the pants legs and shirt sleeves with the heavy iron. She even ironed his garrison cap and webbed waist belt and tuck-in necktie, and shined his shoes and belt buckle. She made him a big breakfast of eggs and biscuits and gravy, and then walked him back down to the bus station. While waiting, they held hands.

"Will you write to me, Iver?" Rita asked. She handed him a piece of her own fragrant stationary on which she had written her name and her Aunt's address.

"I will, Rita. And I'll see you again real soon," Iver said as he folded the note and put it into his shirt pocket. "I won't be able to forget you."

He boarded the northbound, weather-faded yellow Clipper Motorcoach bound for Farmington and waved to her out of the half open window; she waved back happily and continued waving until long after the bus rumbled off out of sight. When the bus sped past the last building on the edge of the town, he took the paper from his pocket, unfolded it, and smelled it deeply; then he casually wadded it up into a tight little ball and tossed it out of the window, where it landed in the sallow mustard pods and rag weeds thriving beside the roadway. Feeling a great sense of peacefulness, he laid back and rested in the hard leather seat and closed his eyes. And because he still felt a little hung over, he immediately went to sleep.

Four hours and forty-seven minutes later, the bus pulled into the Farmington Bus Terminal . . . actually Stan's Cafe, which doubled as the bus depot. In the hot, early afternoon sun, Iver stood in front of the red brick building facade that formed the southwest corner of Dakota Street and First Avenue, blinking the sleep from his eyes and looking down the familiar, quiet main street he knew as home. Rosecran's IGA . . . the New Farmington Hotel . . . Louie Anderson's Barbershop . . . Roscoe's Five-and-Dime . . . Foss Drugs . . . the Ideal Bar and Grille. Little had changed since he left . . . except that the town now seemed so small. Yet life cycles and human patterns still remained the same. Harvest time lay several weeks off; in the lull between planting and tilling and shocking and harvesting, most of the townsfolk were out haying . . . cutting the hay from surrounding meadows and fields to store as winter feed for their livestock. As a result, the dusty streets and sidewalks were nearly empty as Iver looked around long and hard for any familiar face . . . listened for any recognizable voice to let him know that he indeed had returned *home*. After being on the road for three long days, with his body all stiff and sore from the arduous trip, he decided to stop off at the Ideal before continuing on to his home . . . to see if some old acquaintances might be there.

When Iver entered the familiar dark, mildew-smelling interior of the Ideal, just a few of the regulars were sitting around in the cool interior; the only person that recognized him was Smiley Edwards, a retired farmer who had long since become a professional at occupying his own barstool, prominently situated at the end of the bar, closest to the door. As Iver sauntered in, Smiley narrowed his one good eye against the light that leaked in from the bright afternoon, outlining Iver's tall frame against the dim interior; slowly the old man scratched the stubble of his gray beard. After a few moments of uncertainty, however, a smile revealed his tobacco stained teeth and he lifted his slightly curled hand to his lined forehead in somewhat of a semi-salute.

"Iver! Iver Lambson, you old sonofagun! How the hell are ya?!" Smiley latched onto Iver, patting him on the shoulder and pulling him down onto the barstool beside him. "Someone said you was dead!"

"Hullo, Smiley," Iver said slowly as he slapped the old man lightly on the shoulder. "How ya been?"

The two old acquaintances spent the next few hours gabbing, but mostly Smiley spent the time catching Iver up on all that had happened in the years since the young man had left. Most everyone in Farmington considered Smiley to be the Ideal's historian. Folks called him Smiley because of his artificial smile: the right corner of his mouth had become drawn up towards the slit where his right eye had been, in somewhat of a perpetual smirk or smile. When he was seventeen, his brother accidently stuck him in the right eye with the outer prong of a pitchfork, poking out his right-side vision forever. Many believed, though, that Smiley could see more with one eye than most could see with two. Smiley droned on most of the afternoon, telling Iver way more than he really wanted to know. But as long as Smiley kept buying the bottles of cool Schlitz beer, Iver feigned interest in the old man's nothing stories.

"Yeah, ya 'member Sol Samuelson, 'ey? Last winter he was tryin' to start his Waterloo tractor, tryin', ya know, to turn 'er over with a spanner wrench. And when she sparked, see, the wrench flew off of the crankshaft and broke Ol' Sol's jaw. Knocked out all the teeth on the right side, see, and his whole mouth swelled up somepin' fierce! Left a big scar on his face! Knocked him a bit silly, too, fur sure!"

When Smiley paused to light a cigarette, Iver rose from the stool slowly. Having tarried too long, he became more anxious to get home. "Thanks for the beer, Smiley! I gotta move on and go see the family. Been quite awhile since I been with 'em." Iver shook Smiley's old hand and gave him a "So long" before going out into the still heavy heat and sunlight of the afternoon, narrowing his eyes to adjust to the brightness.

Iver gathered up the bag he had checked at Stan's and began walking home, traveling slowly down the gravel edge of Highway 2, balancing the sagging duffle over his right shoulder. No cars or pickups happened along to give him a lift and soon large dark rings appeared under the armpits of his poplin uniform and streams of sweat traced down his forehead and face from underneath his garrison cap. Rita's press job had disappeared, but the good feeling provided by the afternoon of beer sustained him, as well as alleviated any apprehensions he may have had at seeing his family again after such a long time. When he reached the dirt road entrance to the familiar rundown farmhouse, he sat down for a bit and rested on the duffle bag, then took a reinforcing drink from his flask and lit a cigarette.

From his vantage point high in the cottonwood tree, Dewey was the first to notice the man turn the corner and stop to sit down. Even though the far off figure appeared as merely a light brown speck in the distance, Dewey knew instantly that the apparition could only be their father. But he said nothing. Then Duane, who sat swinging aimlessly on the ancient tire swing that hung from the cottonwood, twisting back and forth, his toes dragging figure eights in the dirt, spied him. "Ma! Ma! It's him! He's here!" he cried, ejecting from the swing. Lloyd and Leeland and Darrell all emerged running from various locations in the yard and in the house and began scrambling about, jumping up and down excitedly. They then all picked up in unison Duane's chant of "He's here! He's here!" All except Dewey, however. Not sharing his brothers' sense of glee and excitement, Dewey climbed down out of the tree and listlessly walked off toward the barn, looking down dejectedly and kicking at nothing in particular on the ground with his stubbed big toe.

Cora came to the tattered front screen door, looked out with narrowed eyes, straining to see what had excited her brood. Finally she stepped out onto the porch in order to get a better view. She held up her thin hand above her eyes so as to shade off the glare of the ambient sunlight, trying to make out reality in the shimmering heat rising up from the dirt of the desolate road. "Naw, that ain't him," she said weakly. "That's justa bush." Her voice had an almost imperceptible edge of uncertainty, so the children began running wildly around the front yard.

"Is so! Is so! It's him!" Duane, Lloyd, and Leeland ran several circles around the cottonwood tree and then their wild momentum carried them down the road, off towards their father, who became more and more distinguishable as he emerged from the distortion of the heat waves. The dirt of the roadway, made hot by the relentless Dakota sun, burned the bottoms of their bare feet, so they ran hopping from one spot of shade to the next, lifting their legs high and yelling in excitement and pain.

Cora stood still . . . almost paralyzed . . . frozen in and by time. She had all but forgotten the telegram and the date that he said he would arrive, just figuring the message to be another one of her husband's cruel hoaxes. She had been disappointed by him and his crazy ideas too often in the past and had vowed she would not allow herself to be tricked another time. But he had indeed arrived and her growing shock quickly replaced her resolve. Little Darrell moved in along the porch unnoticed, standing hidden behind her left side, looking out at the approaching man from the back of his mother's thin hip.

Iver made his way to the porch, his children trailing behind him. In their innocence, they had become more subdued. He threw his duffle to the porch and a small puff of road dust rose from it. "Hullo, Cora, Darlin'," he said huskily, confidently, as though an eternity had not passed between them.

At first Cora could only stand uncomprehendingly, rigid and speechless. Then she reached out and touched the arm of his brown uniform shirt, pinching the damp fold of the material, just above the elbow. "Iver . . . . Iv. . .," Cora said and then she began to feel faint.

"It's me, Cora." Iver caught her around the waist as her knees started to gradually buckle beneath her. He attempted to kiss her passionately, but he only found dry lips, so he helped her inside the house. As she sat on the floor and leaned her back against a wall, Iver knelt beside her and fanned her with his garrison cap.

After the initial excitement of seeing their father, and of seeing their mother swoon, the boys quieted down quite a bit. They had all stood slack-jawed for a few moments and then followed the reunited couple into the house. Dewey, on the other hand, retreated further into the barn and burrowed deeply, animal like, into the small pile of upper loft hay, staying there until later that night, sometimes crying quietly in fear, other times clenching his teeth and fists tightly.

Cora recovered after several minutes, rose to her knees and then stood shakily for a few moments. Even though she still remained quite pale and unsteady, she went to the kitchen and brought Iver a jar of warm water. He sat down tiredly in the overstuffed chair in the living room, the one with the large burn hole and the stuffing poking out of it in a number of places. Several minutes of silence passed before Iver finally broke the discomfiture of the scene.

"Well, Cora, how you been?"

" Fine, I guess," she answered with a good deal of uncertainty.

"Didn't you get my telegram?"

"Yeah, but . . . ."

"Well, you gave me quite a scare!"

Several more awkward moments went by before Iver could think of something to say. Again noticing his sons standing off at the other end of the room, he motioned them towards him with his hand.

"My, you boys are quite a crew! You been takin' good care of your Ma?" He spoke slowly, carefully, in a deep, almost frightening voice. After his short, abrupt statement and question, Iver crooked his jaw slightly to the left, as he often did when faced with a perplexing or unfamiliar situation; he then looked somewhat proudly at the boys, who now stood in a semi-circle several feet away. "How many of you are there now?"

"Five," responded Duane.

"This here's Darrell," said Cora, as she stepped forward and gently pulled the small, red-headed child out from the lineup towards his father. "You ain't never seen 'em, nor he you."

Due to the intense experience of the afternoon, her thin voice still cracked a little. With a good deal of hesitation, Iver sat forward a bit and put his large hand up so that his fingers just barely brushed the child's bright red hair; then he removed his hand quickly away.

Iver slowly eyeballed the four and asked, "Where's the other? That must be Dewey. Where's he at?"

"He's out hidin' in the barn. He doan like you," volunteered Lloyd.

"That's nonsense," Cora said quickly, tempering the child's words. "He'll be in after a bit. Iver, honey, you look tired. Why don't you go inta the bedroom and rest a bit."

She retrieved her bottle of gin from beneath the kitchen sink, along with the only two jar glasses in the cupboard, and they both walked off together into Cora's bedroom and closed the door. From inside the room the brothers heard the parents' muffled, happy voices and then the heavy scraping sound of the large dresser being moved over to secure the door. With that the brothers all left to go look for Dewey, who had hidden himself so well that they couldn't have found him for a million years. He watched them stealthily from his lair, cursing their folly under his breath; he angrily decided that the next time they were together he would give each of his siblings a deliberate and hard sock for acting so stupid around their old man.

The afternoon had dwindled into early evening when the parents finally emerged from the room, both appearing to be in somewhat boisterous spirits. Cora lit a lamp and when her four youngest children came in she directed them to make themselves something to eat because she and Iver were going down to the American Legion to celebrate Iver's homecoming. After his mother and father departed, Dewey finally left his hiding place and came back to the house; he immediately delivered a punishing sock to each of the brothers' shoulder and told them roughly why. He then picked the lock on Iver's duffle bag and the boys gleefully rummaged through their father's military belongings, boosting two bright red packages of Pall Mall cigarettes.

For the first time in a long while Cora was somewhat happy. She went to town with Iver that evening and he wore a new, clean, hardly wrinkled uniform he had retrieved from his duffle, which made him look manly and rugged. She looked lovingly at him . . . as if he had never left . . . had never deserted her and her children. Down the dirt road they walked, with Cora proudly clutching her man close, both her arms wrapped tightly, proudly around his strong forearm.

"Cora, honey, I never stopped thinkin' about ya . . . lovin' ya."

"I know, Iver. It'll be okay now."

"I could just never get ahead enough. Everything seemed to be working against me all the time. Geez, I missed you and them kids real bad."

"We missed you too, Iver." She held his hand more tightly, never doubting for a moment his veracity.

When they arrived at the Farmington American Legion Hall, the regulars received Iver well and made him and Cora more than welcome. Word of his return spread quickly and soon quite a few of the members came down to the hall; throughout the evening they provided a seemingly endless supply of free, strong drinks for Iver and his woman. Given the rich history and tradition of the Legion Post, the Farmington legionnaires, most assuredly, knew how to recognize and take care of their own—past, present, and future—and certainly Iver was no exception.

The Charley "Coot" Carlson American Legion Post #169 truly stood as a tribute to the town's warriors. The fraternal group acquired its name from the eighth mayor of Farmington, who had enlisted in the United States Army and shipped out to Europe with the American Expeditionary Force in 1917. While serving as a first lieutenant in the quartermaster corps, he became a casualty of the war when a horse-drawn artillery caisson ran over him just east of Chateau-Thierry, in late May of 1918. Because Carlson had been posthumously awarded the Congressional Order of the Silver Star, the town of Farmington established the post on July 4th, 1929, to honor his name and his memory. After receiving official affiliation with the national American Legion, Post #169 held its first meeting in the basement beneath the Dakota Theater, which earlier in the century had been the town opera house because of the building's naturally good acoustics. And thus the valorous men of Farmington had a legitimate place to socialize on Wednesday evenings. Volunteers from the community, many of whom were veterans of the big war, revamped the musty, mildewed room, transforming the damp concrete walls with much remodeling and painting, all of which were labors of love and patriotism. The new post included a wide room with tables and folding chairs, a podium, a brand new American flag, pole, and brass stand, a large kitchen, and a very impressive bar. All of the post's activities were announced in big red letters on the old theater's white marquee. Ed Haggarty, who owned the building and donated the basement facilities, started the club and appointed Gordy Miller as the first manager. Over the years Gordy proved to be one of the best managers ever; one of his most innovative projects involved establishing ongoing lutefisk dinners every Friday night at the Legion during the long winter months, to which the whole community was invited. During Legion meeting nights, held every second and fourth Wednesday of the month, the Ladies Auxiliary supplied a pot luck meal, with the main course being a pleasant hot dish of macaroni, tomato, hamburger, and onions, with lefse and fresh baked bread on the side. Ed, of course, named himself life-long Sergeant-of-Arms for the post.

The Legion Hall housed the Sons of Norway Lodge and the Post sponsored Farmington Boy Scout Troop 113, which always had anywhere from ten to thirty young scouts. The boys of Farmington, seeking so hard to emulate the bravery and discipline of their veteran mentors, learned how to

march and formed a drum and bugle corp. After the cow-
ardly attack on Pearl Harbor by the "sneaky Japs," the role
and mission of the Boy Scouts changed drastically. The
Scout meetings on Monday evenings in the Legion Hall
were expanded to include air raid alerts, disaster drills, first
aid training, and even methods of spotting sneaky saboteurs.
After all, there were three large fuel storage tanks on the
edge of town. The members of the Legion Post, because
most were veterans, suspended their communal drinking
for one evening each week and assisted the young scouts
with making bandages for pretend gaping wounds, as well
as practicing how to splint broken appendages. Billy Birdsong, fully expecting to one day to achieve the rank of Eagle
Scout, stood out as a leader among his peers. During the
Farmington paper and scrap metal drive, held to support the
war effort, he bullied and relentlessly drove his subordinate
scouts and was consequently awarded a merit badge for his
stellar efforts in helping the troop bale and ship twenty-
six tons of various materials for recycling. The Post also
honored Scoutmaster Corky Iverson by throwing a party in
his honor one evening at the Legion Hall, during which he
became quite drunk, right along with the Legion members.

Many Memorial Days, military funerals, and July
Fourths were celebrated in the American Legion Post #169
hall, but America's entry into World War II had significant
meaning for the members of the organization. The numerous Farmington young men who recently had been drafted
by or enlisted in the military seemed to symbolize the tra-
ditions and rich heritage the Legion Post stood for. Thus
during the first several days after he had returned home,
Iver became well recognized at the Legion Hall; because he

had disappeared for such a long time, and had come back to Farmington proudly wearing a military uniform, he came to be viewed as somewhat of a hero. Free drinks remained the order of the day for Iver and Cora, a kindness which the couple took full advantage of during the time they were back together, once more in love. Iver received many encouraging slaps on his broad back for his bravery in volunteering for the elite paratrooper unit. He never tired of relating the tales of his Homeric adventures since he had left the small town. And when asked about his family, about his five boys, he boasted of his manhood, of his ability to produce male children. "I ain't shootin' no blanks!" he bragged proudly, loudly to the older men and few ladies at the Legion Hall one night, drunkenly, overtly attempting to accentuate his masculinity as he tried to make time with the women folk who were present. Though Cora stood at not too far of a distance from him, and though the bearer of the children that Iver boasted of, she stood silently in the shadows as he came on to Mildred Dipple and put his hand on her knee, massaging it firmly. Cora didn't really seem to mind awfully much, as long as her old friend Earl Lempkey kept bringing her drinks.

The couple, in their newly rediscovered bliss, only came home periodically for the first six days of Iver's furlough. They spent a good share of the week reminiscing and socializing down at the Legion Hall . . . catching up on old times. As such, the newly reunited couple stayed away from the farmhouse most of the time, which the children did not mind at all. Iver's boys weren't exactly taken by him and they silently stood their distance whenever he was around. After the first day, the father spoke only a few words to his children and thereafter never really said anything nice to them. Besides, as Leeland reported, the father's breath stunk sourly and so they kept a good deal of "escape" room between themselves and the man. As a result of all of this, on the few occasions where they all found themselves together as a family, Iver could not stand the awkward silence, with the children seeming to continually be staring at him from the corners of their eyes. He could not wait to leave for town.

Iver particularly did not like being around Darrell . . . did not think much of the boy. Late one evening, when the boys were going to bed, Darrell came up and wrapped his arms around Iver's leg. Iver promptly pried the little child off of him and rather roughly pushed him aside, telling him, "Go on up ta bed, now. Leave me alone."

On the seventh morning of his father's visit, when Dewey awoke and his parents were still sleeping, the boy silently crept into their stale smelling bedroom and went through his father's pockets, where he found two crumpled dollar bills. When the two parents left later that day, Dewey rounded up his brothers and walked down to the town in the early afternoon heat, the money held tightly in his fist. The darkness of the Dakota Theater provided cool relief from the hot outside. After legally paying admission for all of them, Dewey had enough left over to buy a sack of goobers and a package of black liquorices that darkened their mouths. They sat down in the very front row, staring up at the bright screen and passing the treats back and forth, sharing them equally as the motion pictures lit up their faces. The Saturday afternoon program had a double feature of *Flying Tigers* and *Dive Bomber*, preceded by cartoons and Pantheon Newsreels. Before the main attractions, the brothers laughed gleefully at the cartoons: Bugs Bunny in *You're a Sap, Jap* and *Nip the Nips*. They then stared intently as the rooster crowed to announce the grainy news clips of the raging war in Europe and the South Pacific, as well as the news briefs showing the innovative use of paratroopers in battle. As the narrator spoke, the screen showed a sky full of German Blitzkrieg paratroopers and then American soldiers jumping off of platforms, learning how to land and roll as they trained with simulated parachute jumps for future airborne action against the Axis enemies.

Watching the news clips and the full-length movies, with the black and white and gray actions flashing on his angelic face, Dewey became inspired as he thought about his mother and father sitting together in the room below them. Perhaps he had even gained a new respect for Iver. Still not understanding why the man had abandoned them in the past, Dewey decided that it must have somehow been his fault that his father had left. Maybe because he was the firstborn . . . and so he should be the one to try to make his father love him . . . love them. From his mother's talk, he knew his father would soon be leaving. So that evening, when his parents came home, the boy went directly, fearlessly up to Iver and asked him about the paratroopers. Iver became puzzled . . . even suspicious . . . because those were practically the first words that Dewey had spoken to him since his arrival. However distrustful he may have been, the father smiled wryly, cautiously gladdened by the opportunity to bond with his eldest son. Wanting to impress the boy, he bragged about all facets of the upcoming paratrooper training that he would be going through. Dewey, pursuing his childish change of heart, naively, desperately hoped to somehow ingratiate himself, and even his brothers, to their father . . . to make up for his shortcomings that had driven his father away. He came up with a miraculous idea: as a way of paying homage to the father, the brothers also would become little paratroopers.

Late the next morning, after the parents had once more left for town, Dewey called his bothers to action. The large cottonwood tree in the front yard, which had served as the site of so many battles and adventures, became Fort Benning, Georgia. One big branch projecting out from the main trunk, about fifteen feet from the hardened ground, served as the jumping off point. Dewey and Duane eagerly tied two lines of clothesline rope to the tree and also to a dusty, inflated inner tube the boys had stolen a month before from the Farmers Union and hidden in the barn for future unknown adventures. Dewey encouraged Duane to be the first paratrooper to try out the training device and Duane reluctantly agreed. He hoisted the inner tube to the branch, lowered himself inside the narrow opening, grasped on tightly to the sides, and pushed off. When Duane reached the end of the lines, the tube recoiled back up into the air, sharply jarring his teeth and jaw. The tube continued bouncing for several moments, weaving about in all directions as the brothers gleefully danced around the successful test of the project. Dewey was next and his "jump" proved equally successful, as was Lloyd's. The three alternated jumps for the next several hours until their heads ached from all the violent bouncing.

As a respite they collectively decided that Leeland should have a turn . . . jumping from the tree would be the event that truly determined his entrance into the Lambson brotherhood. Reluctantly Lee climbed to the "jumping off branch," where he pondered for several minutes as to whether or not he really wanted to participate in the rite of passage ceremony. Then realizing that in the eyes of his brothers there could be no turning back, he prepared for his rapid descent. As he carefully, hesitantly placed himself inside the tube and scooted towards the point of no return, he wrapped his left arm twice around the rope for greater security. But before Dewey could yell out not to do such a stupid thing, Leeland pushed off over the edge; gravity did the rest. The tube pulled the lines taut when Leeland reached the bottom and in so doing lacerated his wrist and broke his arm in two places. With the first bounce, Leeland began screaming loudly and when the tube finally stopped recoiling he fell to the ground crying.

The brothers quickly gathered around injured Leeland, who held his broken arm close to his chest, moaned and weeping unceasingly. "You're wounded, Lee. The medics will be comin' soon!" Dewey told him excitedly, hoping that some dramatic overtones might help calm the situation. Unable to see the drama, though, Leeland could only emit a relentless combination of modulating cries and moans. Not knowing exactly what to do, the brothers propped him up against the tree and waited for something to happen.

An hour later, in the late afternoon sun, as Iver and Cora walked unsteadily along the roadway leading home, they argued vehemently over some crude, seductive comment . . . a lurid suggestion, as a matter of fact . . . that Iver had made to Alma Ingsted, which Cora and several other folks overheard. But when they came into view of the farmyard, the couple could tell something was wrong and began to run toward their children, albeit in a staggering way. When the parents arrived, breathless, Dewey immediately stepped forward, sensing that there would surely be a measure of understanding from them.

"We was playin' paratrooper, see, and Leela..." was all the explanation he could get out before Iver hit him across the mouth with the solid back of his hand, splitting his young son's upper and lower lips. A rush of blood choked out the remainder of the boy's explanation. The force of the unexpected blow caused both father and son to stumble backwards from each other for a few steps; for a moment they just stared at each other.

"Ya little bastards! Can't even leave you alone for five minutes!" Iver yelled wildly, and then he set to chasing the children drunkenly around the yard. "I'll teach ya a thing or two!" Pulling off his belt, he swung it around over his head, striking out at the three oldest children as they ran in circles, the dust following them in gray puffs. But the youngsters were too quick for him in his drunken state and they finally escaped by outflanking him and running like crazy out into the fields beyond the barn.

When things calmed down a bit Cora gathered up Leeland and Darrell, hurried over to the frightful Indian neighbor's house, and begged him to drive the two parents, the shaking, nearly hysterical Leeland, and the whimpering Darrell into town. Doc Christianson set Leeland's arm, but it had been broken in such a way that even though the doctor set it all right, the boy never did have full use of it again. While Doc Christianson treated Leeland, Cora and small Darrell sat in the outer room; Iver could not take listening to the screams of the injured child, so he left and went back down to the Legion, where he became quite drunk. The Indian patiently, quietly waited outside for the business to be finished, retrieved Iver from the Legion, and then drove the four back to the farmhouse. During the trip he looked sadly at Leeland, who sat close to him, resting fitfully in his mother's lap, jerking awake every few minutes from his medicine-induced sleep. Reaching out, he briefly, gently patted the restless child's knee. Iver sat next to Cora, pressed against the passenger door . . . rigid, fuming . . . holding Darrell stiffly as the car bounced down the road.

When they arrived back at the farm, after the Indian had driven off, Iver immediately ran through the house and back out into the yard, yelling, no, screaming out his oldest children's names, warning them to show themselves or else. He truly felt it his fatherly responsibility to discipline the miscreants by beating them soundly. But the three sat out in the darkness of the fields, hardly breathing, watching him from afar, too afraid to move. He sensed that they were out there somewhere and this infuriated him even more. Finally he went into the house and took his wrath out on Cora as she tended to Leeland and Darrell.

"You're a hellofa rotten mother, ya are! Spoiling them kids like ya do!" he yelled. Pushing her roughly up against the kitchen wall, he held his fist close to her face. "No wonder they can never behave! It's all yur fault!" he screamed at her, his enraged red face just a few inches from hers.

Cora somehow sidestepped him and went upstairs to put Darrell and Leeland to bed, but when she came down again Iver followed her from room to room. He continued to berate Cora for not having been a good mother, shoving her roughly around in the small kitchen, saying that she could not even control her own children. Cora crossed her skinny arms in front of her face but could not defend herself against the verbal and physical onslaught. To finally vent his rage, he hit her solidly between the eyes with his hard, closed fist; the sudden and unexpected blow pushed her backward sharply, awkwardly and she landed sitting upright and dazed on the kitchen floor. Upstairs Darrell slept deeply, but Leeland woke to a sound akin to someone slapping a side of beef and he began crying softly again, whimpering through the opiate elixir that Doc Christianson had earlier given the boy for his pain. Walking briskly into Cora's bedroom, Iver began throwing his belongings into the duffle bag, raging all the while at his wife, who had followed him into the room while holding an old towel to her face. Even then she clung to him, begging him not to leave . . . to stay for the remainder of his furlough . . . telling him that everything would be all right, that she would make the children mind if he would just stay a bit longer. But he merely shoved her roughly onto the bed.

The sounds of violence reached the three brothers hiding in the fields as only muffled noises and shouts coming from inside the house. But they knew better than to return, even after Iver left with his duffle slung angrily over his shoulder. They laid silently and watched him slam the front door and walk on back along the road he had come, on to the main highway where he hitched a ride back down to Jamestown. They slept out in the fields, lying in the low grass and still warm earth until morning. When they finally did go home, Cora sat forlorn in the front room, trying to hide her broken nose and blackened eyes behind her slender white hand, which shook as it held the bloody towel. Rocking back and forth, she grieved over Iver and at the same time prayed silently, asking that she not be pregnant again. Though battered and tired, she still mustered enough strength to scream loudly at the brothers when they came in, blaming them in a clogged, nasal voice for the incident the night before. She gathered them in the kitchen where she chastised them long and hard for driving her husband from the house. Awkwardly raising her left hand, which held the thick, threatening switch, she made them swear not to ever tell anyone about what had happened.

With her broken face and cracking voice, with her raging eyes and threatening arm held rigid and high, the memory of their mother's countenance that day remained with the brothers for a good long time.

Chapter Five—Into the Darkness

The start of the Lambson boys' inevitable undoing occurred on a cold and misty Sunday afternoon in early November of 1942, in plain sight of most of the community. Their drama played itself out on a day that started out with a light rain falling on Farmington and on the surrounding farms and prairie lands and countryside, an icy cold rain . . . the kind of chilly, rainy morning that often times blankets the whole land with a sense of dreary despondency . . . that shrouds one's very soul. A small crowd of townsfolk had braved the weather and gathered down at the large turret-shaped petroleum tanks in the storage yard of Warren Johnson's Standard Oil Company, at the western end of town, to witness and experience and participate in the growing excitement. The three white petroleum storage tanks stood side-by-side and held the entire supply of regular grade gasoline that fueled the tractors and trucks and cars of the farming community—the rationed life blood of the town. Each of the tanks was twenty foot tall and sixty foot in diameter, with a steel walkway that slanted up along the side to a catwalk; the narrow catwalk led around part of the rim and terminated at a metal control valve and large red turn-wheel. This valve provided the focal point of all of the mounting anticipation and suspense . . . the communal sense that something out of the ordinary was about to happen.

Dewey sat at the very top of the stairway, at the end of the catwalk, pointing the long barrel of a .38 pistol directly at the flow check valve, all the while wincing at the sporadic, almost ice-like drops of rain that pelted his young face. The rain made the tanks and the walkways cold and extremely slippery, diluting the red droplets of blood that trailed him up the steps. As he watched the drops dissolve, the cut on the calve of his leg began to ache more sharply, so he pealed back the bloody, muddy slit in his pants leg and felt the wound with his free hand. His young face grimaced in pain as he pressed on the mushy gash, which began to ooze again. Besides almost falling off of the wet stairway several times, Dewey had nearly dropped the .38 pistol as he brandished the weapon menacingly at the people staring up at him. Now the gun grew even heavier in his hand and dizziness engulfed him.

Sheriff Wilt stood off at a distance, behind the protection of his new black and white Ford patrol car, on the muddy ground not far from Dewey's perch. The domed red light on the roof revolved around inexorably, brightly in the grayness of the day, keeping the people at a distance; the sheriff left the light flashing in order to stress the gravity of the situation. For each time the sheriff would move closer to the tank, Dewey's warm, sweaty palm and fingers would grasp the pistol butt tighter and aim it carefully at the control valve and gauge that regulated the flow of gasoline through the pipe attached below it. Once, to emphasize his determination, Dewey held the pistol grip in both hands and squeezed the trigger, slowly moving back the hammer almost to the release position. Sheriff Wilt, along with the small but growing group of townspeople and local authorities that had formed behind him, moved back several steps in unison. Dewey knew he had control of the situation and gently eased back the finger pressure on the trigger.

"Ya better get on down from there, boy, before someone gets hurt!" Sheriff Wilt yelled up at the young criminal.

"Get your fat ass away from me or I'll blow us all to Kingdom Come!" Dewey screamed down at the sheriff. Imagination played a big part of Dewey's behavior; his perception of the situation involved an elaborate storyline of "cops 'n robbers"; as long as he successfully held the authorities at bay, the robbers would prevail.

"You people all get back now, ya hear. If that kid shoots, we could all go up. Get on back, now." At the sheriff's authoritative directive, everyone scuffled back about three yards and continued their hushed analysis and critique of the crisis and the sheriff's handling of it. As news of the dramatic incident spread around the town, the crowd continued to swell. Folks even began to come in from the outlying farms as word of the standoff increased.

"Where's his old lady at? Someone go find her!" he said to no one in particular as he half turned towards the crowd.

"No one's been able to locate her, Ben," someone said from the semicircle of curious onlookers, who continuously shifted and moved about restlessly in order to thwart the cold. "Lester said she's gone off ta Fargo with Earl Lempkey."

"Figured as much," muttered the sheriff, nodding knowingly.

Sheriff Wilt walked away a few steps so that he could reassess the situation. The autumnal sun would soon set behind the dark clouds; the temperature would drop quickly with the cold rain and increasing wind and darkness. The sheriff retrieved his wool jacket from the back seat of his patrol car and put it on. Because the boy wore only a light shirt and no coat, the sheriff knew that the freezing elements and growing darkness would soon dampen the youngster's heated passion. Through his squinted eyes he could see that Dewey's chin had begun quivering and he had lowered, just a bit, the hand tightly gripping the pistol. He decided to wait the boy out.

"What the hell's he doin' with that the gun up there?" Sheriff Wilt asked of his deputy Denny Jenkins, who had gradually worked his way up to the sheriff's side. "Go ast Vernon Reynolds if he's sure that damn thing's loaded"

"Already did and he said 'Yup.' Vernon said it's always loaded and ready to go."

"Shit. Idiot damn kid," the sheriff muttered to himself as he truly knew that he had a situation. "This time he's done it for sure!"

Sheriff Wilt had more than a good deal of contact with Dewey and his brothers for the past weeks and months and even years. The burglary at Farmer's Union Service Station and Restaurant just down the street only served as the culmination of the Lambson brothers' misbehavior. Now he knew that the wisest thing, and perhaps the only thing he could do, was just wait the boy out. In actuality, finally having a resolution at hand for the mischievous boy and his younger brothers proved to be a relief for the sheriff.

Since their father's visit and hasty departure nearly five months earlier, the Lambson boys had become rapidly and progressively more unmanageable. After her face had healed, and perhaps in celebration that she had not again become pregnant as a result of Iver's visit, Cora began to socialize once more, taking advantage of the friendships she had created during Iver's brief visit. Because she had met several male acquaintances at the Farmington American Legion, she spent quite a bit of time there and seldom returned home, except late at night, after the Legion had closed. Meanwhile Sheriff Wilt received various citizen reports that the boys had broken into several homes in Farmington, and the surrounding area, in their ongoing search for food. They had entered the Jensen home, on the outskirts of town, when the happy family went to Bismarck for a week. Walter Jensen immediately filed a complaint when he and his family arrived home after their holiday away. According to Walt Jensen's police report, "While inside the home the criminals emptied contents of the spice and flour and other containers and spread them all over the kitchen floor; as well, they upset the cupboards, rummaged through all of the closets, and generally turned the house upside down." Sherriff Wilt knew immediately that the Lambson kids were probably the culprits because the deed seemed typical of their type of mischief; in addition, he had also discovered what he suspected to be one of the boys' small, beaten-down shoes on the front door stoop of the Jensen place. For once he found Cora at home when he went out to the farm to question her and her sons, so he put her in the patrol car and took her directly to the City Attorney's office. With a good deal of satisfaction that the crime had been solved so efficiently, City Attorney Elvik summarily gave Cora the option of setting the Jensen place right again or going to jail. While the Jensons stayed with relatives, Cora spent an entire day cleaning their place. All the next day, feeling justifiably angry at the misbehavior of her children, Cora continually slapped at them all, leaving red marks on their young cheeks and skinny, bare arms.

After the Jensen incident many of the townspeople of Farmington were no longer willing to put up with the Lambson children and demanded that the local officials—Sheriff Wilt and the city attorney, specifically—do something about the situation, without delay! The two officials, with the assistance of Reverend Driskoll, paid a call on Cora Lambson and delivered her an ultimatum: she must stay at home, become a responsible parent, and do something about her delinquent children, or else face possible criminal charges. The attitude put forth by the three local authorities implied harsh consequences if the negligent mother did not "straighten up" and conform to the norms of the community.

Being given this directive, Cora found her options limited. As the result of her questionable friendship with Red Elgin, the little remaining relationship she had with Iver's family deteriorated completely. Nels, having found limited success as a welder in the Portland shipyards, had sold the farm and moved Inga to Gresham, Oregon; Cora hadn't heard a word from them since they left. Their daughters Adell, Clara, and Edith—Iver's sisters—had married and moved off to start their own families and careers. Adell finally married Hal Bigley and moved to Langdon; when business improved and Ed Cropper's grocery chain expanded to Walhalla, he and Clara wed and set up residence there; Edith became a spinster teacher in Fargo. Long before the family had gone their separate ways, however, Edith had once summarized the failed marriage between her brother and Cora to her good friend and confidant Pearl Anderson: "We all knew that Iver done wrong, but he has also had a awful lot to put up with, being married to that spoiled girl at nineteen. A girl her own people could not get along with." Later on that same week Clara had sadly said to her sisters, "Too bad he was such a weakling and took to liquor. He might notta been so blind and maybe listened to what we had to say." Pearl, as well as Adell and Edith, all had nodded their heads in affirmation of Clara's "perspicacity."

Given these circumstances, and fancying a severe illness coming on, Cora decided to ship the boys off to her stepparents, George and Marian Wills, over in Harveyville. George Wills remained sullenly reluctant to become involved with the troublesome and troubled youths, but under Mother Wills' unrelenting pleading, and against his better judgment, he drove down to Farmington, loaded all of the boys up in his 1937 Studebaker Suburban, and headed off north without even telling Cora goodbye. On the return trip to Harveyville, he hunched over the wide steering wheel while the five brothers bounced around on the seats in the back of the wood paneled station wagon. He sorely wished all the way that he had brought the Ford coupe so that they all could have ridden in the rumble seat. When they at last pulled into the front yard of the Wills' farm, Marian gathered the youngsters up into her large bosom and kissed them in welcome; with her own five children fully grown and gone their separate ways, she missed the tender embraces of little ones. Meanwhile, George walked silently, immediately into the house, already regretting his decision to accede to his wife's wishes. Over the years he had come to closely associate the children's presence with bad luck . . . no good ever came from them being around.

For the last few weeks of August, after the boys left their mother and stayed with their grandparents, things went quite well. The five came to relish the security and relative freedom of the older people's home. Both George and Marian remained ever busy, George with directing the harvest and Marian with the feeding of the threshing crews. As the threshing machine worked farther and farther from the farm, Marian worked the cook car, which always remained near the center of the harvesting activities. The two old people would leave early in the morning and be gone most of the day. Marian loaded Leeland and Darrell into the cook car, which very much resembled a small boxcar on wheels, and which contained the wood burning cook stove, various cooking and serving equipment, and a long counter. The grandparents had quickly given up on taking Dewey and Duane and Lloyd with them—in the fields the three proved to be more trouble than help. Instead Grandpa Wills assigned them numerous chores to do around the farmstead: milk the cows, feed the chickens, gather eggs, and hoe the garden. But they soon found that without much effort they could always manage to finish these menial tasks quickly and then make their way into Harveyville, walking in amongst the tall haystacks and weaving through and around the bundles of sweet smelling alfalfa sitting out in the fields that lined the dirt road into town. Once in town the three brothers would wander down the warm and friendly streets, unhampered by their past and truly free.

Harveyville's Main Street, which paralleled the Great Northern railroad tracks, served as the primary thoroughfare of the small town. The community itself had several dozen houses that lined Main and First and Second Street, as well as Park and Michigan avenue and the fairly new Winnipeg Avenue beyond that; the houses on Main and First and Second Streets faced north and south and those on Park and Michigan and Winnipeg Avenues faced east and west. Chicken wire fences surrounded most of the yards of the framed homes and ran the length of the narrow sidewalks that fronted the rows of comfortable yet plain homes. Patches of peonies and pansies, and sometimes irises and gladiolas and pastel colored sweet peas, would knit their flowers into a fragrant, multi-colored patchwork array, with hues of yellow and red, purple and pink, and white and orange all woven into the wire sections of the fences. Lars and Annie Glendon, along with their four plump, happy children—two boys and two girls—occupied the house on the western end of Main Street. Lars, the extremely able manager of the Farmers Elevator, certainly was well known and equally well respected in the small community; Annie, a sturdy woman, kept active in the American Lutheran Church, where she played the organ, sang in and led the church's choir, taught Sunday school, and in addition to everything else, religiously cared for the altar linens. The Glendon household stood next to John Galvin Park—a grassy rectangle that occupied one entire block of the city, and marked the end of the residential area of Harveyville. Numerous evergreens and elms, as well as some ash and cottonwood trees, provided shimmering shade for the picnic area and playground. Their combined limbs and leaves created a cool canopy for the teeter-totter and the squeaky swing set and the merry-go-round in the center of the park. Further west lay the business district: Baird's Lumberyard and General Store, Rose's Café, Peachy's saloon, Vorheis' Blacksmith and Livery Shop, the Great Northern Train Depot, and Odegaard's Drug Store, and then the several large grain elevators that loomed tall and businesslike on the town's outskirts. Across the wide street stood the Farmers Mercantile Bank, the Palms Hotel, and the Fowler building, which housed the D. Orvik Law Office, the United States Post Office, the Taft County Assessors' Office, the fire hall, and the city offices. Further down the roadway were the Harveyville Meat Market and Locker, Adley's Creamery, and the Polar Ice Company with its cool, oil impregnated, dark-brown wood building and gray, corrugated tin roof.

Because no history came with the boys, they could roam the town freely. When Dewey, Duane, and Lloyd came to town, they would spend the day doing nothing, exploring the deep ditches and high weeds that paralleled the railroad tracks, where the summer grasses and tiger lilies grew hip-high, with brownish heads that could be split open and used for itching powder. They liked Baird's Lumberyard and General Store best, though, where they could roam undetected through the depths of the lumber yard, with its high stacks of pine wood stockpiled along the west outside wall of the hardware store. Wide, watershed eaves extended far out over the diagonal supports that ran from the ground to the roof's edge, thus providing ample protection from the weather in keeping the lumber dry. The best grades of cut wood were kept in the uppermost tiers and this area afforded the brothers a cool and secretive place to play during the warm summer days, as well as a sheltered nook during heavy afternoon rainstorms. A pungent smell of resin permeated the lumberyard . . . the same resin that made their hands sticky as the three youngsters clambered to the topmost tiers of smooth, precut wood.

One day, up in the secure niche, Dewey pulled out the crushed, half-empty package of Lucky Strikes he had pilfered from Earl, one of Grandpa Wills' temporary thrashing hands who housed themselves in the Will's barn. Earl worked as the tractor man, skillfully operating the old Romley that pulled the threshing rig. Sometimes he would run the separator, too. Earl played the mouth organ and had taken a liking to Dewey.

"Whatcha got, Dew?" asked Duane as he and Lloyd gathered close. Dewey casually lit one of the white, deformed cigarettes, coughed several times as the strong smoke filled his lungs, and reveled in the dizziness that followed. After a few more puffs, he passed the cigarette on to his brothers, who shared in the great experience. The boys lit two more cigarettes and lay listless in their dizzy, altered state. Unfortunately, one of the smoldering butts, or perhaps one of the matches they had used, fell down below into sawdust pit for the lumber yard's chop saw and a small fire began to spread rapidly. Hank, the day foreman, smelled the smoke and quickly sounded the alarm. From their vantage point the boys watched with wide eyes the excitement below. The Harveyville volunteer firemen quickly mustered and the city fire truck appeared and put out the smoldering sawdust and half-burned stack of two-by-fours, thus averting a major fire that probably would have burned half of the town to the ground. The boys looked on in amazement and fascination for three hours and never were discovered. The consensus of the crowd that had gathered outside the lumberyard was that the fire could best be attributed to probably the actions of some careless customer; when the crowd's curiosity had been amply satisfied, they returned to their mundane tasks and the boys climbed down from their perch, happy and satisfied with the day's events.

During the brothers' stay in Harveyville, Baird's continued to be a drawing point for them. Sometimes on Saturday all five of them would saunter into the town, presenting a united front of curiosity. Baird's General Store offered a magical cornucopia of merchandise to see and touch and smell and experience. The shelves, always fully stocked, offered a wide variety of gadgets and necessities and small appliances . . . everything a farm or town family needed for day-to-day living. The hardware section contained barrels of nails and orderly, segregated compartments of numerous-sized nuts and bolts and screws and tacks, as well as a variety of hinges and hasps, buckles and springs, and hundreds of miscellaneous small metal fasteners. Along the walls hung the large and small tools of the farm: braces and bits, spade shovels, hoes, hammers and hatchets, axes and picks, large-toothed and small toothed saws, bastard files and rat-tailed hasps, pliers and wheel pullers, small sickles and large scythes. To the rear of the store lay a wealth of household goods and utensils: stove pokers and coal shuttles and ash pans, ten-quart galvanized buckets, two-gallon milking pails and corresponding three-legged stools, rugs and horse blankets, corrugated washboards and flyswatters, copper kettles and coffee percolators, stoneware pots and metal baking pans and cookie sheets and flattening irons. Towards the front lay the aisles and racks of clothes and pungent-smelling leather goods. The entire inside of the store contained the heartbeat of the town . . . the abundance of wares and gadgets, both electrical and mechanical, needed for the survival of its people.

Within such a broad array of products and gear, the boys became artful at petty theft and boosting things from the general store. Lloyd and Leeland and Darrell would enter the store and hurriedly go off in different directions. This suspicious activity would immediately draw the clerk's attention to them; meanwhile, Dewey and Duane, already deep inside the aisles, would grab handfuls of whatever they could find and stuff the merchandise into their baggy pockets.

One morning Dewey even boldly stole a small vial of Chantilly perfume for Irma Wilkey; he considered her his "girlfriend" because she often gave Dewey and his brothers butterscotch candy and various other treats whenever they came to town. Irma, who some claimed to be an illiterate, sixth-grade dropout, waitressed down at Rose's Café; she couldn't count very well and made change for the customers by memorizing the number of penny, nickel, dime, and quarter combinations needed to make change for each meal listed on the menu. Price changes always required a good deal of retraining for Irma, so the owner eventually made her the cook. But she certainly favored the Lambson boys. A kindly and heavy-chested woman, Irma never married and thus had no children of her own, so she always greeted the boys happily by hugging their faces into her abundant bodice. Whenever Grandma Marian gave the boys each a nickel for doing their chores, they would head to town and go straight to Rose's to spend it on candy corn and pralines; Irma always gave them ten times what the pittance of their allowance would buy. They would go to the back of the restaurant and gain Irma's attention by throwing a pebble or two against the back door to make their presence known. She would patiently come out, make the exchange, and send them away satisfied, with loads of sweets and sloppy kisses for all of them. "Yeah, you goot kits!" she would tell them kindly. Sometimes she would sneak them out choke-cherry jam covered bread slices, or heavy tapioca with rich whipped cream atop of it, or slices of delicious peach or blueberry pie, which they ate ravenously with their dirt-smudged hands.

For the most part the boys remained fairly well behaved during their stay in Harveyville. Provided with full stomachs with which to nourish their growing bodies, they pretty much obeyed their two grandparents and generally respected the old people's wishes. As a result, they continually delighted in their new circumstances.

The boys' contentedness connected well with and some ways even mirrored the spirit and temper of the town. The oppressive heat of the summer gradually became moderated by the approach of fall, which heralded the fast approaching end to the harvest season. A festive mood . . . almost a holiday atmosphere . . . infused the streets of Harveyville. Even though war raged throughout the world, creating myriad local and regional and national hardships, the completion of the harvest provided the townsfolk with a feeling of hope . . . of optimism. The harvest had become intricately woven into the history of the farming community and its citizens; the timeless tradition of reaping what had been sown had long ago become permanently etched into the soul of the people. Another year of planting had been successfully completed and a feeling of joyousness and satisfaction saturated the air. On Saturday afternoons families would gradually gather on the green lawn of John Galvin Park in the middle of the town, spreading blankets or checkered tablecloths under the gently moving leaves of the shady trees, all the while swatting at the mosquitoes that gathered thick in the sultry air. Each family would secure a spot and begin unloading the heavy-laden picnic baskets, while the children ran off to play. In the very center of the park stood a solid, six-sided wooden gazebo, stilted four feet above the grass and draped with the red, white, and blue bunting left over from the 4th of July celebration. From this elevated position the Harvey-ville Ingenuity Band, under the sponsorship of the Farmers and Merchants Bank and with J. R. Richardson as the conductor, provided the music of waltzes, polkas, and foxtrots when the evening breezes began.

Labor Day, 1942, fell on one such Sunday, so the spell-binding orator R. F. K. O'Henry was invited to town to deliver a political speech about the war, and the tyranny of the Nazis and their Axis allies, in hopes of heightening the spirit and patriotism of the townsfolk. George Wills, though not much of a political activist, eagerly gathered Marian and the five boys up and took them to town to hear the event. They arrived somewhat late, and thus had to remain on the outer periphery of the crowd. Because of this, Dewey, Duane, and Lloyd easily slipped away from their grandparents. With a great deal of curiosity the three Lambson boys went around to the rear of the gazebo and snuck in the small door-like entrance that had been cut into the lattice work skirting the structure. Moving quietly along the small, narrow crawl space to just below the front of the stage, they could look out undiscovered through the diagonal slats and watch the listening, smiling people as they enthusiastically cheered and applauded the orator's main points. After the rousing speech, the Ingenuity Band began playing. In their excitement of wanting to see what real families did on such occasions, the boys watched out at the Glendons, who managed to sit prominently in the front of the semi-circle of townsfolk. Lars sat flanked by a son on each side, with his daughter nestled into his lap as his feet kept time to Benny Goodman's "There'll Be Some Changes Made"; sitting close by, his wife Annie kept their nearly walking infant daughter, who had a pink bow tied into her wispy blond hair, confined within her outstretched legs and helped the baby clap its tiny fat hands. Earlier, on the way in, the boys had snuck fistfuls of ham and sweetmeats and sticks of fresh bread from Grandma Wills' picnic basket and stuffed the food into their pockets; now, feeling truly part of the event, they hungrily ate the foods and joyfully watched the festivities from the security of their lair. However, after a time Lars noticed movement behind the skirting slats and heard the boys' quiet laughter and singing and chattering. Sure that they could be up to no good—perhaps playing with fire and thus inviting a catastrophe—Lars sprung quickly into civic action. Jumping up, he moved with great certainty around to the rear of the gazebo, rousted the boys from their vantage point, and drew them to the front of the crowd; when the band stopped in mid-song, he asked loudly what family the miscreant children belonged to. With much chagrin, Grandpa Wills reluctantly came forward, making his way through the seated families, to claim his charges; not wanting to become any more of a spectacle before the townsfolk, he herded them roughly off to the dusty Studebaker Suburban where he waited, his back to the crowd, while Grandma Marian hurriedly gathered up the picnic materials and joined them. Not realizing that they had once more become the focus of a town's silent scorn, or that they had even done anything wrong, the boys happily got into the car. Grandpa Wills slammed the door and drove off silently towards home; Grandma Marian just looked out the passenger window at the passing town, not wanting to say anything that might provoke an angry outburst from her obviously upset husband.

"Why we gotta leave so soon, Gramma?" asked Leeland.

"Yeah, how come?" chimed in Lloyd.

"We was just startin' to have fun!" added Duane.

"Hush, now," their grandmother said softly. "You boys just sit back and *try* to behave."

When no further answers or conversation came from the two silent guardians sitting in the front seat, the boys began excitedly discussing the many marvelous things they had seen and then began singing snippets of the songs they had heard earlier.

Grandpa Wills angrily forbade the boys from ever going back downtown. But for them the on-going weather of the Indian summer prolonged the festive mood of harvest time they had experienced that afternoon. The evenings remained warm and silently pleasant as the sun dimmed and faded orange into the western prairies. Grandma and Grandpa Wills, aged and fatigued by their history of hard farm labors, always slumped off to bed almost immediately after dinner and were deeply asleep by dusk. Though expected to follow the same schedule, the boys were unable to fall asleep as quickly as their grandparents. Often they would lay awake, full and contented, discussing the day's events, or plan-ning the morrow's promise, or talking about their mother

Cora . . . wondering where she was and why they never heard from her.

One night, a few evenings following the Labor Day adventure, while Leeland and Darrell slept soundly, Dewey and Duane and Lloyd remained wide awake. Particularly restless that evening, they decided to do some "moonlight" exploring. The window of their second story bedroom stayed open to catch the temperate evening breezes, allowing the three brothers an avenue of escape. They quietly climbed over the window sill, crept along the slanted roof, shinnied part way down the creaky rain gutter, leaped over to the outstretched limb of the elm tree growing beside the house, and then inched their way down the trunk to solid ground. At last free of the stifling confines of the farmstead and of the stolid grandparents, they laughed and joked and playfully shoved each other as they ran off into the nearby fields towards Stan Baumgaard's place, the Wills' nearest neighbor. The newly tilled ground sunk softly beneath their shoes as the brightness of the harvest moon lit their pathway. Once at the Baumgaard's they began to explore the packed watermelon patch, which lay at the edge of the green, fertile garden, a few hundred feet from the farmhouse. After smashing two fat melons on the ground to open them up, they eagerly began to scoop the liquid mush from the green shells, relishing the sweet taste and the rich smell and feel of the sticky pink pulp. Soon the noise of the party woke up the farmer's dog, which began barking long and woefully. Lights came on in the house and almost immediately Farmer Baumgaard came out into the spray of light spilling out from the house into the yard. The three boys picked up a whole melon each and immediately lit out for home, running hard as Baumgaard fired off his shotgun, which was filled with rock salt, in the direction of the rapidly departing boys. The flash and blast made the boys run harder until Lloyd, who blindly led the way, ran directly into the almost-invisible, three-strand, barbed wire fence that bordered the watermelon patch. The top strand caught Lloyd chest-high, with the sharp barbs tearing his shirt and cutting into his small chest. This abrupt, stopping action thrust him backwards, knocking him to the ground with a good deal of force, violently driving the wind from his lungs. But Lloyd's selfless act saved Dewey and Duane from the same fate, so they gladly dropped their spoils, picked up their gasping, grasping brother, navigated through the wires, and limped him back home.

Later that same evening the constable came to the Will's house, knocking forcefully on the front door for several minutes until he at last roused the old couple. Seems that Stan Baumgaard had seen the watermelon thieves running off towards the Wills' farm and, naturally assuming the Lambson kids to be the wrongdoers, had called in the law. Accompanied by the constable, the tired, unsteady grandparents went upstairs only to find the boys sleeping innocently in their beds, immersed in the covers. Marian Wills assured the constable that there had been a mistake made; she swore to him several times that the children had gone to bed and had been in the house all evening. With no proof, the constable and Stan left, not entirely convinced that the older three boys had not been fully involved in the mischief. Also being skeptical of the boys' innocence, George Wills did his own investigation early the next morning, while the children still slept soundly. Carefully pulling back the covers revealed their faces and hands still gray-brown and sticky. As well, he found Lloyd's torn and bloodied shirt stuffed under the boys' mattress. Further inspection revealed tiny bits of rock salt embedded in the inside of the cuffs of Dewey and Darrell's bib overalls, along with stringy watermelon pulp and black pits clinging tellingly to all of their pants legs. Grandfather Wills grew more and more irritated, sure that his grandchildren continued to give him a bad name in town, and thus became further determined to send the boys on back to their mother as soon as possible.

Yet the brothers continued to truly enjoy their visit at the Wills' place. With the harvest completed, every one of the town's children returned to school, the opening of which had been delayed because the young folks had been needed in the fields that year, what with the number of young men off to war. The Lambson boys, however, became exempt from any school attendance and thus were pretty much free to do what they wanted. Grandpa Wills had made his mind up that the boys were already far behind in their education and would probably only cause more trouble in the local school. Therefore, using the excuse that he did not really know the duration of their stay, which he hoped would be short, he arbitrarily decided against their attending school at Harveyville.

"They needn't bother enrolling in the school," he told Marian sharply. "They can help me with the end-of-harvest chores that need doin'. I got alotta tillin' to do before the first snows set in. Besides..." He said, looking severely at his wife, "they need to get on back home. You talked to Cora yet?"

"I've sent her several letters, George, but she doesn't never...."

" Call 'er, then!"

"You know she don't have no phone."

"Baaaa! She needs to come get these kids, dammit! I rue the day I ever saw her! She ain't no fit wife or mother or nothin'!"

So not having to attend school, and having nothing else to do, the curious boys would intently follow their grandfather around, keeping him from doing his own work. The boys certainly could not be considered lazy, but rather they lacked direction, which Grandpa George was in no way ready to provide them, busy as he was with his own hard work. Finally, in addition to their regular chores, he ordered them to load freshly cut and bailed shocks of hay onto a flatbed wagon for storage in the barn. Not knowing anything about the process of shocking hay, the boys, shortly after beginning the task, merely left for other more interesting pursuits. Later that same day Grandpa Wills came by and found their pitchforks lying beside the wagon and them gone. After that he pretty much gave up and just tried to ignore them, even when they would follow him around intently and then come up to him and ask their numerous innocent questions.

"Whatcha doin', Grampa?" asked Leeland one day as Grandpa Wills bent over the grinding wheel, absorbed in sharpening a harrow disc. When Leeland received no answer, he asked the question over and over several times until he finally got a response. The other brothers stood off at a distance, curiously watching to see what Grandpa Wills would say and do.

"Nothin', Goddammit!" the old man finally responded angrily as he stood up. "At least nothin' that concerns you! And don't call me 'Grampa'," he told Leeland meanly as he moved off to other more important tasks. "You kids go on and find somethin' ta do! Get outta my hair!" He waved them off collectively without looking back.

This one, unequivocal gesture seemed to the boys to essentially free them from their obligation to the mean old man and the demands of his chore-ridden farm, and in reality gave them the freedom to roam the confines of their world, particularly the delightfully smelly Christian Holt & Co. Stockyards, where the wooden loading shoots for the animals led up to a spur off the main railroad tracks.

Dewey often enjoyed losing his younger brothers and going off by himself to the gently rolling hills beyond the yards. There he had discovered myriad prairie dog colonies that pockmarked the open grasslands with acres and acres of bunkered-up holes. Lone prairie dog sentinels, serving as pickets on the periphery of the community, perched nervously up on their small haunches, would squeal out an alarm whenever a circling hawk, or a skulking fox, or the curious boy approached too closely to the burrows. The darting, dun-colored rodents, tails held high and rigid, would race for the protection of the cool openings, each making sure that the young entered first. And as dictated by the process of natural selection, there would always be a small, scared one or two of the creatures that could not move fast enough, or faltered in fear, and thus fell victim to the hawk or to the fox or to Dewey. Using the slingshot he had secretly brought along with him from Farmington, he would expertly pick the laggards off one by one. Crafted from one of the firm "y" branches from high up in the cottonwood tree at home, with a section of inner tube tightly tied to each end of the fork providing ample force to launch nickel-size stones, the weapon proved accurate and highly lethal to small prey. For long hours he would lie still in wait on the edge of the rodent community, hardly breathing. After the excitement of Dewey's initial raid, the prairie dogs would soon begin to peer up over the edges of their bunkers, their heads darting side to side; he would launch a pellet and more likely than not hit his target. Sometimes he would silently give the rodents names before releasing the missile and smile in satisfaction when it found its mark. Finally, satiated with his marksmanship, he would rise, brush himself off, idle over to the stockyards, and then walk back to the Wills' place far beyond.

Through the waning summer and the early fall, there always seemed to be some sort of intriguing activity or inviting adventure going on in the general vicinity of the yards. For example, one day the boys sat on the yard's long split-rail fence and watched excitedly as a set of diesel engines pulling a seemingly endless line of flatbed cars of M3A1 Steward Light Tanks, bound from Detroit to Seattle for shipment to the Pacific theater, swished by them, fanning a gentle breeze past their excited faces. Standing up on the fence, they cheered and waved their arms; Dewey affirmed loudly, happily, that the event indeed represented a good omen for them.

The only real difficulty the youngsters had during those free times of late September and early October, at least what they considered to be trouble, lay in their ongoing feud with the Merriman kids, who lived on the outskirts of town, close to the stockyards. The Merriman boys hated the Lambson boys, envying their freedom from the responsibility of school attendance. Invariably after school the Merrimans would

come by the stockyards on their way home from the schoolyard and a dirt-clod war, or perhaps a regular fist fight, would
erupt. Clayton, Clinton, and Frankie, the cross-eyed one,
mirrored Dewey, Duane, and Lloyd in age. Rumor around
town had it that Sam Merriman, a widower, often beat his
children with a razor strap when they misbehaved, so they
were reputed to be a "bunch of tough cookies." Clayton had
somewhat of a pushed in face, as though he had run headlong
into a brick wall or someone had hit him full force with a
pan-faced shovel; his lips actually curled up towards his flattened nose. With these distinguishing features, along with
his large, protruding ears, he certainly offered a hardened
demeanor. But because there were only three Merrimans
and five Lambsons in any given engagement, the Merrimans
usually sustained the worst in such frays, although they had
once caught Leeland by himself, hit him in the head with
a small rock, and then beat the heck out of him. Thereafter, relishing the superiority the Lambsons held in any given
confrontation with the Merrimans, Dewey would arrange
so their paths crossed as often as possible—the dominance
they had, after all, proved to be the only power and influence the brothers could exert over other people. Whenever
a confrontation arose, Dewey would always make light of
Clayton's physical appearance. "Hey, monkey face," he
would holler challengingly at Clayton when he saw the boys
ambling toward them in the distance. "Is your momma an
ape?" The fact that his mother had died giving birth to a
breached Frankie infuriated Clayton even more and his flat
face became bright red with frustrated anger and hurt. Then
the Merrimans and Lambsons would go at each other with
warrior-like intensity.

One chilly afternoon, when the cool wind from the north came as a harbinger of the fast approaching winter, the five Lambsons, idling down at the stockyards, waited patiently for the appearance of the Merrimans and for the subsequent afternoon wars, all the while talking boldly about what they would do to their adversaries. The boys sat along the plank fence, getting splinters in their butts every time they moved, anxious for something to happen. In one of the nearby pens wallowed a large, dusty pink slaughter hog with wispy tufts of wire-like hair poking out of its leather-rough hide. The rooting and snorting drew their curiosity, so they left their uncomfortable perch, sauntered over, and looked in between the rails of the fence at the stinking brown mud of the large pen.

"Bet I could ride that big, fat bastard!" asserted Dewey.

"Shoot, he must weight two three hundrit pounds! He'd roll over and squash the guts right outta ya!" snorted Duane.

Dewey considered Duane's statement to be a challenge . . . he now felt compelled to ride the weighty animal in order to maintain his position in his brothers' eyes. For quite a while he sat on the rail, looking intensely at the ominous creature and its surroundings, studying it, looking intently for its weak point. Finally his dark brown eyes fell upon a rusty block and tackle dangling from the roof of the pen, with a long piece of weathered rope drooping from the rig; the device moved slightly in the wind, intriguing Dewey.

"Come on!" Dewey suddenly commanded and the four brothers followed excitedly as he went over and jumped down into the soft muck.

The pig squealed loudly as the boys chased it around the pen. After a bit they were able to find a length of leather strapping, fashion a lasso, and rope the pig's hind legs. With the animal thus disabled, Dewey loosened the rope from the block-and-tackle and looped it around the pig's fat neck. In unison the boys strained at the course, dark hemp line, which cut into their hands and left tiny splinters. The rusty pulley squeaked under the heavy load and the mighty battle, and the sounds blended in nicely with the pig's screams. All five of the brothers pulled on the rope and when the pig flailed, the weight of its body would sometimes pull them off of the ground all at once, making them all laugh joyously. Finally the combined weight of all of their young bodies prevailed, enabling them to raise the front quarter of the animal up off of the ground gradually. Following several more minutes of supreme effort, the pig's head and front feet rose high off the ground, with its body supported only by its bound hind legs. The pig thrashed around wildly when they looped, cinched, and tied off the rope to the top rail of the pen. Sweating and tired, their hands all raw from rope burns, the brothers leaned back against the rails of the fence and rested.

"Yeeeehawwww!" screamed Dewey suddenly, loudly, as he ran over and mounted the pig at the small of its bowed back and wrapped his arms around the pig's neck as it began to buck. "Okay, Duane, let 'er loose!"

Duane ran over and released the hobble rope from the animal's rear legs. The pig reacted with even more furor and for quite a while Dewey delightfully pretended like the animal was bucking him wildly, all the while hanging on tightly to the taut rope holding the pig in place. Both Duane and Lloyd screamed for their turn, but Dewey would not yield and just ignored them. He continued to yell loudly and flailed away relentlessly at the animal's flanks with the imaginary cowboy hat that he pretended to grip tightly in his small hand. The animal did keep thrashing around wildly for quite some time, but its resistance became less and less until there finally was no more movement at all. Whether due to a broken back or strangulation, the animal at last hung limply beneath Dewey, its rear cleft-hooved feet dug into the dirt and mud. Dewey dismounted slowly, not realizing what he had done.

"Damn, oh dear! Look at what ya done!" said Duane

"I didn't mean ta . . . ." Dewey murmured.

"Dang . . . we lynched 'er," observed Lloyd as he nudged the huge, limp carcass with a short length of stick. All of the brothers walked around the dead pig in wonder, poking it now and then, as if the action might somehow bring the animal back to life. That is when the reality of death and the magnitude of their deed finally reached them, almost in unison.

"Shit, let's get the heck outta here!" cried Duane and they all lit out for home.

When they arrived at the farm they nervously tried to pretend that nothing had happened, at which they were somewhat successful. Unfortunately, the Merriman boys had been coming home from school and watched the entire cruel event from the corner of the corral. Though they thoroughly enjoyed seeing the lynching, and they even admired Dewey for his wild rowdiness, nothing could have pleased them more than to be able to tell the owner of the stockyards, Mr. P. Everett Wolfe, what had happened to the murdered animal and, more importantly, who had done it. Consequently, later that evening, the town constable, accompanied by the angry Mr. Wolfe, showed up once more at the

Wills' farm to get an accounting of that afternoon's incident. Grandpa Wills had no evidence to support the boys' claim of innocence and so had to accede to Mr. Wolfe's demand that Wills pay for the hanged pig. The pig turned out to be a purebred Duroc, and the cost to Grandfather Wills for its death amounted to $72.50, for which he was required to sign a handwritten promissory note for payment to Mr. Wolfe. Wolfe and the constable left, somewhat placated, but Wolfe mumbled loudly, so George could hear, about how he would eventually get even with Wills. Grandpa Wills, infuriated by the whole string of incidents, remained silent and resolute, yet in so doing decided he had had quite enough.

Despite the vehement protestations of Grandma Marian, early the very next morning, he loaded the youngsters up in the rumble seat of the Ford coupe. Before he drove off, Grandma Marian stuffed their light jackets and a basket of food in amongst them. The ride back to Farmington was cold and the boys huddled against one another. When they arrived at the Lambson farmhouse, Grandpa Wills dropped them off even though Cora was not at home. After entering the house and not finding his adopted daughter, he hustled them out of the rumble seat and got back in the car. Leaning out the window, he pointed his finger at them and said gruffly, "And tell yur ma not to call us anymore! We don't want anything more to do with her!" He drove off quickly, leaving them standing in the desolate front yard, watching him in bewilderment, not knowing exactly what they were supposed to do.

Initially glad to see their home, the boys wandered about the house and the barn and happily scampered up into the cottonwood and swung comfortably and lazily in the tire swing for the better part of a day. However, the boys quickly became despondent when they found the place, as always, totally barren of food. Even the warm ice box contained nothing, not even any of Cora's beer, and no bottle of clear gin lay hidden in the cupboard below the sink. To Dewey, this emptiness indicated both that his mother hadn't been there for awhile and that she probably would not return any time soon. A moment of panic shook Dewey, almost overcoming him, but he knew he must shake it off and do so quickly. He had no other option but to care for his younger brothers. Within a very short time—the next day, as a matter of fact—when their mother had not returned and the provisions Grandma Miriam had sent were gone, they had no choice but to resort to their old, known, reliable ways of satisfying their growing hunger. And because they had been fed so well and regularly for the previous two months, their hunger became ravenous . . . almost all consuming. Dewey began to formulate a concrete plan for their survival.

On the Friday following their return, which was almost two full days without any substantial food, Dewey decided to act, regardless of how reckless their crimes might become or what the consequences would be. Dewey and Duane had found enough scraps from the corners of the cupboards to make a terrible tasting gruel . . . a recipe that Dewey had acquired from the hobos down at the camp; the bums had jokingly called it "Robin Hood porridge"—a gumbo made from anything anyone could find or steal. But because the boys' soup was composed mostly of hot water, it did little to alleviate the rumbling in their stomachs. Consequently all that day they fanned out in a "scouting" party, as Dewey put it. "We need to sneak out and see what kinda supplies we can get holda. We're escaped American prisoners in Germany, tryin' to survive, see," he said to his brothers, a great deal of excitement in his voice. "So don't get caught!" But as hard as he tried, the brothers had grown so hungry that they could pretend very little drama into the forays. At the end of the day they all returned tiredly to the cold farmhouse, with only a few meager, pilfered provisions, and reported that in all of the houses they spied on people were busy laying in stores of food for the coming winter. Autumn had ended abruptly and winter bore steadily down upon them; the days grew shorter and the nights became increasingly colder.

Based upon the gathered intelligence, Dewey chose the Widow Ruth Ulrud's place, one of the last homes on the outskirts of town. He had crept up to her window and watched cautiously as her wispy frame moved slowly from room to room, so he knew the layout of her house. Their hunger had become an ache, so in the morning they left early and made their way to the widow's place, where they laid in wait in the field to the east of her house, hoping that she would venture off into the town. At about 10:45 she left for the Saturday meeting of the Zion Lutheran Community Church Ladies Aid Society, the benevolent social organization whose members so prided themselves on having a long and well recognized history of concern for the needs of others. The meeting that particular morning, being held over at Rachael Stump's place, had been convened as a "stitching session" in which the dedicated women members worked hard to sew quilts and knit woolen scarves for the poor; the ladies were in the midst of a heated competition with the Catholic Women's Society to see which organization could do the most for those less fortunate.

Once sure she had left and would not be returning any time soon, the young burglars let themselves in though the unlocked back door. The place had a warm, inviting, cinnamon-like smell to it, so they took their time while they plundered her larder. Ruth Ulrud must have stayed for coffee after the end of the gathering, chatting her lonely emptiness away with her lady friends, because the boys had long since departed when she arrived home. With them they had carted off a plate of meat, six potatoes, a large jar of rhubarb jam, a loaf of homemade bread, two cans of sweet corn, a box of matches, and several yellow-white cakes of paraffin. At least those are the items that the widow listed in her burglary report to the sheriff later that afternoon.

Unfortunately, the Lambson boys had never been very good criminals. Or perhaps their ever-present hunger clouded their sense of carefulness. But it seems that every time they would commit a break in, they would invariably leave something behind that belonged to them . . . an identifiable piece of clothing or something else that interfered with them being good and successful criminals. Besides that, though, whenever any petty larceny occurred in the small town, the Lambson boys usually became the first suspects: either the authorities suspected them or else found incriminating proof that inevitably pointed to the youngsters. In the Widow Ulrud's case, the evidence was a series of small, muddy footprints, of various sizes, leading in from the field behind her house. And this time Leeland had dropped a small, black head warmer he had saved from the previous winter.

Sheriff Wilt had his suspicions right away when the widow called to inform him that someone had broken into her place and stolen a sizeable amount of food. The food became the first best indication of the Lambsons' probable involvement, but when he went out to her place and investigated, he saw the small footprints and ransacked foodstuffs, along with the woolen cap that could only fit a child's cold head, and immediately named the brothers as the culprits. Though the boys had not been around for the past two months, and because the town had suffered no burglaries during that time, Sheriff Wilt surmised it could only be the brothers . . . they must have somehow returned to the town. So again, as he had done numerous times before, Sheriff Wilt drove the lonesome road out to the Lambson farm. To his surprise, though, he could find no one there. Walking through the empty house, he quickly concluded that no one had been there for some time; completing his investigation, he surmised that, given the barrenness of the house, no one would be returning soon. He must have been wrong, he thought, deeply perplexed.

But the brothers, hidden away in the barn, watched his movements intently as he wandered around the farmyard, looking for anything suspicious. In the upper loft of the barn they had constructed a lean-to shelter with wood and doors they scavenged from the floor below; when they were all gathered within their "hideout," their combined body heat kept them warm. And as in the past, whenever the brothers broke into any place, they always took all of the food they could find, carried it off bundled in their small arms, and hid it, along with themselves, in the upper loft of the barn. Doing so not only added to their provisions, but also hid them and any of their incriminating evidence from snooping investigators. This time they had done the same with the

Widow Ulrud's spoils. But in the middle of their feasting on the plunder, when they heard the approach of a slow moving car, they had scurried to look out cautiously from the top floor door of the barn. When they saw the sheriff, they quietly retreated to the shelter and burrowed themselves and their food in the shadows.

"Nobody make a peep or I'll beat the snot outta ya!" Dewey had whispered harshly to them and then they listened and waited fearfully. Slowly and silently they ate while Dewey crawled over and looked out of the small crack by the lower door hinge, watching out into the gathering darkness of the cold afternoon.

Sheriff Wilt poked around a bit and then looked up at the barn, directly at Dewey, before moving his gaze to where the other brothers lay hidden; but the sheriff could see nothing. He left after several minutes, but they waited for about two hours before going back into the house to gather the frayed and torn woolen blankets from their bed and then return to the security of the barn. The heating oil and lamp fuel canisters inside the house all sat empty, so the boys made a small fireplace in their protective nest; using an inverted, tarnished hubcap, they burned twisted scraps of straw that had collected from the corners of the barn and a few scraps of wood wrestled from the walls. Soon they huddled together tightly, wrapped in the urine-smelling comforters, finishing off the remains of their plunder and wondering what to do with the paraffin . . . that is, if the small, round cakes of wax might be edible. Eventually they discovered that the paraffin could be melted into the fire to keep it burning.

Before the warmth and light of the fire died, Dewey completed his bold plan. Given the success of their raid on the widow's place, and because their concerns remained focused on their own pressing needs, the brothers unanimously agreed with Dewey's suggestion that they immediately strike again. He suggested that they rise before daybreak and try their luck at the Farmers' Union Service Station and Restaurant, which would no doubt be closed on Sunday. They had made several successful raids there in the past few years, so the store presented a viable target.

In the early morning cold and dew, they made their way down the quiet streets of Farmington until they came to the darkened restaurant. Off to the east, heavy, red-gray clouds filling the skies signaled the approach of the first fall storm. Before the brightly reddening morning had matured into full dawn, they approached the Farmers' Union, broke out a painted window in the back bathroom of the restaurant with a chunk of lumber, and quietly entered the relative warmth of the brick structure. After warming themselves and cautiously exploring the building, they all sat down behind the counter and feasted on donuts and coconut cream pie and milk until they could eat no more. Then, rested and re-energized, the youngsters spent the remainder of the morning playing "business," a game in which they commenced to upset everything on the counters and the tables. Much to his delight, Duane was the first to figure out how to ring open the cash register. But Dewey quickly elbowed him aside and began stuffing all of the bills into their pockets, with the immediate intention of escaping the town and going to find their dad. Their joyful, unfettered pillaging of the restaurant then progressed into a game of throwing at each other and at the walls the remaining desserts that they had been unable to eat. Slipping and skidding on the meringue and pudding and broken pie crusts that lay smeared all across the tile floors, they could actually play ice hockey, which they had only been able to observe other children doing on the frozen local ponds during the winter.

That's when Dewey found the gun. Slowly he pulled it from the drawer below the register, mesmerized by his newly acquired power; he held it up like a prized spoil of war . . . a trophy. "Dang, lookit this!" he said in amazement. The brothers all crowded around him as he held the gun in one hand and kept his brothers at bay with the other. The weapon felt heavy, yet good in his grip. He felt a strange energy exuding from the .38 caliber pistol.

"Shoot it! Shoot it!" Lloyd shouted encouragingly as he excitedly jumped up and down, but he calmed down when Dewey gave him the stare. "Shudup or I'll shoot you!" he said, thus reinforcing the seriousness of the occasion by momentarily pressing the barrel of the weapon into his younger brother's small chest and then raising it again.

The bothers crowded closer around Dewey as he tried to spin the pistol around on his trigger finger. The weight of the gun, though, collapsed his finger and the gun fell with a thud to the tile floor. When it stopped spinning, they all dove for it, but Dewey emerged from the pile with the gun held high over his head, out of the reach of his brothers. "You guys get back," he warned, "or I'll blow yur heads off!"

As the boys huddled around their brother, their attention suddenly and collectively became drawn to a metallic noise at the front door. Vernon Haugenford had come to do some reconciling after church services. They heard his keys in the lock and instinctively began to scatter. All except Dewey, that is.

"What the hell!" exclaimed Vernon as he stepped into the mess of his vandalized restaurant and found the small boy pointing the rather large pistol directly at him. "Wai… Wai…" he stammered at Dewey. Holding up his right hand defensively towards the long, shaking barrel of the gun, he slowly backed out the door and closed it.

Vernon hustled off over to the fire hall and called Sheriff Wilt, and not even five minutes elapsed before the two slowly pushed open the front door and hesitantly peered in. Dewey had herded the brothers back to the restroom and helped them to escape out the window. To throw the trail off of his brothers and further delay the authorities, Dewey waited until Vernon and the Sheriff cautiously entered the semi-dark interior.

"Goddamned it, Ben, I'm tellin' ya! He was pointin' that gun straight at me!"

"Hush up, Vern! He's only a kid!"

Dewey closed and locked the bathroom door, breathing quiet and shallow, hoping to give his brothers enough time to get away. But the scraping noise of the tight door bolt entering the catch drew the sheriff's attention to the bathroom and the two men moved slowly, warily towards the sound.

"Come on outta there boy, before ya get inta more trouble." The sheriff twisted the worn white door knob and then shook the door roughly. "Come on, open up!"

Dewey looked out of the broken window and he could see his brothers in the far distance heading for home. Raising the gun, he started to fire a round through the wooden door, just to scare them off, but his shaking hands would not allow him to squeeze the rigid trigger. Still clutching the pistol tightly, he stood up on first the toilet and then the dirty sink so he could boost himself out of the window headfirst. But as he freed himself of the window frame, a rather sizeable shard of glass still embedded in the gray, cracked putty sliced through his pants and cut into the calf of his leg. He hardly noticed the wound, yet it was large enough to leave a trail of blood along the road as he made his escape to the Johnson's Standard Oil Company on the edge of town.

"I can't let them damn Nazi Japs catch me," he thought as he gripped the gun even more tightly. The coagulated blood had slowed to a mere trickle as he climbed the steps of the fuel storage tank and tried to hide on the catwalk. But below he could see the sheriff's car pull up with its red light on, and the sheriff and his deputy get out. Then a growing crowd of curious townsfolk fresh from church services began to gather, drawn to the scene by the flashing red beacon from the town's only fire engine, which had now been called into action.

After his initial bravado and his standoff with the town of Farmington, the day turned out to be a very long one for Dewey; as the afternoon matured his prospects for a satisfactory settlement of the situation diminished. With the setting of the sun the sleety rain became more intense. His cold clothes, which could become no wetter, hung from his slight body, weighing upon him. The ache in his torn leg gradually grew into full blown pain. Looking down into the growing darkness, the figures below became less and less distinguishable, and thus more threatening. His small body began to shake with hypothermia to the point where hugging himself and pounding his arms against his freezing body would do no good. In fact, in the process of trying to do so to keep warm, he dropped the gun. The weapon skipped down, bouncing and clanking along the steel grated steps, and without discharging landed in the mud below. When Dewey saw Sheriff Wilt walk over and pick up the gun, he knew the adventure had truly ended.

A few more minutes of not knowing what to do passed. Then still hugging and clutching his shoulders with arms across his chest, he sheepishly, slowly limped over and descended into the twilight darkness, down to the cold people below. Too cold. Too wet. His teeth chattered together uncontrollably and he began to cry, softly at first, and then more strongly, making his shoulders shake. He held his chin down to his chest and soon his slobber and snot blended with the rain running down his face. Though his narrow shoulders shook with sadness and despair, no sound came from him. His long dark hair had become matted and it streaked down his forehead, much as it must have on the day of his birth. A wet, crying beginning. His mother might have held him tightly and cooed and touched his dark, damp hair then . . . at his delivery . . . perhaps gently pressed him close to her breast in order to ease his newborn crying. Broken, he wished she were there to touch his face. No one, save for his mother, had ever seen him cry before and he tried unsuccessfully to hide his sorrow and shame.

Sheriff Wilt met Dewey at the bottom of the steps and wrapped his warm wool jacket around the child. "It's okay, boy. It's over now," he said as he gently patted Dewey's quivering shoulder.

Dewey shook off the sheriff's hand as he forced himself to toughen up and stop sniveling . . . stop bawling. No one should see his tears, least of all his brothers. And now most of the town stood by watching him . . . judging him.

He steeled himself and straightened to look at his keepers toughly . . . contemptuously.

Being pretty much a small town, Farmington had no juvenile facilities. Therefore, after he had rounded all up the remaining Lambson brothers, and after Dewey had his leg stitched, Sheriff Wilt decided to make the boys, at least Dewey, Duane, and Lloyd, spend the night in the city jail. That, he reasoned, might make them more aware of the consequences of such antisocial behavior. Wilt locked the three oldest criminals up and then took Leeland and Darrell home with him. Fortunately for him and his wife, and the town in general, Cora came home from Fargo two days later and the townsfolk could be rid of the responsibility for the children. The town officials agreed among themselves that certainly the experience and the jail time should have taught the boys a collective lesson, so the Lambson brothers were subsequently all released back into their mother's custody.

When the Widow Ulrud found out it was "them Lambson boys" that broke into her place, she was not at all surprised. In fact she discussed the matter with the other ladies of the Aid Society over glasses of sherry at the next week's knitting session and they reached somewhat of a consensus.

"What do you expect from them? They're of Lambson stock! What else could you imagine from the ilk of that ol' horse thief Nels and his good-for-nothin' son Iver," Sara Birdsong surmised.

"Yes, quite so. Quite so."

"None of 'em is any good."

"Especially the eldest . . . that Dewey."

"He'll probably be in jail by the time he's sixteen!"

"Yes, yes! No doubt!"

"They're all headed for trouble!"

"I pray that they get exactly what they deserve."

"Yes…yes."

"It's good that the sheriff locked them up for awhile . . . . Give 'em a taste of what life's really like," Widow Ulrud finally said indignantly.

"Yeah, dats da vay of it!" stated Lena Elvik, who held her knitting up close to her old eyes.

Her statement drew a chorus of "Amens!" from the others as they all nodded their heads in agreement, sympathetic to the trauma their dear old friend had suffered . . . the violation she had so courageously faced and overcome.

Chapter Six— Redemptions

In the early spring of 1943, March 20th to be exact, Mr. Wilford Hiebert, the Executive Secretary at the Neilson County Social Services Office, sat in his office reading a disturbing letter he had recently received concerning Cora Lambson and her children. Actually, Mr. Hiebert had known of Mrs. Lambson, as well as her situation and behavior, for a long period of time. Indeed, he had discussed the Lambson file with his superior, Hyram Welty, several times and both of them remained at a loss as to what to do. Therefore Mr. Hiebert exhibited little surprise when the good and socially responsible Reverend Driskoll contacted him regarding Cora and the future of her children. In fact, he felt more than relieved upon receiving the message, for Reverend Driskoll wanted care of the children to be taken over by the Lutheran Welfare Society, which had a regional office in nearby Grand Forks. Mr. Hiebert's professional view held that churches had always been, and should continue to remain, the welfare system for the society, especially in terms of errant adolescents. The State had no business interfering with the way that people raised their children. The organized church, no matter what denomination, maintained a much better position for handling such ethical matters. Consequently, Wilford completely sympathized with his colleague and good friend.

Cora had tearfully confessed to Reverend Driskoll when he had last visited her that she felt herself even more of a pariah in Farmington since the incident with Dewey and the handgun and the petroleum storage tank. Also, according to the good reverend, she stated she could no longer care for her family on the monthly $156.00 Service Men's Dependents Allotment she received from the U. S. Army. These circumstances, along with other on-going difficulties with her children, led to her health becoming quite poorly. Therefore she had decided to separate herself from her boys for the time being . . . probably about nine or ten months or so until she could get on her feet better. A gentleman she recently met in Fargo—he being a new boyfriend, no doubt—had suggested that the South would do her health "a world of good." Her male acquaintance had also informed her that numerous jobs would be available at a new dehydration plant being built in Charlotte and had graciously offered to help get her a position. Therefore, Cora was moving to North Carolina within the week, *"without them damned kids!"* She flatly told the reverend that the Lutheran Welfare Society would have to take care of the children . . . they were no longer, as she saw the situation, her responsibility . . . she needed to take care of herself above all else. She emphasized, though, that when she satisfactorily reestablished herself and recovered her health and well being, she would most assuredly send for them without hesitation.

Reverend Driskoll tried to discuss with Cora the desirability of her staying and working locally, and then placing her children in homes where they would receive daily care and where she could have them at home with her in the evenings. He told her, "I discourage you from parting with your

175

God-given children unless it is absolutely necessary." He then discussed with her all of the undesirable features of her plan, both for herself and the children, especially if she and the children and Iver ever hoped to again be reunited as a family in a God-blessed home.

But Cora remained steadfast in her plans and in fact played her trump card. At the request of Grandma Wills, the Catholic priest from the Harveyville Blessed Savior Church traveled all the way over to Farmington so as to try and talk Mrs. Lambson into sending her children to the Catholic school in Fargo, where she could have them taken care of for $75.00 a month. Mrs. Lambson had, after all, received a strong, correct Catholic upbringing; but because all of the children—or at least Dewey and Duane—were previously baptized as Lutheran, she wanted only the best religious upbringing for them. She then told Reverend Driskoll flatly, "But if I have to, I'll give 'em over to the Catholics."

This became the deciding factor for Reverend Driskoll. He told Cora that he would personally see to it that the boys were all taken in, at least temporarily, by the Lutheran Welfare Society. He went directly back to his parish office and typed a letter to his good friend. Reverend Driskoll's letter read as follows:

Mr. Wilford Hiebert
Executive Secretary
Neilson County Social Services
Farmington, North Dakota
Dear Wilford:

I am quite in a quandary as to the children of Cora Lambson. Her wayward brood has been in and out of trouble for the past several years, with an increasing degree of severity. I have prayed regularly for the youngsters, but now more direct intervention is needed.

The county worker that you assigned to her case stopped in to see me twice before talking directly with Mrs. Lambson. The worker seems staunchly opposed to the idea of taking the woman's children from her, for this relieves her of all of her motherly and parental responsibilities and frees her to cavort around and do as she wishes. However, if the children stay with their mother, I sincerely believe that their condition can only worsen and the youngsters will become more deeply involved with the civil authorities, to no good end.

I am not accusing Mrs. Lambson of anything, for it is not my place to judge. However, adequate concern for her children has been lacking for the previous several years and even now they are not being given the care they deserve. From my point of view I strongly believe that doing anything for the five striplings while they still are young will be far better than ignoring the situation and doing nothing. And even if Mrs. Lambson does choose to carry on in a matter not befitting her maternal instincts, at least we will be trying to do something and not sitting back on our haunches and watching while those youngsters destroy themselves. Perhaps, too, if Mrs. Lambson is dealt with in a kindly way, and her children are taken care at the Lake Charles Lutheran Home in Grand Forks, she might truly have a Christian change of heart. Mrs. Lambson, as far as I have heard, is a good worker, but in my opinion she severely lacks the self discipline capabilities needed to look out for herself and her charges. I truly believe that with a little help and some good Christian guidance and intervention, she will be able to redeem herself and become a good mother.

At any rate, Wil, I am requesting that you personally make a call to Hyram Welty. If Neilson County cannot act on behalf of the Lambson children, it will be almost imperative for us, the Lutheran Welfare Society, to do what we can to take them. I assure you that the LWS can do a far better job than either the Catholics or the State in bringing these boys to a good end. I write as I do simply to stress the urgency that <u>something</u> must be done soon, without having to call in the law later on. I am in daily contact with the High Reverend Ethedge Daniels, Director of the Society's office in Grand Forks. At the direction and authorization of your office, I can have the children transported to the Lutheran Children's Receiving Home immediately.

I anxiously await your immediate reply.

Your friend and fellow servant,

Rev. Paul Driskoll

Sitting hunched over his broad oak desk, Wilford Hiebert understood his friend's letter and the ensuing dilemma. His elbows leaned tiredly on the desktop pad and showed that his Sunday-black suit barely fit his sagging shoulders.

His eyebrows furrowed up into his forehead, further displacing and thus accentuating his grayish brown toupee. The deep blue of his eyes highlighted his pasty face and his smile collapsed into his jutting chin. He nodded his head knowingly and decided to act immediately, given the gravity of the situation and the mother's capriciousness. Later that same week, Reverend Driskoll received an emergency telephone call from Mr. Hyram Welty requesting that the Lutheran Welfare Society come as quickly as possible to pick up the Lambson children. City authorities in Farmington were in the process of turning over the youngsters to the Grand Forks Juvenile Court, thus making them wards of the State of North Dakota. Welty assured the good reverend that all the necessary paperwork would be submitted to the proper authorities and that custody of the children would be granted to the LWS in the very near future.

Reverend Driskoll gave an extended prayer of thanks to God for the intervention of Wilford Hiebert and then realized he had to act immediately. Rather than have the children become property of the North Dakota State Court System and consequently be sent to the State Juvenile Correction Facility in Mandan, Reverend Driskoll contacted Director Ethedge Daniels and informed him of the decision of the Neilson County Social Services. Without hesitation, Director Daniels dispatched Clarissa Ann Clementson, the chief welfare worker at the Grand Forks LWS Office, to go to Farmington. Her instructions from the director were precise: pick up the five Lambson children and take them directly back to the Lake Charles Lutheran Children's Receiving Home in Grand Forks, "*without fail!*" As she spoke to her superior over the telephone, she recognized the imperative tone in his voice and reacted accordingly. Dutifully she quickly arranged her schedule so she could depart for Farmington the very next morning.

Reverend Driskoll, trusting that God would see the plan through, drove out to the Lambson farm and delivered the news. Cora became increasingly giddy with the resolution and assured the reverend that the boys would be all ready to leave. But even though Reverend Driskoll had made the trip out to the farmstead intentionally to notify Mrs. Lambson in advance of the LWS decision and that the worker would be coming for the children the following morning, the youngsters were far from being ready when Miss Clementson came at 10 a.m. the next day. The arrival of the young, pretty, smartly dressed social worker seemed somewhat of a surprise to Cora, who looked at her blankly from behind the raggedy screen door. Realizing the tenuousness of the plan, and that she would need Cora's cooperation in order to get custody of the children, the social worker remained patient and pleasant and ignored the smell of alcohol coming from the mother.

She smiled and spoke forcefully: "I'm Clarissa Clementson from the Lutheran Welfare Society. Reverend Driskoll said you would be expecting me. Are the boys ready to leave?"

"Dunno. Yeah, I guess."

"Well, where are they?"

"Playin' out back or o'er in the field somewhere, I s'pose," Cora looked beyond Miss Clementson and nodded her chin out towards the large cottonwood tree, in the general direction of the morning.

"Well, let's get them ready and we'll be off!"

"I forgot ya was comin'...."

"Yes, yes, that's fine. Come along now. Call them in, please, so we can tell them."

After finally rounding the youngsters up from the distant muddy fields, Cora, with Miss Clementson standing tall and staunch behind her for support, told the boys of the relocation arrangements. "This here nice lady is going to take you all to another home . . . in Grand Forks . . . where you'll be stayin' for a little while." Cora paused for a moment, then went on hesitantly: "I'm gonna go away for awhile so I can get better." Cora somewhat expected an outburst of disobedience, or misbehavior, or even rebellion from her sons, or perhaps anger or bawling from them, but instead all of the youngsters just stood on the porch, staring at her blankly, awaiting instructions.

Miss Clementson made sure that each child was adequately cleaned up, albeit in a cold-water bath, and after quite some effort and searching, gathered up enough clothes for them. While Cora stood and watched, the young woman rummaged through the burlap bag of used clothing until she somehow found enough shirts, pants, underwear, socks, and shoes to fit the brothers. Then the worker helped to get them all dressed and ready, thereby becoming somewhat acquainted with each in turn.

"Geez, yur pretty, mam!" said Leeland as she helped him button his too-large red checkered wool shirt. He reached out and touched the finger waves of her short, dark brown hair and the sleeves of her gray, light wool, business dress. He stared long into her hazel eyes. "You smell good, too!"

"Well, thank you, young man!" When she fastened the top shirt button at his neck, she tenderly chucked his chin with her curled finger. Moving on to the next one in line, the smallest, she gently removed his thumb from his mouth and helped him put his shirt on. She made a mental note that the youngster's top teeth had begun to protrude outward from what must be continuous thumb sucking.

"Me Darrell," he said to her softly. When he reached out and tentatively touched her full face and her smooth fore-head, then traced his fingertip lightly down her red-rouged cheeks, she smiled deeply at him, looking straight into his eyes, and he knew he could trust her. "What you name?" he asked softly, innocently, almost inaudibly.

"I'm Miss Clementson," she answered and then whispered softly, "But you can call me Clarissa." She smiled once more at him, more deeply this time, and her shining eyes looked intuitively into his. Because of her training and experience in the field of social work, children held a special favor for Clarissa Clementson; indeed, she bore a sharp disdain for all of those that abused them in any way.

After an hour and a half, she and the five brothers gathered on the front porch, finally ready to leave. Cora stood just outside the door. Though the boys did not know exactly what was happening, they seemed to sense something positive would soon be transpiring and so began to look forward to the trip to their new home in Grand Forks. Mrs. Lambson told the social worker that she planned to pack immediately after her sons' departure and to leave Farmington for Chicago, and from thence to travel by train with her companion to Charlotte, North Carolina. So she generously offered the little bit of remaining food and canned goods to the Receiving Home and said she would send a box of clothing for the children as soon as she had time to wash, iron, and mend everything. The box, though, would never be sent.

At the social worker's quiet direction, the brothers happily piled into the car, and at the point of no return, Miss Clementson cleverly resolved the final element of the agreement. She produced a formal looking letter that had been precisely typed on a Lutheran Welfare Society letterhead. The letter contained a petition asking the Lutheran Welfare Society to assume temporary guardianship of the five Lambson children . . . a document which needed to be signed by the mother. Part of the agreement stipulated that each month $104, two-thirds of her government allotment—those monies allocated by the U. S. Army to insure the welfare and care of her and her children—would regularly be turned over to the agency as a payment for the keeping of the children.

"I din' know that was part 'a the deal," Cora began to complain.

However, having no empathy or sympathy, and even less patience for the woman, Miss Clementson quickly cut her off by moving closer to the mother, their bodies almost touching, and pushing the letter more forcefully towards her. The social worker, with her neat, no-nonsense business attire and permanent-waved brunette hair, certainly represented authority to the unsophisticated mother. "The children can stay, if that is what you wish," she said in her steady, public voice. The firmness in the young lady's tone intimated that the restless children could just as easily exit the car, and so the mother grudgingly scrawled her name on the bottom of the document.

With the transfer finished satisfactorily, Miss Clementson curtly suggested that the boys' mother keep the agency informed as to her future plans and whereabouts. But just as with the promised box of food and clean clothes, the agency would never receive any of the $104 subsistence checks that Cora had agreed to send to help support her children. At any rate, with the signing of the agreement, the deed had been done.

Though the separation was supposedly only temporary in nature, Cora would not directly impose herself on the boys' lives again for quite a long while. And even though they did receive letters from their mother periodically, none of the boys ever openly admitted they missed her, although Dewey would come to dream about her sometimes lovely, sometimes haunting image in the coming months and years, often awakening in the middle of the night in a cold sweat after having dreamt about her.

As the car pulled away from the farmhouse, turning around slowly in the yard and heading for the dirt road, they drove once more past the barren-looking mother. Miss Clementson noted how frail and woeful the woman appeared as she stood slight and almost invisible beside the tall, spreading, still winter-dead cottonwood tree. Cora raised her white, empty arms and waved her thin hands over her head in sluggish goodbye until her visage disappeared in the rear view mirror.

The car bumped steadily along the road with Darrell sitting beside Miss Clementson; again sucking his thumb, he nestled himself closer to her, as though burrowing himself into the warm safety of her body. She gently put her arm around him after she had shifted into high gear and the agency-owned Chevy gently rolled down along the dirt and mud road. Leeland sat beside Darrell and she included him in the embrace as well. Looking back in the mirror, and adjusting it slightly downward, she could see Dewey and Duane and Lloyd with their arms crossed on the top edge of the wide front seat, their chins all resting on top of their folded hands.

"Can you really drive this thing?" asked Lloyd cautiously, daring to break the initial silence. The question seemed to hang in the air. But she answered it with a laughing "Yes, of course!" and her casual reply released some sort of a floodgate. Immediately they all joined excitedly in the conversation, each competing for a position of recognition as the auto made the turn out onto Highway 2.

"How old 're you, mam?"

"Will ya let me shift the gears?"

"Ya, me too! Me too! Can I, huh?"

"How fast does this thing go?"

"When will we be there?"

"Quit hittin'! Ya big jerk!"

"Have ya ever wrecked?"

"Are ya married?"

"Do ya got a boyfriend?"

"Can I be your boyfriend if ya don got one?"

"When's lunch?"

"Look it how Leeland can bend back his broke arm! Look it, look it! Gawd, that's neat! Do it again, Lee! See!"

"She said Darrell could call her Clarissa, huh, Clarissa! I heared her tell 'im so."

"Can we call ya Clarissa, too?!"

"Yeah, can we? Can we?"

"Clarissa! Clarissa! Clarissa!" became their wild, rhythmic, unison chant as they bounced about in the seats.

The car had driven several miles before the thoroughly confused and befuddled Miss Clementson could get the boys calmed down. In fact, on Highway 2 she had actually made a left turn instead of a right and not until they reached the half-way point to Devils Lake did she realize that she had gone seventeen miles in the wrong direction. They all laughed joyfully at the error and once they had turned around and were headed the right way, back towards Grand Forks, things seemed to settle down. As she drove along she reached into a brown paper sack and distributed chokecherry jam-and-butter sandwiches she had made and carefully wrapped in waxed paper that morning, and this quieted them a bit. The quickness with which the food disappeared amazed her, so she also gave them the two sandwiches she had prepared for herself. All the while the young worker's social training allowed her to observe more closely her new charges and she began to make myriad mental notes.

Observing the Lambson boys had already proven to be extremely interesting and no doubt would provide ample substance for an enlightening case study, Miss Clementson concluded; she intently watched their faces and expressions, and studied particularly the three oldest boys' reflection in the rear-view mirror. She wondered greatly why none of them had turned around to wave goodbye to their mother as she stood thin in the farmyard. Not one of them shed a tear upon leaving her. No sad words. No embraces or anything. No questions about or objections to the separation. No sad lamentations or words of regret or temporization. They had not even looked back as the car drove off, not a one.

All during the trip into Grand Forks there was no end to the questions they asked, in a rapid fire way, about what this or that was and what their new home would be like. Just as with the young and bright Miss Clementson, nothing seemed to escape their observation either. Whenever a bird or a pheasant flew up suddenly from along the side the road, they would all in a loud chorus of rifle reports pretend they were shooting it, holding out their small arms as though they were supporting a rifle. In spite of their young ages, they had traveled widely around and beyond the town, establishing certain favorite hangouts and swimming holes within the area; they described in detail to the fascinated Miss Clementson about their affinity for the bums' camp and about going swimming down at Hollecker pond.

"We goed swimmin' nekked there," Lloyd said excitedly, trying to convey descriptively the wonderful freedom of the pond. The boys all snickered as he said the word "nekked" and the social worker began to love the innocence of the youngsters.

"Yeah, but playin' Mud King down at Hollecker Pond is the funnest, though" added Duane, not wanting to be outdone.

"Goodness! What is Mud King?"

"One of us is chose to be Mud King and the rest of us all crown him with handsfulla mud 'til he can't take it no more."

"Gracious me! That does sound like fun!" Clarissa said excitedly as she began to hand out oatmeal cookies from the lunch bag. After distributing the treat, she neatly folded the paper sack and stowed it away in the glove box for another day.

Continuing their journey to a new beginning, the boys munched on the delicacies and secretively told their new confidant about their junkyard playground and their mother's friends and the Indian across the highway and their father the army man. The social worker continued to be taken aback by the depth and breadth of their young experiences and gathered more notes in her mind than she could keep. They truly were like five lost sheep . . . and she felt deeply, almost as a religious experience, the God-directed mission of bringing the lost ones back into the fold . . . of taking them to a better place.

During a brief lull in the commotion and talk, she felt a slight, subtle brushing movement against the hair on the back of her neck. Darrell had gently reached up and taken hold of her right earlobe between his thumb and forefinger, rubbing it softly. "You got 'feel ears,' mam. Me like you," he said and then he began contentedly sucking his other thumb.

* * *

The hour-and-a-half drive passed quickly and soon the mud-spattered black Chevy rolled to a stop in front of the Lake Charles Lutheran Children's Home. Miss Clementson set the handbrake and turned off the ignition, and the joy of the ride seemed to end quite abruptly. The boys walked silently, morosely in front of the social worker and the bond between them and the pretty young woman quickly dissipated. The full implication of what was happening, of the profound change . . . of their leaving the familiarity of their mother and the farmhouse, began to settle on them as a group. The unfamiliarity of the situation unnerved all of the brothers . . . at least with their mother they knew what they could expect. But as they approached the new unknown, they all seemed to collectively understand that turning back and returning to the farmstead, and to their mother, would never again be offered as an option to them.

They looked around them, scrutinizing everything, "sizing it up" as they walked reluctantly toward the large, white house. Stepping slowly, resolutely up the four cement steps of the stoop, they opened the storm door and the heavy front door, and then entered the home. Almost instantly the brothers made their presence known. Once past the front entry, they instinctively split up and went exploring in different directions as they normally did, quickly working past the introduction of the house parents, Mr. and Mrs. Rykker. The two older authority figures and the social worker, along with several of the other resident boys sitting in the front room, could only watch in amazement and perplexity as the Lambsons exhibited no control whatsoever. In their unrestricted fit of exploration Dewey found a bearskin rug on the floor of Mr. Rykker's office/den and wrapping it around himself began to chase his brothers ferociously about the house, growling loudly through the mouth of the bear's head. Everyone watched in disbelief . . . all, to a person, quite stupefied, even almost paralyzed, by the boys' extraordinary behavior, especially Dewey's. Finally Joel Hopkins, the oldest of the boys in residence, tackled Dewey and held him pinned tightly on the floor until the youngster's exuberance at last subsided. Several hours passed before order could once more be restored in the home, much later in the evening.

During the first few weeks of the newcomers' stay, every member of the Receiving Home had to assist in keeping watch over "them Lambson kids" until the five brothers finally became able to find their places and learn how to conduct themselves in a normal home environment. At the end of April, Mr. Rykker wrote the following in his initial report to his superiors at the Lutheran Welfare Society downtown office:

April 14, 1943
My Dear Reverend Daniels and Miss Clementson:
 You have truly bestowed upon us and our house five <u>wild Indians</u>. The Lambson children have been a rather trying group of boys, as it seems they were entirely without training and no doubt have been given little care and supervision in their short lives. They are not used to having controls or having adults or other people tell them what to do and how to do it. Up until now they have apparently done pretty much what they pleased. Their attitude has also had an impact on the other thirteen kids here, who are up to fifteen and sixteen years of age, and the house has become somewhat unmanageable. I am afraid that I will need to apply some harsher measures and if those are not successful, I don't really know if we will be able to keep the brothers.
Yours in Christ Jesus,
Norvel Rykker

Because she had been assigned as the permanent Lutheran Welfare Society caseworker for the Lambsons, Miss Clementson also received a carbon copy of the report, the contents of which disturbed her greatly. She had become quite attached to the boys and visited them as often as she could.

The close proximity of her office, located in the downtown area, to the Lake Charles Receiving Home allowed her to monitor the boys' progress, or non-progress, on a routine basis. When not out of town or involved in other business for the LWS, she would often visit them during the lunch hour and take them sugar cookies and red, succulent apples. As summer started to blossom, she took them and other children from the home, as frequently as possible, to Meyers Park, located several blocks away, down by the fast flowing Red River.

As each boy's birthday came, she would arrange a party as a special occasion, paying for it from her own meager resources. Dewey and Duane's birthdays had already passed, so she started with Leeland's on May 15th, then with Lloyd's on June 12th, followed by Darrell's on August 7th.

Because the Lambsons had never heard of such an activity as a birthday party, and because the experience was particularly unique for the brothers, all of the other children in the home put much energy and planning into each event, busily arranging games and setting up decorations. At the close of Leeland's party in May, Duane had exclaimed, "I never see'd nothin' like this!" He just looked around incredulously as he stood in the mess of multicolor wrapping paper and bright streamer remnants of his brother's celebration.

At his party, Lloyd's eyes went wide as he watched and watched the nine brightly burning candles that had been stuck into the heavy frosting of the cake; he seemed to be barely breathing as he gazed intently at the flickering flames. Enthralled, he refused to blow the candles out, even with the strong shouts of encouragement given by the other children gathered excitedly around the kitchen table. "Make a wish an' blow 'em out!" they all coaxed. But the youngster remained hypnotized by the fire; besides, he didn't really know what making a wish entailed. Dewey finally had to blow them out for his little brother; he gave Lloyd a sharp cuff behind the head for "actin' so stupid," an inappropriate deed for which Miss Clementson scolded him mightily. And for the first time in his life, a contrite Dewey actually apologized for his behavior.

Miss Clementson, amazed to find that the concept of birthdays and parties had been so foreign to the five brothers, made copious notes concerning their strange reactions. After the party for Darrell, later that evening in her office she wrote a note in the boys' LWS cumulative file:

Lambson Children Observation, August 7th, 1943

The whole idea of having birthday parties has certainly been a curiosity for the boys—the games and the cake and the presents from the other children and everything else. Darrell received a blue metal truck, as well as a coloring book from me and a box of crayons from Mr. and Mrs. Rykker. The other children in the home gave him a harmonica and a bright plaid shirt. So far none of the five boys can believe that someone would just give them presents for no reason and they were all quite skeptical at first. Dewey in particular was very standoffish for some reason during Leeland's birthday in May, and somewhat so after Lloyd's birthday in June. But today he joined in vigorously with all the others. Helen Rykker made a large vanilla sheet cake, with thick white frosting, and the boys all willingly participated in churning the homemade ice cream. They were all quite delighted. I think this might be an important turning point in their young lives! I pray that it is!

C. A. Clementson
Chief Welfare Worker, LWS

All through the summer Miss Clementson paid special attention to her charges, giving them books and pencils and colors and blank sheets of paper at every opportunity, for she felt it crucial that the boys be prepared for school in the fall. Whether due to her special attention, or the birthday parties, or just the freedom of summer having a calming effect on them, the Lambson brothers' attitudes began to change for the better. In fact, in early September, Mr. Rykker penned a follow up letter—a somewhat tentative addendum—to his first report:

Reverend Daniels and Miss Clementson
RE: follow-up to initial evaluation report on the Lambson children

The Lambson boys were such a difficult bunch to handle and initially they seemed to have completely upset the whole household. Now, however, they have adapted somewhat to the home environment and might turn out to be good boys after all! Their behavior has continued to improve throughout the summer, especially since the birthday parties that we gave them. They are now registered in school and seem to be integrating well into the education system. Time will tell, but we continue to pray for their redemption.

Yours Truly,

N. Rykker

Pleased by Mr. Rykker's second report, Miss Clementson continued to be encouraged about the boys' progress. Her ongoing interest in and certainly affection for the brothers—particularly Darrell—continued to grow. "My little ones!" she had begun calling them. After conferring with Director Daniels, she again called on the Receiving Home during the first week of October, but this time for a more official visit—to not only see how the boys were getting along, but also to formally confer with Mr. and Mrs. Rykker.

Miss Clementson began the meeting by explaining how pleased the Lutheran Welfare Society was that the brothers all appeared to be happy and contented in their new surroundings. The social worker conceded that getting those boys adjusted to the life and routine of a well-ordered home must have been a daunting task for the Rykkers. The house mother, Helen, agreed and readily admitted that she feared at first that the situation with the Lambsons would certainly be more than she could handle; but with patient directions, and Miss Clementson's constant encouragement and support, the boys quickly began to improve in their habits. Norvel added that they all seemed to be learning to play with others without being destructive. Miss Clementson also noted that their table manners already showed much improvement. Both of the Rykkers had become exceptionally proud of the fact that even though the three older boys were enrolled in classes far below their age level, they attended school regularly and there had been no difficulty in getting them to return home each day after classes had ended. The house mother did report that they all continued to have very real problems with their constant nighttime bed wetting, but the boys showed a little progress in that area as well.

When Miss Clementson visited again two weeks later, Mr. and Mrs. Rykker both agreed enthusiastically that since the previous meeting the boys exhibited even more improvement in their behavior and had begun to be a real part of the family at the home. Dewey had encountered some difficulties in adjusting to the rules of the school; he had, in fact, been already involved in two fights. Duane, though, performed especially well in his classes and Mrs. Rykker was pleased with his behavior at the home. She felt that she would be able to particularly win his confidence and help him to develop along the right channels. Duane promised Mrs. Rykker to work for some A's for the next marking period. He loved to read; Miss Clementson and Mrs. Rykker both suggested that that specific interest should be capitalized on. Whenever Duane had simple reading material, he remained content and would read indefinitely. Duane also got along splendidly with everyone. He naturally exhibited a more likeable personality than his bothers and seemed more congenial towards the other children. He was also a willing worker. Dewey remained to be the hardest to handle, but he, as well, seemed to be making progress in the home.

Mr. Rykker noted many of these observations in his third progress report, submitted to LWS in early November:

. . . . Duane continues to be doing very well. However, Dewey is stubborn by nature and somewhat of a bully. He is also a disciplinary problem in school. Frequently his teacher has had to isolate him from his class by placing him in the hall or the cloak closet for long periods of time. Hopefully these measures will work and I will not have to use the hose on him or Lloyd again. Lloyd got into trouble for playing with matches out in the field behind the home. Leeland and Darrell, both very good little boys, are still not able to go to school. Leeland is particularly quiet and unassuming and usually entertains himself. Darrell has already become the favorite in the home, which is natural because he is the youngest child here. He is very affectionate and a friend to everyone. And everyone loves to tussle his bright-red hair . . . they all feel it is somehow lucky to do so. He does, however, have a persistent, annoying habit of continually sucking his thumb, and putting objects in his mouth. Also, he always carries around a dirty piece of felt that he rubs against his cheek and that he calls his "ung-gung." He should not be doing this at four years old, but we cannot seem to break the habit. We pray that he will be rid of these problems before he starts school.

My wife Helen would like to report that the boys had their first Halloween several nights ago. Each one had a mask and a Jack-O-Lantern and they were allowed to go and visit the neighborhood where they were given treats. There also was a special dinner prepared for them when they returned home after their neighborhood visits. Though they were excited by all of the frightening costumes, the Halloween holiday itself was a strange one for the boys . . . they maintain that they had never participated in this type of festivity before, which is extremely hard for me to fathom. They still cannot believe that people would just give them so much candy and cookies for noth-ing—unless such gifts involve some sort of larceny. We are anxious to see their reactions to the upcoming holidays—Thanksgiving and Christmas. As always, we continue to pray for the Lord's intervention in directing them along the proper Christian paths.

      Respectfully submitted 11/7/1943
      Norvel Rykker

Thanksgiving came with as much surprise and joy to the boys as Halloween; they had heard about such holidays but never experienced them before, so therefore did not know what such occasions involved. When Mrs. Rykker prepared and set out the feast, the boys became transfixed by the entire process. As they sat before the well-laden table, with its succulent variety of potatoes and vegetables and roasted tur-key and pumpkin pies, their eyes and their mouths remained wide open in disbelief for several minutes. Overcome by the abundance, or perhaps by the haunting memory of past hunger, they stuffed themselves until they could eat no more; later they became sick and groaned happily late into the evening. Oddly enough, the boys found a new comfort in the satiation and in the surfeit surroundings of the home, but more so from the constancy and security they had come to know.

The Christmas holidays evoked just as much of a fusion of pleasure and disbelief from the Lambsons. Christmas meant games, candy, fruit, nuts, and playing outside in the snow. The older boys in the home showed the brothers how to make skis out of barrel slats and took them skiing on nearby Christian Hill and sledding down the natural drifts accumulating up against the bowing wooden fence beside the home. Dewey, Duane, and Lloyd even went with Mr. Rykker to buy the Yule tree. They watched in amazement as Rykker placed the huge, fragrant tree right in the very center of the front room and then symbolically decorated it with popcorn and cranberry chains, which they gleefully helped to make. On Christmas morning they carefully unwrapped the gifts joyfully handed to them by a smiling Mrs. Rykker—those gifts purchased by the Lutheran Welfare Society. All of the children in the home equally received two articles of clothes and a toy. The Lambson brothers remained still very much suspect of the concept of giving . . . of how they deserved to get something special for doing nothing. Or, indeed, that someone would freely do such a bizarre thing.

On Christmas night, at the full dinner table, the house master delivered grace and reminded all present at the table to be ever thankful for all they had received. During the meal, while everyone busily consumed the feast, Dewey asked innocently, "Should I be thankful for my Ma, Mr. Rykker? After she left us and all?"

Surprised by the theologically rich question, Mr. Rykker remained quiet for a few moments, his fork held half raised to his mouth. "Well, yes, I suppose," he stammered. "Yes, be thankful that she saw fit to send you to the home here . . . that she wants you to be well taken care of. I suppose . . . ."

He finished his meal in somewhat quiet reflection, watching all of his charges as they ate.

After dinner, still pondering Dewey's question and thus seeing an opportunity for some religious instruction, Mr. Rykker tried to explain the story of Christ's birth and the concepts of forgiveness and redemption to the brothers. But the tale lay far beyond the boys' realm of understanding and they soon lost interest as they played with and exchanged the toys they had received. But the five all agreed that they did not believe in the crazy notion of Santa Claus, although they laughed delightedly at the drawings of the red-suited, white-bearded, silly-looking old man pictured on the Christmas cards hanging from the fireplace mantle.

At the end of the holiday season, Miss Clementson noted in her observation journal that, in all, the Lambson children, who had heretofore never known that holidays such as Halloween, Thanksgiving, and Christmas actually existed, happily and fully participated in these occasions with gusto and seemed to be adapting to and flourishing in their new situation. She noted as well that no money or card or letter or even presents had come from the boys' mother. Reverend Daniels, since the boys' arrival at the home, had been vigorously trying to locate Cora and collect the money she already owed LWS, but with no success. In closing her notation, the young woman questioned how a woman . . . a mother . . . could forsake such beautiful and vibrant children; then, in a more professional vein, she erased the personal, reflective, overly subjective passage and signed the revised entry.

Soon after the first of the year, when Duane became seriously ill with pneumonia, the boys' physical well being was given careful attention. Early in February Miss Clementson scheduled a collective appointment and Mrs. Rykker herded the boys into the doctor's office at the appointed time. Dr. Halverson gave them all physical examinations and proceeded to administer to them amass all of their small pox, diphtheria and whooping cough immunizations. The boys, however, never in their collective memory having had to receive so many painful injections at one time, needed to be chased around the examination room and out through the waiting area. In a throwback to their previous existence, the five used all means available to resist the forces of authority, yelling and screaming as though creatures in the wild—much to the amazement of the several ill patients waiting to see the doctor. The bewildered nurse hastily called Miss Clementson on the telephone and the young social worker quickly came over to somewhat restore order in the doctor's office. Finally, under Miss Clementson's supervision, the nurse and doctor and Mrs. Rykker subdued each boy individually, one at a time, in order for the inoculations to take place.

Dr. Halverson, much exhausted from the afternoon excitement in his office, dictated a report that evening:

TO: Miss Clarissa Clementson, Lutheran Welfare Society
FROM: Jacob Halverson, MD
RE: Medical Evaluation of five Lambson children, February 8, 1944

The Lambson boys seem to be in fairly good shape and have been given all necessary shots. In two months they should be brought in for tuberculosis tests. I could find no obvious causes for the boys' enuresis. I suspect, though, that this can be attributed to their past family history, based upon what you have told me. Continued training should help in this area. My main concern, however, is that all of them have numerous carious teeth and these soon will cause them various health problems. I suggest that dental care also be provided for them as soon as possible. Overall, though, the lads seem to be in fine health. Yours, Dr. J. Halverson

p.s. — In the future would you please see that no more than two of the boys come to the office at the same time. Thank you!

The lot of the Lambson children improved progressively with each passing day and with the approach of spring. In February, March, and April, all survived numerous visits to various dentists in the Grand Forks area. Mr. and Mrs. Rykker had learned quickly to divide and conquer the five boys by taking them individually to the different appointments. In April all of their tuberculosis tests appeared negative. The house parents even noted a marked improvement in the problem of enuresis. They reported to Miss Clementson that the boys took a good deal of pride and responsibility in overcoming that persistent, odious habit.

In early April Miss Clementson was delighted to learn that, through the efforts of Reverend Driskoll and his friend Wilford Hiebert, temporary guardianship of the boys had been granted to the Lutheran Welfare Society, by a Court Order issued by the Honorable Daniel B. Holt, District Judge, dated April 17, 1944. According to Director Daniels, the Lambson case had been litigated by Mrs. Madison, North

Dakota State Juvenile Commissioner, based upon Cora Lambson's abandonment of her children and her failure to help defer the financial cost for the care of the children. Commissioner Madison's letter of findings and determination had just recently been received at the LWS office:

Director Ethedge Daniels
Lutheran Welfare Society
Grand Forks, North Dakota

Dear Director Daniels —

Enclosed herewith you will find a notarized copy of the Consent, Findings of Fact, and Recommendations of the State Juvenile Commissioner, and Order Appointing Guardian ad litem. The Juvenile Division of the Welfare Department of the State of North Dakota, as the results of a Show Cause Hearing, has determined that custody of the children of Iver and Cora Lambson (children Dewey, Duane, Lloyd, Leeland, and Darrell) now resides with the Lutheran Welfare Society, Grand Forks, North Dakota. The originals of the official papers have been filed in Neilson County.

We have also written a letter to the United States Office of Dependency Benefits with reference to the G.I. allotment for these children, a copy of which we have forwarded to the Clerk of Court of Neilson County, asking him to enclose a certified copy of the order and forward to that office for us. The mother of the children is hereby ordered to make restitution to the Lutheran Welfare Society, as well as to

Neilson County, for all funds accrued in the care of her children.

Martha M. Madison
Juvenile Commissioner
State of North Dakota

With this official notification, the mother, Cora Lambson, finally became officially relieved of her maternal duties. However, the letter did not completely release her from the burden of her financial responsibilities, and therein lay the problem that again worked to the detriment of her sons. The courts and the Lutheran Welfare Society both had been looking for Cora because of her ongoing failure, or maybe just refusal, to send the $104 from the monthly allotment checks she received from the United States Army—the money desperately needed by the LWS to contribute to the adequate care of the children. Reverend Driskoll strongly suspected that she was using the money for her own selfish purposes and Director Daniels heartily supported this supposition. Both officials agreed that the situation made the financial support for the five children much, much more difficult.

At Director Daniel's request, Reverend Driskoll once again wrote to his friend Wilford Hiebert in hopes of getting further financial assistance from Neilson County:

Dear Wilford —

I am herewith enclosing correspondence which I have had with the War Department regarding the allotment for the Lambson children, who, as you know, are now under our care. I do not know just where Mrs. Lambson is, so I cannot get the information from her regarding her intentions. In discussing the allotment with Mr. Woodson, the official I spoke with, he felt that it would simplify matters and safeguard our interest if the allotment could come directly to us. I need to have either Mr. or Mrs. Lambson's authorization to do this. However, Mr. Lambson is currently serving in the European theater of the war and we have not been able to make contact with him. In addition, we do not have Mrs. Lambson's present or former address as she seems to be continually traveling from one state to another and she suggested that we not write to her.

The cost of care for the five boys has presented the agency with a deficit. Caring for them has well surpassed any monies we have received. The mother's allotment would have helped to offset the expenses substantially, but as I mentioned, she has refused to endorse the government checks over to us. The subsidy that Neilson County has provided—five dollars per month, per child—has been helpful, but we are, out of sheer necessity, requesting more funding. Because we are unable to receive state funds, would it be possible, Wil, for your office to double the allotted sum that is coming to the agency? If this request is at all feasible, please let me know as soon as you are able to.

Yours in Christ Jesus,
Reverend Paul Driskoll

The good reverend thought that invoking the Lord and Savior's name and then formally signing the request would add credence and import to the appeal, but it did not. Wilford promptly notified his friend that his request for more county funding was not possible. The amount that could be allotted for each child had earlier been set by county officials, so therefore his "hands were tied" in the matter.

Miss Clementson became extremely dismayed when she received Reverend Driskoll's note detailing Neilson County's denial of further supplemental funding. Director Daniels had forwarded the message on to her, along with a memo summarizing the agency's decision . . . the older boys would need to leave the receiving home for other, more economical arrangements. The cost of caring for the Lambsons, unfortunately, had been a strong and determining factor in the decision to split up the brothers. At the end of the school year, the four older children would be transferred from Lake Charles Lutheran Children's Home and sent to other homes. Mr. and Mrs. Rykker and the Lutheran Welfare Society jointly determined that they no longer had the resources to offset the burden of the Lambson children and the decision would be best for all concerned. Having guardianship of the children would allow the LWS to board them with willing Lutheran families in the area.

Late one Sunday evening, in the middling warmth of June, Clarissa sat at her cluttered desk, in her bare white office, the walls adorned by only a wooden cross and a painting of Jesus inviting little children unto him; a mess of paperwork and files, and a well-used Smith Corona typewriter lay before her. She remembered once again Cora Lambson's reluctance to sign the agreement with the Lutheran Welfare

Society; though Clarissa considered herself a Christian of deep faith and commitment, she could find little forgiveness in her heart for the woman . . . the mother . . . who abandoned her children with such callous indifference . . . who so casually, indifferently shirked her filial responsibilities. As a professional, Miss Clementson had in the past tried her best not to become emotionally involved in the lives of her clients; but where the Lambson boys were concerned, she somehow felt an overwhelming sense of personal commitment to them. They had all made remarkable progress during the short fourteen months they had been at the Children's Home . . . all seemingly for naught. If they had a bit more sustained time of stability, they would be all right. She knew that to be true, both intellectually and emotionally. But now that appeared impossible, thanks once again to the actions of their mother. So, though she felt little confidence in any plan to divide the brothers up, their circumstances offered her little choice; she had at last decided that she must steel herself to the reality of the situation.

With a good deal of sadness, she replied to Reverend Driskoll's note:

June 15, 1944
My Dear Reverend Driskoll,
    As you perhaps know, the capacity in our Lake Charles Receiving Home is small, and certainly the need is great. So in order to serve more children we must sometimes move children out from there into other boarding homes, whenever suitable accommodations are found and when we feel that those children are ready to go into family homes. We feel that

for older boys farm homes as a rule are preferred as there are more things there for them to be interested in and to busy themselves with. Therefore, at the end of June, after the close of school, Dewey and Duane will be placed in the Erlingsrude home in Devils Lake. Likewise, Lloyd and Leeland will be going to the Thompson farmstead in Grafton. Darrell, because of his age, will be kept here at the receiving home in Grand Forks. As you know, we want only what is best for these youngsters. Our prayers go along with them.

Yours in faith,
Clarissa Clementson

After sealing and addressing the envelope, Clarissa experienced a crisis of confidence . . . indeed, of faith. Even since her early childhood, on through confirmation, she knew well she had a Christian calling. Immediately following high school, with the support of her parents and local minister, she had entered Gale Divinity College. The constant influence of Bible study and the Word of God, along with the guidance of truly Christian teachers and fellow students, crystallized her desire to be a lifetime servant of the Lord. At first she wanted to be a Christian educator, and then later a missionary. Finally, in her senior year, she decided that becoming a welfare worker in the Lutheran Church was her true mission in life. The years of religious fellowship and spiritual retreat had forged her resolve to dedicate her life to Christ, to the church, and to others in need. But those years of spiritual seclusion had also given her an idealistic worldview, which changed drastically when she went to work at the agency. The few successes she experienced in her work were far overshadowed by the situations in which she had little influence or control . . . the Lambson children being the most pronounced. The evils of the world always seemed to prevail, no matter how hard one tried, or how much faith one had. Honestly, she did not know how long she could maintain.

She sat the pen aside and began praying vigorously, relentlessly for the well-being of her special children, and of the children of the world, clasping her hands and pressing them to her pale lips, her hazel eyes raised sadly towards the rough hewn crucifix hanging on the wall before her. "Please come down from the cross, Christ Jesus, and rescue these children . . . this community . . . this troubled world." She held tightly in her hands the small, smooth wooden cross that had been given out at the previous Easter Sunrise Service and after a very long while she fell into a troubled, fitful, trancelike sleep right there at her desk.

By the first of July the LWS finalized and approved the plan; preparations had been carefully completed for the removal and dispersing of the youngsters. However, though the scheme to separate them may have been a practical, well-planned-out one, the implementation turned out to be extremely difficult: the Lambsons' departure from the Lake Charles Lutheran Children's Home proved to be much, much more difficult than their arrival. The brothers were never outright informed of the change in their circumstances until the day the plan was to be carried out. Rather, the Rykkers merely told them to gather their clothes for a summer trip to the countryside.

When Miss Clementson arrived at the Receiving Home early on the Tuesday morning of their transfer, she had already resolved to be strong. The LWS's decision had been a Godly one and must be abided by. There could be no questioning of the decision. But as soon as the boys had been gathered together in the front of the home, her resolve began to crumble. She tried to focus on the deed at hand by supervising the transfer in a businesslike way, bustling about and hovering over them, making sure the separation went smoothly. Yet try as she might, her heart broke as the Rykkers split the children up and began herding them off towards the two awaiting LWS cars. And then the betrayal became evident.

"Hey, how come we gotta ride in two different cars?"

"You said we uz only gonna be gone two weeks! How come you puttin' alla our stuff in the trunk?"

"Hey, why ain't Darrell comin'?"

"What's going on?!"

When no answers came forth, the boys all became even more nervously suspicious of what was about to transpire, suspecting foul play. Collectively they all slowed and then, in resistance, began leaning back, twisting and pulling at the hands that tightly gripped their wrists.

"Where ya takin' us?!"

"What the heck!"

"Lemme go! Lemme go!"

Realizing suddenly that the Rykkers had not had the foresight, or perhaps the courage, to tell the boys about the arranged separation, Miss Clementson, in a very unprofessional manner, began to sob.

Dewey refused to move another step until he found out the truth about their leaving in separate cars, about Darrell staying, about the reason for Miss Clementson's sudden weeping. He finally broke free from Mr. Rykker's firm grip, jerking his hand downward and away from the man's grasp as he ran back to the social worker, his supposed friend and advocate. "Hey! Where we goin'?! Where they takin' us?! Where're Lloyd and Leeland goin'?!" he yelled at her. "Why's Darrell not leavin'?!"

In an attempt to bring calm to the hurtful situation, she knelt down, took his set and angry chin in her hand, and started explaining the transfer to him in as simple and caring words as possible, all the while looking earnestly at him. He stared back intently, angrily into her tearing eyes, looking for answers that she could never provide.

"Dewey, try to understand," she began purposefully, hoping to bring reason to the increasingly desperate situation. "We can't keep you boys here at the home any longer."

"Yeah, so?!" Dewey almost yelled in defiance.

"Well, you and Duane are going to live with some nice folks on a farm near Devils Lake." She hesitated a moment, again trying to remain steadfast, and she felt Dewey tense. "Darrell is staying here and Lloyd and Leeland are going to another farm with th . . ."

Dewey sharply slapped her cool hand away from his face. Mr. Rykker came back quickly and secured Dewey's wrist again, then began shepherding them all towards the idling agency cars. But Dewey started fighting violently, flailing his free arm and fist wildly. The other boys launched into hysterical wailing and crying; instinctively resorting to previous tactics of escape and self-preservation, they pulled in different direction in a desperate attempt to scatter.

"We ain't goin'!"

"I don wanna leave here!"

"We ain't done nothing!'"

"We'll be good! Honest!"

"Ya said ya liked us! Ya lied!"

"Ya damned liers!"

"Let us go back ta Ma!"

"We'll never see each other again!"

"They're gonna kill us! They're gonna kill us!"

"Dewwwwwey! Help! Dewwwwwey!"

The Rykkers, having learned from past experiences, had made certain that enough reinforcements were present to control the situation; an adult was assigned to individually restrain each of the Lambsons. Although the brothers pulled hard against the hands that held them firmly, they could not break away. During the commotion, Miss Clementson became unceremoniously elbowed off to the sidelines of the skirmish, where she just stood helplessly watching and weeping. She extended her hand slightly towards Dewey as he began to kick and punch at anybody within reach.

"You dang sonsabitches! Ya ain't takin' my brothers! Ya ain't gonna...."

Mr. Rykker, though somewhat elderly, could still muster up a good deal of strength. Grabbing Dewey's right arm at the elbow, he clinched it painfully. "It's for your own good, boy. Get in the car with your brother."

Even though Dewey kicked him in the shin several times, and in the groin once, Mr. Rykker wrapped his arms tightly around Dewey from behind and wrestled him towards the open rear door of the waiting black Chevy, pushing him roughly into the back seat with Duane, who sat rigid with fear. Another worker sat in between them and forced his bulk down on the struggling Dewey. When Mr. Rykker slammed the door, the LWS driver immediately stepped on the gas pedal and the car containing Dewey and Duane sped off towards Devils Lake. The vehicle whined in first gear until the driver ground the transmission into second and then into third; lurching forward several times, the car sharply turned the corner at the bottom of Christian Hill and disappeared into time and change. The swift and forceful restraint of Dewey, and his and Duane's hasty departure, quickly and surely broke the backbone of any resistance the five might have collectively mustered. Lloyd and Leeland submitted docilely to their fate. Fighting back tears . . . whimpering, even . . . they submissively entered the second agency Chevy, which spirited them away to the Thompson's in Grafton, miles in the opposite direction. Their sad faces gazed out of the rear window, staring back forlornly at Miss Clementson and the Rykkers.

Darrell could only look on, standing and waving good-bye uncomprehendingly at his brothers' sudden departure into the new summer morning heat. Miss Clementson picked him up and held him tightly for a long while after his brothers' rude departure, telling him softly, over and over again, that everything would be all right. Nothing in all of her training and work, or perhaps even life experience, had prepared her for an event as traumatic and tragic as the one she had just experienced.

* * *

Time did not bring relief to the young social worker. A persistent sadness and guilt—a growing jadedness—engulfed her in the days and weeks that followed the boys' removal from the receiving home, dogging her during the whole length of her days and often late into her nights. Indeed, she continually felt that she had, even in following the rules of the agency, deceived and forsaken those who had trusted her. In fact, many nights during the sweltering, humid summer, she would lay awake in her stark living quarters adjacent to the agency, sweating profusely as she dreamt about the Lambsons.

Not until the first part of August could Miss Clementson bring herself to visit Dewey and Duane at the Erlingsrudes' farm. But she deemed it to be her duty . . . she had received two wrinkled letters from the boys' mother in North Carolina. She felt that delivering the letters might possibly gain her access back into their confidence, especially with Dewey, whom she felt she had most betrayed. She left Grand Forks in the early morning and headed towards Devils Lake, traveling west on Highway 2. Her sense of heavy-heartedness worsened when she drove through Farmington and out past the house where she had picked them up the previous year. Vivid memories distracted her . . . memories of Cora . . . of the children's quality of innocence . . . their questions and innate sense of curiosity . . . the feeling that she had rescued them from a cruel fate . . . the ultimate reality that she had not. The ride for her became very long and sad.

She arrived in Devils Lake in mid-morning, still deeply mired in guilt and depression. After buying the boys some socks and underwear and a small bag of red and yellow and green hard candy in town, she drove along several miles of dirt country road before finally arriving at the farmstead. In the lull between planting and harvest, the entire countryside seemed lazy and peaceful. The Erlingsrude spread, evidently a prosperous one, included a spacious and pleasantly white farmhouse, a large barn and adjoining pump building, a hog house, a chicken coop, three granaries, and a machine shop and tool shed.

Mrs. Erlingsrude, pre-middle-aged and rather slight for a farm wife, invited the young social worker in for lemonade, sent for the boys to come in from their chores, and proceeded to give a full report on their activities and progress. "The boys seem to be getting along here *tolerably* well since their arrival," she began slowly, putting perhaps too much emphasis on the word "tolerably."

The almost disingenuous manner of the woman somewhat irritated Clarissa, but she knew the importance of maintaining her composure. "Well, I am very glad to hear that. The agency certainly hopes that they will fit in," Clarissa responded, letting the stolid agency woman in her show through. However, she knew from Mrs. Erlingsrude's tone that much more remained to be said.

A short while passed before the boys entered the front room and sat on the edge of the floral couch. Neither spoke or even acknowledged Clarissa but instead stared down at the darkness of the braided oval rug beneath their feet. She looked at Dewey and smiled, but he just looked down more intently into his hanging hands, inspecting and picking at the growing calluses. Duane sort of smiled when she said hello to them, but then gazed over at Dewey and then down at the floor.

Mrs. Erlingsrude laced the parlor conversation with a litany of subtle grievances, all of which Miss Clementson deftly deflected with a series of non-committal, limited "agency" answers. The foster mother spoke openly to the social worker about the boys' conduct, as though they weren't even present . . . as though they were invisible . . . non-entities.

"The whole problem is that Dewey just doesn't listen very well." She didn't make the statement in a mean sort of way . . . just spoke it somewhat matter-of-factly. But she did glare a bit at Dewey immediately after she made the statement.

"I'm sure that they are just settling in. Please give it a little time, Mrs. Erlingsrude. The agency sincerely hopes that this placement will work well for both you and the boys, just as the others have in the past. And we hope that the funds are adequate support for their stay here."

"We'll see. We'll see."

The wife finally excused herself so she could finish preparing lunch for the group. After giving them their paper bags of candy and clothes, Clarissa asked the boys about their stay at the new home and about their welfare. They in turn answered her in a series of non-committal, single-word responses, never looking up and making eye contact with their former advocate.

Soon Big John Erlingsrude, a man not much older than his wife, but who overwhelmed her in physical stature, came into the kitchen from the yard, washed up, and roughly scraped his chair up to the well-provisioned table that his wife had been busy setting for him, the children, and the social worker. With the noon meal set before them, he delivered a solemn grace, rigidly holding his clenched hands and interwoven fingers tightly to his half-sunburned, half-white forehead. With the completion of the blessing, the talk around the meal at the kitchen table fell to a superficial discussion by the three adults of the weather, the crops, the war, and the general condition of the Devils Lake community, while the boys sat quietly eating their meal.

"As soon as you boys are done talkin' with the lady, you get out and get them chores finished. We got lots ta do." Mr. Erlingsrude concluded his meal and left abruptly. He had been utilizing agency children to help around the farm for the past several years and knew well how to best employ them.

After lunch Clarissa gathered up the two brothers and the three all went out onto the porch. They sat in the cool mid-afternoon shade, swinging slowly back and forth on the creaking swing, Miss Clementson in the middle, a brother on each side. Perhaps because the Erlingsrudes were not present, the initial sullenness and lack of response by the children seemed to dissipate somewhat. They even began to once again warm to her and her friendly smile. She asked in a silent prayer that they might somehow have forgiven her.

"How're my brothers?" asked Dewey, finally looking directly at her.

"They are fine and miss you both very much. It won't be long until you are back together again," Miss Clementson reassured them. "I have some letters for you . . . from your momma." The two brothers, who had never received mail before, eagerly tore open the envelopes and between them they deciphered their mother's words. The longest of the two letters, and the most recent, having been post marked only two weeks prior, read:

Charlotte, North Carolina
July 1, 1944
Dear Boys:
    Was surely glad to receive the LWS letter as I have been so worried as to what had happened to you all. But I sure was glad to hear you all are happy. I never got the letter til yesterday as I guess it had been sent back because I have been changing addresses lately. I get so terribly lonesome for my boys. I've been working and this is such a wonderful country here in North Carolina. Very glad to hear that you boys are having such a good time and are going to Sunday School. Please send me some pictures if you have any as I have some friends that would love to see you and all the pictures I did have burnt up in the fire I had last month when I lost all my clothes. Please remember that I love you with all of my heart. I know that you must be lonely too but sometimes thats the way this world runs.
                            Your loving momma,
                            Cora Lambson

When they had finished the letter the two boys sat quietly for quite some time, looking out onto the flat, timeless prairie farmland.
    "What a buncha hooie," Duane said at last, but not really in a nasty way.

"You be quiet! Maw's comin' back ta get us! Just you wait!" Dewey blurted out.

"Ain't neither!"

"Is too! You shutup!"

"Don't have ta!"

"She's comin' ta get us! Take us outta this stink hole!"

Dewey reached across Clarissa and roughly punched his brother hard in the center of his narrow chest, jarring the slow back and forth movement of the swing so that it swung all askew. Then the angry boy jumped off, grabbed up the two letters, and silently trekked off towards the open fields, his head lowered, his chin almost down on his chest as he bit into his lower lip.

The swing righted itself after awhile and settled once again into its slow, rhythmic back-and-forth movement. Many minutes of silent, subtle swinging went by until Duane at last quit rubbing the sore spot on his chest and spoke. "Miss Clementson . . . Clarissa . . . can I tell ya sumpthin'? Show you sumpthin'? Over in the barn?"

"Why, yes, certainly, Duane. You know, I very much want to be a friend to you and your brothers."

She placed her hand gently over his and they got up from the swing. Duane took her hand, interlocking his fingers with hers, and guided her down the porch, across the farm-yard and over to the barn. When they entered the semidark-ness, he released her gentle grip and went ahead of her. "It's really neat," he whispered as he motioned her on and guided her to a far corner of the warm, stuffy building, where small shafts of sunlight crept in through the cracked joints of the wooden walls. When their eyes had adjusted to the dim-ness, he pointed, with contained excitement, to a litter of several multicolored kittens and a mother cat, all of which he seemed extremely fond of. The kittens lay lazily around the mother, who had burrowed a soft, safe home in the straw for her young.

"I found this ere litter just after she borned 'em. Fact they was still wet . . . . She was lickin' 'em off . . . cleanin' 'em." Duane sat down on his haunches beside the cat family and remained quiet for a bit, so she sat down next to him. He carried on a very normal, natural conversation with Clarissa about the kittens and about various things concerning life on the Erlingsrude farm. Then the boy turned to her, very serious.

"I think I know why Dewey's sa hateful."

"Why, do you suppose?" She gently moved a lock of dark brown hair back off his forehead and he sat down closer to her.

"Well . . . ya see . . . ." He paused, searching for words. "Can I tell ya a story? A real secret story?" he finally asked without turning towards the girl.

"Yes, of course," she answered softly, encouragingly. "I'd love to hear it."

"Well, me and Dewey was cleaning out the storage room over there by the machine shed." He stopped for a few moments; half turning, he pointed to the outbuilding across the yard, then continued in earnest. "Then Dewey dumped some pails of junk out onta the porch and there was an ol' bat in one of 'em. A small ol' black one that flopped all around like crazy in the daylight. Me and Dewey was just watchin' it."

He stopped for a few moments, trying to find the right words. Miss Clementson sat transfixed by what the boy tried to relate to her. Finally Duane picked up and began petting the only calico kitten in the litter. With each stroke the kitten bit playfully at his hand. "This 'ere kitty was on the porch with us and when it saw the bat it went right up and swatted it hard. And then the bat got real mad and bit the kitty on its back leg . . . right here." Dewey looked up shyly into Miss Clementson's face. He handed the kitten to Clarissa, who felt its rear leg and then stroked its soft fur until it fell asleep.

"It really is a beautiful kitten. Does it have a name?"

"Nope . . . not yet." He kind of snickered a bit before continuing with his tale. "Anyway, when the bat bit it, the kitty jus' jumped straight up in the air and squealed like hell . . . I mean heck. Scared, it was! Just kept bellerin'. After awhile the big ol' momma cat here comes out of the barn, runnin' full hard, right across the yard and under the fence and right up to where we was. An' then she stopped and stood real still, lookin' deadly at that bat."

Duane gave a brief, self-conscious laugh and paused in embarrassment; then he looked up to see if the young woman was still listening. He continued on intently, stopping every once in awhile, trying to comprehend the significance of his own words. "Then she walked right up, real slow, see . . . and swatted the bat down and bit it hard, right in the back of the neck . . . right 'ere . . . and kilt it dead." Pausing again for several moments, he strained to explain the incident and why relating the enigmatic tale to the young woman somehow provided him with a small degree of understanding. Slowly he shook his head back and forth.

Finally he went on, looking off to the yard. "Then when the momma cat left, this 'ere kitty started hitting the dead bat around and around the porch . . . like *he* had kilt it! The kitty swatted it for a long time before takin' it into his mouth and tossin' it around and up and down . . . then he walked back toward the barn with the bat in his mouth . . . walkin' real proud like. Me and Dewey just stood an' watched the whole danged thing."

The boy stopped abruptly, as though looking for just the precise words to complete his metaphoric tale . . . searching for an end to a story. "We couldn't figure it out . . . why the momma'd do that . . . . Then when I looked over at Dewey, he was sorta cryin', ya know. When I asked him what was wrong, he shoved me down on the ground and walked off."

A few more moments of stillness passed during which Duane took the kitten back from his silenced friend and began stroking the soft tan and white fur of its back and then its small paws. The kitten rolled over on its back and its sharp claws dug lightly into Duane's rough finger to hold it still for playful biting with its sharp teeth. "This 'ere cat's mine. Mr. Erlingsrude already said I could have 'im. I'm gonna take care of 'im good." Duane put the cat back down gently next to its mother and stood up. "I'm gonna name 'em Champ! Whadda ya think?"

"Yes, I think that would be a nice name." Miss Clementson sadly knew the story had ended. Nothing more needed to be said.

As the two left the barn and walked back towards the farmhouse, out across the warm and sunny yard, the young woman choked back the desolation that had welled up deep inside her. In her sad helplessness, she drew Duane close to her before they arrived at the house, stroking his soft hair as he also began to sob harshly.

"Don't say nothin' to Dewey . . . or tell him I tol' ya the story, okay? He'll beat me up for sure."

Chapter Seven–
Revelations

Seems fitting that the conclusion of the Lambson children's tale of waywardness should end with Dewey. He had been, after all, the lynchpin of the group and thus the lightning rod for many of the undeserved troubles that befell the brothers . . . the innocents.

On a wintery afternoon in March of 1949, Dewey Lambson sat forlorn and alone on his iron bunk at the State Reform School in Mandan, running his hand reflectively across the coarse wool of the blanket. From the first floor window of the three-storied, stolid, red brick Morton Main building he could look out onto the surrounding structures that formed a quadrangle around the open assembly area. A pair of flagpoles stood in the center of the quasi-parade ground, held in place by a tripod pile of white-washed rocks. The American and North Dakota State flags flapped rigid in the strong north wind, the latter flag flown just below the former. Because of his seniority, Dewey had first choice of the largest footlocker and the bottom rack in the three-bed tier, only one of many bunks stacked warehouse-like in rows. He would often just stare down at the cold, starkly gray linoleum floor of the open bay of his and the other young inmates' common living quarters, lamenting where his young life had led him thus far, wondering what his future would be when he was released from the reform school the next month, on his eighteenth birthday.

Given his own circumstances, he frequently speculated about what had become of his four brothers . . . wondering if they, like him, resided in some institution or jail somewhere . . . or if they had found good families to take care of them. For the most part he had lost contact with his siblings in the years that passed since their time together as one in the Lake Charles Receiving Home. Almost five years had gone by since that summer of 1944, when he and his brothers became even more scattered by the powers and people that held life-determining control over them and their existence. His recollection of their young faces and mannerisms had dimmed considerably. Now abandoned and confined deep within the reform school environment, institutionalized into submission and obedience, Dewey often puzzled over the on-going contradiction of his and his brothers' community . . . of their being forsaken by a worthless mother and father . . . of the sneaky duplicity of the Lutheran Welfare Society . . . of the treachery of Miss Clementson . . . of the dreadful hopelessness of the justice system. Great anger still remained within him, especially regarding her betrayal.

The fragmentation, indeed, the total dispersing and separation of the Lambsons . . . that is, the sudden, irreversible shattering of their tenuous bond of brotherhood . . . presents a situation that in and of itself proves exceedingly difficult for an outsider, an interloper, to comprehend, much less explain, given the nature of the community into which the bothers had not asked to be born. The people in that general society collectively seemed to have reduced life to a very simple philosophy—the family and the farm were paramount in living and life. Every new yield and each new birth, as well as each newly turned-under field and every withering death, revealed a brief glimpse of the essence of God. Each new child and every new crop that emerged from the black ground came to symbolize renewal . . . rejuvenation . . . regeneration . . . an ongoing, tangible resurrection of the human spirit. The life cycle provided an ever present sense of stability and routine, of consistency and reliability, of birth and death, of truth and certainty. The two prominent entities of the land and of human existence intertwined to very much serve as all-too-simple metaphors for life's longing for itself, and at the same time came to stand as transcendent truths for the people of Farmington. Yet strangely enough, for the society underpinned by rebirth and restoration, the only solution to the issue of the Lambson children somehow always involved further separating and distancing them from each other. Perhaps the unspoken rational was to fragment the brothers into non-existence . . . to the point where no one would have to explain, and thus justify, what had happened to the youngsters. But probably nobody realized this disjunction more than Miss Clementson, who with the slow passage of time agonized over the treatment of the Lambson boys.

During the several months that followed the Lambsons' abrupt and traumatic departure from the Lake Charles Receiving Home, the reports that Miss Clementson received through Director Daniels confirmed her fears concerning the boys' outcome. A pit of anxiety—of painfully harsh reality—seemed to continually reside in the depths of her stomach; her heart grew sadder and she became increasingly despondent; as time passed she became more profoundly disillusioned with her life's calling.

The case of Darrell Lambson proved to be somewhat of a relief to her . . . a small achievement . . . a bit of an accomplishment, if you will, that tended to temporize a little of the guilt she felt. Because of his young age Darrell had the good fortune to be taken into foster care by a middle-aged couple . . . the Goodwins . . . who farmed a small spread down by Mayville. The Goodwins, both devout Catholics and devoted to the Word, had three daughters, aged ten and twelve and thirteen. However, the couple could no longer have children and wanted to see if they could love a child who wasn't their own, even if the child came to them from a different religious background. With a certain amount of misgivings, the Lutheran Welfare Society, because of the positive economic considerations involved, relented and transferred Darrell to his new home with the Goodwins.

After Darrell's arrival from the Lake Charles Receiving Home, Mrs. Goodwin wrote happily to the LWS:

October 12th, 1944
Dear Director Daniels and Miss Clementson—

Thank you so much for letting Darrell come into our household. We have been truly blessed with the boy!

Upon his arrival Darrell was very quiet at first in our presence, but by the end of the first day he was engaged in playing by himself, occasionally calling our attention to what he was doing. He has since adjusted well to our home and its rules. Our entire family—several aunts, uncles, and cousins included—had been looking forward to his arrival and had purchased an abundance of clothes and toys for him. Charlotte, our oldest daughter, remained home from school in order to be here when Darrell arrived. She has taken charge of him ever since . . . this afternoon she set a small table for him for a tea party. One of the neighbor's children came in to see Darrell and stayed for the whole day. Now that Darrell has come to realize he is going to stay at our house, he does not seem at all unhappy. In fact, he is trying hard to be a part of the family. We have already come to love his gentle nature . . . his angel-like face and red hair. We are even working hard on breaking his thumb sucking so that it won't give him buck teeth and ruin his beautiful smile.

We thank God and the Lutheran Welfare Society for giving us this child! With God's help, we will do our best to give Darrell a good Christian upbringing.

Sincerely Yours,
Alma Goodwin

Subsequent reports to LWS by the Goodwin family indicated that Darrell would most likely be a welcome, valued, and thankfully permanent addition to the Goodwin family.

In fact, during the next several years, the Goodwins tried a number of times to adopt the youngster into the family so that he would be a legal member and they could change his name to theirs permanently. However, the LWS informed the family that Cora Lambson adamantly opposed vacating her parental rights; she rigorously maintained that she would someday return and regain custody of her five sons. Though his name could never be legally changed, Darrell remained a vital part of the family, with the mother and three daughters continually fawning over the lovely, loveable boy, almost to the point of alienating Mr. Goodwin.

The success story of Darrell, though, became cancelled out many times over by the travails of his four brothers. In the next few years Miss Clementson, who had gotten even skinnier with the passage of time, monitored closely the progress of the other Lambson children; she grew increasingly frustrated with not only her but also the Lutheran Agency's inability to change the youngsters' fate . . . to intercede in the course of their young lives in a meaningful way. The circumstances of their upbringing and destiny, sadly enough, remained far beyond her control. Though she felt somehow responsible for the children—certainly a false assumption for anyone in her position to make—she was powerless to intervene and exert any authority in order to bring about a positive resolution to their plight.

Much to Clarissa Clementson's continued disappointment, in early November, after the satisfactory placement of Darrell Lambson, Melva Thompson wrote the Lutheran Welfare Society to say that she and her husband would no longer be able to care for both Leeland and Lloyd Lambson. She penned a very long and frank letter to Director Daniels, which he commented on, initialed, and forwarded to Miss Clementson.

Written in Mrs. Thompson's ornate, slow, deliberate handwriting, the text of her message read as follows:

November 18, 1944
Mr. Ethedge Daniels
Director, Lutheran Welfare Society

Dear Mr. Daniels,

Regrettably, Mr. Thompson and I have decided that we are not in the position to keep both of the Lambson boys at our home.

Leeland gets into mischief whenever he is in Lloyd's company. Leeland has the ability to do work but he is struggling under the influence of his brother. His emotional status and poor habits of work are a hindrance to his progress and to his remaining here at our place. Leeland seems to crave attention and affection and oftentimes wants only to sit on my lap. He continually soils himself and is a weak sort of a child. Lamentably, because he does not have a great amount of endurance, he is not doing too good at working on the farm. With the limited use of his left arm, there are few chores that he is capable of completing. Also, I wonder if he isn't a bit slow mentally. But although Leeland is a very needy child, he IS always pleasant and happy, for the most part.

The main reason for our decision is that the boys seldom do as they are told. A good deal of this can be put on Lloyd, who exerts much control over Leeland. They often play hooky from school. And even though they were specifically forbidden from going into town, they have done so anyway, hanging around down to Bud Wilkerson's barber shop or loitering outside of the pool hall. They like to play around the depot. They seem to like to be at the station when the trains come in and to ask the people for money. This for us is quite embarrassing. In addition, one of our neighbors has recently complained that the boys were rather destructive around her place and that they had thrown eggs on the roof of one of her out buildings. I could see where the contents of the eggs had run down the outside of the wall. Our neighbors are sympathetic with us but they feel that the boys are rather mean. These peaceable folks are not going to put up with them any longer.

Regarding a few other matters, Lloyd took a $1.00 bill the other day from Mr. Thomspon's billfold and some money was also missing from the change that I keep in a Mason jar in the top cupboard in the kitchen. I also would be remiss if I did not mention that there is no noticeable improvement in Lloyd's eyes, that he is still wearing glasses. It is difficult to keep the frames straight as he is always in a fight and the frames are always bent. Most, if not all, of the fights come at his instigation.

Lloyd has one of his permanent front teeth missing, on which he had used a pliers to try and pull it out, and in the process broke the tooth off at the root. I sincerely believe that the motive that prompted the removal of the tooth was the fact that Leeland had a tooth missing and various people had mentioned how cute he looked with his tooth gone. This is just one of many instances of how difficult it is to handle both of these brothers.

Mr. Thompson and I are very fond of the boys and in many ways we are reluctant to let them go. But we feel that since Mr. Thompson's health is somewhat run down at the present time it is advisable to move the boys, at least Lloyd. We would be willing to keep

Leeland for a time and have the youngster continue school here. When not being influenced by Lloyd, Leeland gets along very well with other children. For all of his faults, Leeland is very affectionate, extremely active to the extent of always wiggling. He is also truthful when I ask him a question directly, so therefore I know that we will be able to accomplish something with him if he is able to stay with us. However, you must find a new home for Lloyd.

We anxiously await your decision, which we hope will be in Leeland's favor.

Yours truly,
Melva Thompson

Based upon Mrs. Thompson's report and request, the LWS at length decided that just before Christmas Lloyd should be transferred to the Lutheran Children's Home in Fargo, while Leeland would remain with the Thompsons. Director Daniels, using Miss Clementson as his spokesperson, assured the Thompsons that without Lloyd's bad influence they would be able to control little Leeland much better.

The day before Lloyd left their home, Mr. and Mrs. Thompson sat the youngster down at the kitchen table, with its gingham, red and white checkered tablecloth, and told him how sorry they were that he could no longer stay. However, they told him finally, "Keeping you here is impossible." The two people braced themselves for a possible physical outburst, but none came. "Good! I hate it here, anyway! You two old people are mean and stingy and I hate you, too!" was his only reply as he stomped off up the stairs to gather his belongings. Miss Clementson arrived the next day and Lloyd was completely packed and ready to go. When she appeared at the front door, Lloyd stood there waiting patiently for her, holding his small bundle of clothes tightly, very much ready to leave. As he stepped across the threshold, he turned and shook hands with sobbing Leeland in a gentlemanly way, as though they would not see each other again. Saying not another word to the Thompsons, he turned and walked off to the waiting car.

During the trip from Grafton to Fargo, Lloyd and Clarissa talked almost continuously. He spoke about his mother and asked the social worker if she wanted to see the letter he had received from her three months ago. He confided in her that he never heard from his father because the man was far away at the war, but his mother wanted him to come live with her. In fact, he emphasized, before long she would be coming to get him. The ride, along with the young boy's chatter, reminded Miss Clementson once again of the day she had brought the boys into the welfare system and the memories heaped further sadness upon her soul.

Almost immediately upon his arrival at the Fargo Lutheran Children's Home, the staff there branded Lloyd a "problem child." After one week, the induction worker assessed him in her initial evaluation report as follows:

12/10/1944
Preliminary Induction Report
Client: Lloyd Lambson, transfer from Lutheran Welfare Society, Grand Forks Office

The client is an intelligent, likeable boy but a child that is ready to take advantage of a person at any time that opportunity presents itself. Lloyd is extremely enuretic, which makes him the brunt of the other children's teasing. He is cold to other children and pretty much stays to himself. We talked at length about the Thompsons' report about his unusual interest in knives and during one interview he mentioned an episode that had happened down in the hobo jungles on the outskirts of Grafton. Lloyd had found an old rusty knife in the tall grass and weeds and for some reason he could not explain had taken the knife and cut Leeland several places with it. He seems to show little or no remorse! Indeed, I found the matter-of-fact manner in which he discussed these issues to be quite unnerving!

Wilma Ferguson
LCH Chief Counselor

The social worker ended the report emphatically. The clear, crispness of her prose belied her consternation; however, in frustration she underscored the last sentence of the form, the tip of the pen almost tearing the paper.

Throughout the next several years, until he finally escaped the relentless "help" imposed on him by the welfare system, Lloyd relocated to a variety of settings, all of which never seemed to work out for the restless young man. In May of 1945, he left the Lutheran Children's Home in Fargo and went to work on the Lubinski Farm on the outskirts of Casselton. This arrangement only lasted the summer and then the old farmer promptly hustled Lloyd back to the Children's Home once more. Two-and-a-half years later, when Lloyd had become more uncontrollable, the Children's Home transferred him to the St. Vincent Catholic Charities Home in Bismarck so he might learn a trade. Authorities there, in less than six months, indicated that he "lacked focus and exhibited the behavior pattern of a quitter." Consequently, they summarily put him on a bus and returned him to the authorities in Fargo. Despite numerous different attempts to place him with other farm families, Lloyd somehow always returned to the Lutheran Children's Home in Fargo, where he remained until spring of 1949.

At the age of fifteen, at about the same time as his brother finished languishing in the Mandan correctional facility, Lloyd broke free of the system. The cause of his escape was simple enough. He had snuck out of the Children's Home late one June evening and stayed out overnight, just wandering the streets. One of the junior counselors at the home met him at the front door the next morning and commenced to administer the standard punishment for such infractions, which involved several whacks across the back of the boy's legs with a three-foot length of old one-inch, grayish black rubber hose. Lloyd, however, had been the victim of enough such castigation, so halfway through the punishment he took the hose away from the counselor and hit him in return several times across the head and back and shoulders, screaming all the while "How do *YOU* like it?!" Bolting out the back door, leaving the man on his knees— bent over, covering his head with his arms and hollering empty threats—Lloyd ran down the back alleys as fast as his aching legs would allow him. Reaching the railroad yard south of town, he rested for a bit as he pondered his future. Then, without hesitation, he hopped aboard a slow moving westbound freight train. As the train gathered speed, Lloyd sat at the open boxcar door, his feet dangling over the edge, breathing in the sweet air of freedom; he joyfully waved back at Stocker Brenley, the Great Northern switchman who became the last person from the area to ever see him again. Lloyd, at last released from captivity, began his lifelong pursuit of aimless drifting, his wide smile exposing his missing front tooth.

Leeland, though, never escaped the system, as his older brother Lloyd had. Not too long after Lloyd's departure from their home, the Thompsons, feeling great sympathy for the rather slow, almost pathetic lad, agreed to keep Leeland on indefinitely as a foster child. They took good care of him and he became a pliable, obedient adolescent. However, in the summer of 1949, Leeland, then thirteen, broke his left arm once again in a freak accident on the Thompson farm: while he was helping with the threshing and shocking of the grain, the haying wagon on which he was riding hit a rut, causing a mass of the stacked shocks to shift and slam his arm and shoulder up against the metal bars of the hay rack, pinning the screaming boy there for almost a half hour. X-rays at the Grafton Regional Hospital showed that his shoulder joint sustained merely a sprain; however, the gray-black images also tragically revealed that the first break of Leeland's arm had never been set properly and therefore the second, higher fracture severed several vital nerves, rendering the boy's arm nearly useless. The Thompsons certainly felt sorry for their foster child, but given the severity and permanence of his disability, his use to them on the farm became extremely limited after the accident.

With the help of the Lutheran Welfare Society, the Thompsons shipped Leeland off to the Brimington Vocational Rehabilitation Center, a division of the North Dakota

State Hospital in Jamestown, following his Hearing of Committal. The LWS, as well as the Thompsons, hoped that by institutionalizing him, Leeland would be able to learn a trade and eventually become a productive member of the community. Yet when he arrived at Brimington the lad immediately became labeled "retarded" by many of the other residents of the place, especially the younger inmate patients who simply referred to him as "the retard." From the time he arrived at and began to adjust to the rehabilitation center, the moniker dogged him . . . a situation made worse, no doubt, by the way he favored his lame arm and his inability to defend himself, both physically and verbally.

Certainly the bodily limitations he experienced were exacerbated by his somewhat limited learning capability and intellectual growth; additionally, his emotional inadequacies were further stunted by his ability to learn abstract concepts. And these myriad, persistent factors kept him from benefiting from the general education courses he was placed in at Brimington. For example, during one penmanship lesson, being too afraid to raise his good arm and hand for permission to go to the toilet, he wet himself while repetitiously practicing the letter "L/l" for sixty-five minutes. When the class dismissed for lunch, Lyman Manley, who sat directly behind Leeland, immediately seized the opportunity to call everyone's attention to the yellow puddle beneath Leeland's seat. Screaming loudly, Lyman hopped up and down and excitedly pointed at the darkened crotch of Leeland's trousers, continuing to screech incessantly for five minutes, provoking the other gaping onlookers in the classroom to almost a near riot. Many occasions and instances such as this caused the superiors at Brimington to eventually formalize the boy's reputed psychological condition by typing in the descriptor "not educable" beside his name on the manila institutional file record that documented his life there.

As a result of his cumulative shortcomings, the formal education classes he had been attending and failing were curtailed; instead, Leeland received close instruction in shoe and boot repair. Eventually he became amazingly skilled at mending shoes with the use of only one arm . . . adeptly holding the hobnails in his mouth and working the mallet with his one good hand. The shoe repair and restoration shop provided a fairly substantial source of revenue for Brimington. The Second World War, as well as the Korean Conflict that followed, left the military with mountains of worn, mismatched combat boots, so the institute arranged for a government contract to restore the footwear for war surplus sale. The endless supply of boots, some blood soaked and some still containing scraps of flesh and pieces of bone, were trucked to the institution for sorting and refurbishing, thus giving Leeland's growing abilities as a cobbler lasting value. Though slow, he proved to be a relentless, thorough worker whenever a required task was clearly explained to him in the simplest terms possible. Through his own tenacity, and with the generosity of the vocational center, Leeland remained working and living at Brimington, almost as a testimonial to the institute's capacity to rehabilitate those in need. He had, indeed, finally found a home.

Ironically, the fate of Dewey and Duane mirrored almost the same path as that of their brothers Lloyd and Leeland. After the fall of 1944, the final separation of Dewey and Duane began, which would ultimately complete the fragmentation of the Lambson brothers.

The additional reports that Director Daniels and Miss Clementson received about the two oldest Lambson boys during September of that year proved to be as equally disturbing as the information from the Thompsons involving Lloyd and Leeland. An abrupt, terse, handwritten note from the Erlingsrudes regarding Dewey and Duane offered little encouragement or explanation. Though the Erlingsrudes claimed that they would have liked to do so, they could not possibly keep the two brothers after the harvest season ended, though the couple provided no real concrete reason for the decision. Miss Clementson did not know why for sure, but Director Daniels intimated that the Erlingsrudes wanted to adopt children rather than provide just foster care. And because the LWS informed the Erlingsrudes that Cora Lambson still had parental control over the boys, they decided to "keep looking."

On October 1st, Dewey and Duane were once more abruptly transferred by the LWS, this time from the Erlingsrudes' home to the farmstead of Fred and Dorothy Helges, a young husband and wife who farmed twelve and a half miles south of Devils Lake. Director Daniels and Miss Clementson hoped, and even prayed together in Daniels' office, that the Helgeses, being youthful and perhaps more tolerant than the Erlingsrudes, would be able to have more direct influence on the two boys. Yet only a few months after this transfer, the Helgeses contacted Director Daniels and notified him that they also could no longer keep the boys in their home together because of the boys' behavior, especially the elder brother Dewey.

In the detailed, several-page letter that they sent to the agency, the couple reported in great length their experience with the boys, the substance of which in part read:

> . . . In sharp contrast to Dewey, Duane can best be described as a sensitive youngster who probably thinks deeply about things that have been said to him. He is a very responsible individual. Though anxious to see his mother and his father and his brothers, Duane hasn't been too perturbed when he did not hear from any of them. Dewey, on the other hand, is always quite anxious to hear from his mother, which he never has. He constantly stews about it, almost to the point of obsession.
>
> . . . Dewey is an inveterate bed wetter, even when we paid him ten cents a week not to. The young man is not friendly . . . always on the defensive . . . argumentative . . . unmanageable. We feel that there is a world of difference in the personalities of the two boys. Duane is easy going and is so much less difficult to satisfy. Dewey has obviously brought with him the very same patterns of behavior that he exhibited in the Erlingsrudes' home, from what we understand.
>
> . . . Dewey apparently is a very unhappy and disturbed child and talks a great deal about wanting to be with his mother. Dewey is reluctant and sullen. He never helps with the farm chores unless he is specifically ordered to do so, while Duane seems to know what should be done and goes ahead with the work

on his own accord. Dewey is jealous of Duane and often mistreats him. The boys share the same room and sleep in the same bed. Dewey, however, pushes Duane out of bed at night and forces him to sleep on the floor. He can be very violent. Dewey even threatened Mrs. Helges with a butter knife when she accused him of trying to drown Champ, the calico cat that Duane had brought with him from the Erlingsrudes; the boy's cruel act, as well as his uncalled-for, violent reactions and outbursts, have frightened the Mrs. greatly and has caused us to write to you.

We do like Duane very much and thus Dewey seems to be very jealous of him because of that. However, we are adamant in our claim that we have shown no favoritism where the boys are concerned.

We must insist that there be some sort of resolution to the problem. We have both agreed that we might keep Duane with us. However, if both boys must go in order to be rid of Dewey, so be it. We can certainly try other youngsters from LWS.

We await your immediate response.

Fred and Dorothy Helges

December 2, 1944

The Helgeses' letter to the LWS requesting custody of only Duane pretty much solidified the fates of the two boys. At the end of December, 1944, through the advocacy of the LWS, Dewey was transferred from the Helgeses. Because of his age, a decision was made to send him to the Cass County Adolescent Center in Fargo, where he might get appropriate care. The Helgeses became quite relieved when the LWS notified them of Dewey's scheduled departure, which they emphasized resulted from his own misbehavior, not because they did not like the youngster. But they had, after all, decided to keep Duane, who they felt would be much more pliable and amiable *after* the departure of his older brother and could eventually be trained to be a valuable hand on the farm, as well as an upstanding young man. The qualities that he exhibited heretofore certainly indicated that.

Once rid of Dewey's troublesome influence, Duane did become a completely different youngster. In fact, Duane's behavior improved drastically, so much so that the Helgeses' attitude towards the youngster grew warmer and they tried earnestly to make him feel a part of the family. With the passage of time, especially when the couple began to have their own children, they considered him to be, more or less, part of the growing family; Duane, with a good deal of cautious reluctance, even began to believe the same thing himself, trying in every way possible to ingratiate himself with those around him. Entering his teenage years, the boy grew into a robust and active youngster. Soon he was excelling in school, making up for all of the education he had missed out on in his previously dysfunctional childhood years, as well as becoming good friends with a select few of his fellow schoolmates.

The relationship between Duane and the Helgeses grew stronger because of his quiet obedience and their firm but fair handling of the boy. After awhile, probably a little over two years after Dewey left, the Helgeses wanted more than foster care of Duane and began the adoption procedure for him. However, each time they tried, the LWS regrettably had to turn the couple down. And even though he remained with them throughout his teenage years as a foster charge, whenever the Helgeses tried to adopt the boy formally, legally, Cora Lambson, still very much a malevolent influence, would never consent to relinquishing custody of any of her sons. Just as was the case with Darrell and the Goodwins, Cora would never consent to releasing her possession of any of her children; she hung on tenaciously to her legal parental rights, probably hoping to perhaps leverage some financial benefit at a later date.

Duane did not regret the fact that he probably would never return to live with his natural mother. However, that distinct possibility always remained a part of his existence . . . that is, the truth that he might be forced to leave the stability he had come to know and be condemned to return to the terrible life struggle he and his brothers had once known. This reality, coupled with the fact that he never really could become a true and legal part of the family, remained an unspoken hurt deep within him . . . indeed, a possibility that haunted him all during his time in the Helges household. Additionally, Fred and Dorthy Helges had a total of three natural children after Duane's arrival, which, due to his non-familial status and the on-going, unspoken insecurities within him, continually caused the youngster to spend a good portion of his adolescent years gradually, subtly distancing himself from the Helgeses' fosterage. Though the family did as much as possible to embrace the young fellow, somehow his memories of the past wouldn't allow him to totally realize that acceptance, at least not to his own intense measure of satisfaction and expectation.

During his growing years, because of the difference between his last name and that of his sponsoring family, he became acutely aware of the fact that quite possibly the community held him to be one of those "welfare" children and had failed to accept him—there were, after all, those stares and stage-whispered remarks that revealed an unspoken communal attitude. The schoolyard pranks that are normal to growing boys became magnified out of proportion when played on Duane. In school, and in accomplishing his responsibilities around the farm, he seemed to feel that he must continually "prove" himself in order to be accepted by those around him. He played on the "B" squad on the high school basketball and baseball teams, but could never set himself above the rest in terms of his athletic abilities. His most outstanding accomplishment came with his being elected District Treasurer of the Luther League, a position he tried to fulfill with great maturity and responsibility. And as the LWS noted in Duane's 1947 Annual Evaluation, the teenager seemed to truly exemplify the fact that the only thing children really need is for someone to genuinely care about them.

But the demons of his past remained never far away. Because the Helgeses were not wealthy people, he felt compelled to earn extra money to help pay for his keep, all the time praying that the Lutheran Welfare Society would not deem his foster costs to be too great and thus send him to another home, or worse, return him to his mother, wherever she might be. Though Duane had developed into a tall, hearty young fellow, his friends remained limited and carefully selected. Indeed, undermining and destroying his self confidence required very little effort on anybody's part.

In his young manhood, Duane innocently began to sign his name by using the last name of the Helgeses, particularly in school: Duane Helges rather than Duane Lambson. Given the long history he had with his family, this insignificant linguistic act seemed reasonable. Mr. Helges, however, felt it necessary to counsel his young almost-son about the inadvisability of doing this. Since the assumed name "Duane Helges" was not his real name, and probably never would be since he remained unavailable for adoption, using it could quite possibly cause considerable difficulty for him in the future. To illustrate this, Mr. Helges used the example of Duane's upcoming graduation from high school: the name on the diploma would be different from that he had been using in high school, which would make it difficult for the boy to find references from the community. Duane understood intellectually, but emotionally the illustration hurt him deeply.

Immediately after the almost-father/almost-son talk, Duane went into somewhat of a prolonged period of introspection, almost differential depression; his thoughts turned to escape from the family and the farming community as a balm to his troubled soul. Yet during all of his times of growing restlessness, the family still thought the best of him. They attributed his unruliness to the "growing pains" of youth. The couple, who always considered themselves to be his real parents, remained ever hopeful that the boy-turning-young-man would again become the happy, obedient, pre-teenager they had once known him to be. But in June of 1949, as soon as Duane turned seventeen and finished his final year of schooling, which he was by then failing miserably, he ran off and joined the U. S. Navy. Yet he did not . . . could not tell his supportive parents "goodbye," choosing only to leave them a short note on the pillow of his carefully made bed . . . thanking them for their care and thoughtfulness over the years . . . expressing his deep gratitude to them for being the only family he had ever known. However, he had, he wrote, a desperate need to find himself. In the several years following his departure, infrequently the Helgeses would receive letters from Duane, written in his neat, tight handwriting; the envelopes, which sometimes contained small amounts of money, always bore the postmarks of far off ports of call and briefly told of adventures far beyond the quiet, desperate prairies.

Unlike Duane, or even Lloyd, Dewey with the passage of time became somewhat resigned to his fate. Showing little emotion when he left the Helgeses' home in December of 1944, he merely grunted a goodbye to his brother and his foster parents and submissively accepted his transfer to the Cass County Adolescent Center. For quite a long time after that, he seemed always very moody . . . extremely disconsolate and insecure. For many long hours he dwelt upon the fact that Duane stayed on with the Helgeses while he had been summarily sent away. He continually wondered about what was wrong with him . . . about why nobody, not even his own mother or father, needed or even cared about him. He felt as though he was the only one of his original family that no one wanted or gave a damn about. When he asked the counselors at the center about this, none could give him an answer. And he longed to see his mother . . . to know what had become of her . . . to know why she had left

Three months after Dewey's arrival, Mr. Horace Thydeson, the chief administrator of the Center, wrote the following report to Director Daniels:

4/1/45
Rev. Ethedge Daniels
Lutheran Welfare Society
Grand Forks, North Dakota

The following is a report on the young charge, one Dewey Lambson, who your agency transferred to us in December. The boy is having great difficulty adjusting himself to the group and is continually clamoring for attention, either from the staff or the other resident boys. Though he has improved somewhat, he has been a very hard youngster to handle, more so than any I have had at the center for quite some time. He is stubborn by nature and rather a "ruffian" and a "bully." This attitude is very understandable, coming from a young person of his status and with his background.

He has also been a real disciplinary problem in school. Frequently his teacher has isolated him from his class by placing him for long periods of time alone in the detention room, but to no avail. Dewey's enuresis has not improved. His bed wetting is quite out of control and extremely irritating. I have tried every way I could think of to interest him in quitting. I offered him a dime, but not even money can stop him from this disgusting habit. I made up my mind he would stop his bed wetting and used a rubber hose on him several times, but with no success. "Yeah, so?!" is his favorite expression and he sounds sort of on the defensive when he says it, as though he is challenging anyone that he says it to. He tends to be much more than just a little cynical. If he feels an injustice has been done him he isn't quick to forget most times, while curiously enough sometimes a smile and a little joking or understanding will make him forget. He does have a chip on his shoulder, but he has begun to get along tolerably with the other children in the home, although perhaps he is the brunt of some of the other children's taunting, most probably because of his bedwetting, which quickly brings on a physical confrontation. The other children often try to blame him for many things. He seems to do a lot of thinking and feels things more keenly than the others. He wants to be good but finds it hard.

Additionally, he reported to me that he has had continuous dreams of his mother and says that he constantly dreams that she is coming for him. From my understanding of his background, based on what I have read in his LWS records, the mother is not ready to admit that the things she has done to her son may indeed have caused his emotional and behavioral problems. I wonder if she herself may not realize that her treatment of him makes her responsible for his disobedience and lack of respect for authority. Yet he still talks of her with affection and says he cannot wait for her to come and take him to live with her. This is what I have the most difficulty understanding.

Overall, though, I do like the young fellow and he does have some winning ways. I feel sorry for him and I sincerely hope that the Center will eventually have a beneficial effect on him.

Mr. Horace Thydeson
Cass County Adolescent Center
Fargo, North Dakota

Miss Clementson did not see the report until a month later and when she did she decided to make an unplanned trip to Fargo to visit Dewey at the Center. With her she again carried another letter from the boys' mother, which had been channeled to her through the agency. He appeared less than happy to see his former friend and "protector." When he entered the large front room, which served as the visiting area of the Center, he walked stiffly up to her. The boy, who had grown some since she had last seen him, stood rigid before her, looking askew in order to avoid her eyes, then looking out of the rain-clouded front window, then looking down at her black, patent leather shoes.

"Whadda *you* want?!" He asked meanly, without looking at her. With somewhat of a smirk, he turned slowly towards her, staring meanly at her, hoping his words would hurt her as much as he had been hurt. "What's wrong now? One a my brothers dead, 'er sumphin'?" Dewey's eyes moved down to the floor.

"No, Dewey. I . . . ."

"Well, what's wrong then?" he blurted out, without giving her a chance to finish. "Am I goin' to be put some place else, now? I hope so. I hate this dang burg!"

"No, no, nothing's wrong. Why do you say that?"

"Every time *you* come around, sumphin's wrong . . . or sumphin' bad happens," he snarled. "Every time I see ya I get moved someplace else." He looked at her out of the corner of his eye, hating and loving her . . . feeling immediately sorry for his words . . . blaming her and yet somehow wanting to release her of any responsibility regarding his circumstances. He desperately wanted her . . . or anyone, for that matter . . . to love him . . . to care about him.

Somewhat taken aback, Miss Clementson reached over and touched his shaggy brown hair. He had grown so much. "I just haven't seen you for quite awhile and I was interested in how you are getting along. That's all."

"Why don't ya jus' leave me alone?" He jerked his head away from her outstretched hand and she withdrew it. He snorted loudly and belligerently as he did so, but at the same time didn't make any attempt to leave her.

Miss Clementson turned her head away slightly, chagrined by not only the perceptive nature of his observations but also by the assertiveness of his remark. "I'm sorry, Dewey. It's just been months since I've seen you and I wanted to say hello."

"How're my bothers, then?"

"They're doing well and they said to tell you 'Hi'."

"Yeah, I guess *they're* doin' okay. Heckofa lot better'n me!" Then his voice softened a bit as he realized again that the woman before him had once shown him a good bit of kindness and understanding. "There's a bird here. In a wire cage. A yella one like Miz Rykker had in 'er kitchen at the Home in Grand Forks. Always singin'. It reminds me a bein' back there. With my brothers and all."

After a few moments, Miss Clementson motioned him over, patting the seat beside her, and the two finally sat down on the stiff couch in the middle of the still-winter-warm, still-winter-stuffy room. Several minutes of unnerving quiet followed during which she watched him sadly and he could only look dumbly at his young hands.

"What about my Ma?"

She remembered the letter and withdrew it from her sweater pocket. "I brought this letter for you, from her." She half folded it and pressed it into the white palm of his hand; his fingers gently passed over her hand for a few moments before she withdrew it. Miss Clementson hoped that she would be forgiven by her young friend . . . that she could somehow make up for the past to him and renew his trust in her.

Dewey took his time reading the letter and when he had finished his demeanor changed drastically. A semi-smile crossed over his face. "She's comin' home. She's comin' home real soon." A sense of doubt restrained his actions, but she could see that he still maintained hope that his mother's return would actually come to pass. "You need ta tell my brothers that she's comin' back to get us!" he said to her, somewhat animated. "We're all gonna be together again!"

Miss Clementson took the letter from Dewey and began to read. The scrawled handwriting stated that Cora had divorced "that no-good-for-nothin' father of yours" and planned on marrying a gentleman from Carolina when they returned to North Dakota; she would be headed home soon and she would come and gather up her sons and be a family once more. Miss Clementson handed the letter back to Dewey and visited rather pleasantly with the boy for another hour, trying to help him as much as she could to understand and deal with his circumstances, trying to convince him that the future would brighten for him, regardless of what his mother did.

When the young social worker left later that day, walking out into the cold February afternoon, she immediately began to formulate a last, desperate plan . . . one that might make amends to Dewey for her part in his ongoing loneliness and isolation. She was certain her idea would lead to her young friend finally getting someone who cared for him, hopefully before his mother could come back and reclaim him and his brothers. Because she felt directly responsible for Dewey's plight, he became almost an obsession with Miss Clarissa Clementson; she became more determined than ever that Dewey would be hurt no more. Even though the youngster had presented many problems to his benefactors and had to be closely supervised—the primary reasons why he had not been permanently placed in a boarding house or with a caring family—her resolve now became to find him a permanent, loving home. She again drew on her resources in order to get Dewey transferred to the care of Marvin and Mabel Dahlen, two very good acquaintances of hers who would do just about anything to help her. Though the Dahlens had a grown son of their own, they had over the years been the foster parents of several children from the LWS, two of whom presently resided at their home.

In late June of 1945, she picked up Dewey and his few belonging from the Center and drove him over to Hillsboro to meet his new guardians. She had earlier explained to him that the Dahlens' home would be a better place to stay while he waited for his mother's return. Because he hated the Adolescent Center, he readily agreed. All during the trip the two chatted lightly, as though old friends, and even laughed together a number of times at small things they noticed on the drive. Dewey, somewhat excited about the prospect of again living as part of a real family, at least until his mother came to rescue him and his brothers, once more allowed his friend Clarissa partially back into his confidence.

"What're they like? Are they old? Do they have any kids? How big's the farm?"

"You'll like them. And they'll like you! They are a little bit older. They have one son who is grown up and lives near them with his family. And there are two other LWS boys there now . . . Joel and Steven are their names. Both of them are a bit younger than you." After a moment she paused and then looked earnestly over at her young charge. "But you've got to try real hard to be good, Dewey. It's important. Please prom-ise me that you will. We're out of families that you can go to."

"Yeah, okay. What about my ma? When's she comin' back?"

"Well . . . well, I'm not really sure. When she gets back, you can go and live with her, I guess," Clarissa lied. For the past month she had been constantly pleading with God and Jesus to prevent Cora from coming home to "rescue" Dewey and his brothers. Clarissa prayed fervently, sure in her belief that both would listen and respond favorably to her entreat-ies. "But 'til then you really have to try and be a good boy. Alright? Promise me again, now."

"Okay," Dewey conceded in order to satisfy his newly reconciled friend.

And at first Dewey did try hard . . . real hard. He forced himself to accept and get along with Joel and Steven, who in return showed him how he could "work" old man Dahlen. Marvin Dahlen proved to be a strict disciplinarian and because of this things seemed to be working out well for Dewey. During the initial several months at the Dahlens' Dewey quietly submitted to the firm, stern directions of Mar-vin. The boy actually did not fear the tall, thin man, nor did he really fully respect him; rather Dewey had matured to the point of accepting the fact that he would be much better off by not being so contrary and by letting his defenses down a bit. Marvin also relented a little and even once put his arm around his young charge when the boy did an exemplary job of cleaning out the barn.

Then in August, nearly three months after his arrival, another event transpired that would further alter greatly Dewey's future. On the fifteenth of that month, the Allies declared absolute victory over Japan, finally bringing a complete end to the Second World War. A sense of renewal . . . of optimism . . . spread over all of the land, along with the widespread jubilation and celebration that resulted from the armistice. And from the midst of that hopefulness, out of the shadowy depths of memory, Cora Lambson contacted her eldest son one warm autumn day. She had come back from North Carolina and was presently living in Grand Forks. Only recently having returned, Cora had decided to try to once again get her "beloved" children back. Even though reluctant to do so, Director Daniels grudgingly revealed to her where her children were; after all, she reminded the director, she still *was* their natural mother, in the eyes of God and the law. She especially wanted to contact Dewey, her eldest. She mentioned to the director several times how Dewey had *always* been her "most favorite of them all."

Early one Sunday evening in mid-September, when Dewey sat at the kitchen table, the phone on the wall rang twice, indicating that the incoming party line call was for the Dahlen household. Mrs. Dahlen answered the call in her usual cheerful voice, then without a word she handed the listening piece to Dewey and informed him that the call was from his mother. Without a word, Dewey hesitantly lifted the receiver up to his ear and stood close to the wooden telephone hanging on the wall. Uncertain of the whole process, he stared intently at the speaking tube, as though his mother would be speaking at him from just within the box.

"Hi, Dewey, honey. This is yur momma!"

For several moments the phone line remained silent as Dewey, awestruck, could not even muster up a grunt. Finally he spoke, almost inaudibly, incredulous as to what was happening. "Ma . . . ?"

"Dewey, honey, it's me! *Yur momma!*" She spoke the last two words loud and slow, so as to stress their importance. Dewey heard the voice on the other end hesitate and then crack with emotion. "Oh how I missed my boys. How ya been, honey?"

"Okay, I guess," the boy whispered tentatively.

"Dewey, I am so ashamed of myself for not writing, especially to thank you for your lovely letter and pitture. My, you are getting to be such a big, handsome boy."

"Uh huh," he agreed quietly, mesmerized by the voice from the past, nodding slowly.

"Guess what! I'm back in Grand Forks, now, honey, and I'm achin' with all my heart ta see ya! I had such a terrible cold since before July and I been workin' eight hours a day and it's sorta got me down. Yur new daddy-ta-be is comin' up from Carolina in a few weeks and I want ya to meet him. You'll like him!"

The one-way conversation went on for several minutes, with Dewey nodding his head periodically, his jaw held half open in silent uncertainty . . . even disbelief at what he heard. Finally, with some relief on Dewey's part, his mother brought the call to a close.

"I been workin' with the Lutheran Society to get all of you boys back with me. It ain't gonna be easy, though. I had a little spat with the director there . . . he said he was not sure if I could . . . he didn't like so well some of the things they said was done between us. It made me pretty mad and pretty blue . . . . I guess I hollered at him a bit. But we'll be together soon, honey!"

After a few more minutes of monologue, Dewey finally replied, "Yeah . . . Okay . . . I'll ast her . . . Okay . . . Uh huh . . . Bye." He slowly hung the black ear piece back in its cradle on the wall phone, still mystified by what had just happened to him.

"Was that your mom? Well, ain't that nice. What'd she have to say?" asked Mrs. Dahlen, truly happy for the boy.

Dewey spoke meekly, still not looking directly at the woman. "She wants ta know can you send her ten dollars so that she can take the bus down here to see me next week."

Mrs. Dahlen, quite taken aback by the boy's words, took several moments before she responded. "Well . . . Well, I . . . I'll have to talk it over with Marvin. We'll see."

"She'll call ya tomorrow," he said and then walked slowly upstairs to his room, confused by the myriad thoughts rushing through his head, truly amazed by, and somewhat fearful of, the new turn that his young life had now taken.

Later that night, when Mr. Dahlen returned from Grace Methodist Church, where there had been an elders' meeting, Dewey heard the couple's muffled voices in the kitchen below just before he fell asleep and dreamed long and hard the Cora dream once more. Tossing and kicking at the brown wool blanket, he soiled the bed again, something he hadn't done for several months.

At breakfast next morning, Mrs. Dahlen informed Dewey that they had decided not to send his mother the money. In the first true rage the boy had shown since arriving at the Dahlens' home, Dewey suddenly pushed back violently from the table, spilling his glass of milk and causing the coffee to slosh over the sides of the Dahlens' cups; he began screaming at the pair, to the utter amazement of the two other boys sitting around the table. "You could if ya really wanted ta! You're just a coupla stingy old goats and I hate your guts!" He grabbed the sack lunch on the counter and slammed the door soundly as he left for school. Following the boy's angry display, the pair relented and grudgingly promised to send Cora the money when she called later that morning. Dewey became elated when his guardians gave him the news at dinner that night. After reluctantly offering an apology to his two foster parents, he began making plans, both verbally to the Dahlens and within his own mind, of all of the things he and his mother were going to do and of everything he wanted to tell her.

Yet even though the Dahlens faithfully mailed Cora the bus money, and made specific arrangements for her to visit her son the next weekend, she never showed up. In fact, several weeks passed before Dewey or the Dahlens heard from her again. Cora sent her son a brief note, mailed from North Carolina, which read: "Dewey, honey, I am sorry that I didn't come that weekend. Millie, a new friend of mine, and me went back to N.C. to see your new daddy-to-be, who hasn't been able to leave there yet. When Mommie gets back you and your brothers can all come to live with us. Won't that be just grand? With all my love, your Momma."

In late February of the next year, 1946, when she did finally return, Cora on three occasions called Dewey and told him that she planned on coming up to see him on Tuesday, March 1ˢᵗ, her only day off from the Bronze Boot restaurant where she now worked. The Dahlens allowed Dewey to stay home from school for the special occasion. Mrs. Dahlen even did extra baking for the expected nice visit. But the hours passed as Dewey looked out the front room window, wiping away the fog that formed on the cold window pane from his breath. Mr. and Mrs. Dahlen grew sorely disappointed when the mother did not show up or even call to let them know she would not be coming after all. Late in the afternoon, when night began shrouding the snow-frozen ground of the front yard, Dewey let the musty smelling, gray lace curtains fall back to their closed position. "Ma just lies to me . . . always has. I guess she always will." Turning from his caretakers, he walked upstairs and went to bed.

The next month Mrs. Dahlen sent the following letter to the agency:

April 11ᵗʰ, 1946
Dear Director Daniels—

Once more Dewey was disappointed by his mother. He did not spend the weekend with her in Grand Forks as planned, as she had promised. I got up especially early the day she was going to come and pick him up. I made sure that he was bathed and I shampooed his hair as I do not like to send him off unkempt. I also packed the necessary clothes for him and he was quite excited—could hardly contain himself, he was so happy. However, we waited all

day and into the evening and she did not come . . .
did not even call to let us know if she was still coming or what was happening. Dewey was crestfallen
and Marvin and I were quite disappointed as we were
invited to spend the evening at my husband's brother's home as it was their 24th wedding anniversary,
but we did not go—expecting Mrs. Lambson.

A week ago yesterday Dewey received a phone
call at noon from Mrs. Lambson; she wanted for him
to come to the café here in town. He asked her to
come to the house but she refused to do this and so
Dewey visited her downtown before going to school
at 1 p.m. Dewey did not enjoy the visit as she told
him of their new daddy-to-be and she would be taking him and his brothers again. In fact, as I was later
informed, the two had an angry argument and were
asked to leave the café. Dewey was very upset as he
said he hated his mother and then a bit later sobbed
that he loved her.

This whole situation with Dewey and his mother
is very troubling for us. Not only is it affecting our
family lives, but the lives and behavior of our two
other LWS boys as well. Dewey has asked us if he
couldn't stay with us until his daddy comes home
from the army, as he wanted to live with him. I told
him I could not promise because you (the Lutheran
Welfare Society) had placed him here and we had to
abide with your rules. And I suppose that is why I
am writing to you now.

We feel very sorry for Dewey and we are doing
everything we can for him. During his time here he

has been somewhat troublesome, but we have been able to manage him. However, now that his mother has come back into the picture, he has become much more difficult. As you well know, he was not trained in proper bathroom habits and other acceptable social behaviors before coming here. I use a rubber sheet on his bed (as I have him wash out the soil himself and it has been helpful). Yet I want you to understand what a difficult job it is teaching him what is right. This task is now even more difficult with the continual annoyance of his mother. We want her interference stopped at once as we do not want to hear from her again at all. Mr. Dahlen is becoming particularly annoyed at the problems caused by the presence of the boy's mother and I wholly agree. If the Lutheran Welfare Society cannot intervene to keep her at a distance from Dewey, I fear that we will need to ask to have him taken from our home.

Please respond at your earliest convenience,
Mrs. Mabel Dahlen

When the Dahlens did not receive an answer to their report, especially after several weeks, Mrs. Dahlen felt compelled to write to her good friend Clarissa Clementson, for whom she had done the favor of taking in Dewey. She wrote,

May 14th, 1946
My Dear Clarissa–

It is with much regret that I write this letter. However, I am afraid that the arrangement of Dewey living at our home is no longer possible.

Mr. Dahlen noted to me the other day that Dewey was getting along all right in our home up until last year, when his mother contacted him. Marvin seems to think that Dewey is a very unsociable boy; understanding him and some of the things he has done is difficult. Marvin maintains that Dewey's seeing and talking to his mother these past several months has caused the boy to become restless and unpredictable and he too often acts without thinking. For example, Mrs. Lambson came down to our place twice in the past two weeks to visit Dewey, but when they were together they always quarreled. After his mother left, Dewey just wanted to be alone in his room. (He wet the bed again that night and since then the episodes have increased to almost a nightly occurrence). And then just this weekend he went to Grand Forks to visit her. When he returned Sunday night he was very irritable—disrespectful and "sassy"—even though Marvin threatened him about talking back to me in such a way. Dewey wouldn't apologize until Marvin slapped him good across his smart mouth, which he fully deserved.

The boy's mother continues to disturb him. Dewey is very bitter; he thinks everyone dislikes him. He has admitted to me that he does things he shouldn't do just because Marvin tells him not to and he is not afraid of Marvin. Dewey remains very unhappy and fights with everyone . . . he has even once threatened to kill somebody or anybody. He runs after other children at school and picks up sticks and beats on the small boys when they are on the playground.

In the past few months Dewey has become very much out of hand. We often do not know where he is. He has trouble listening to us and he has been telling the other LWS boys that are with us—Joel and Steven—that they are "dopes" for minding us and doing what we tell them. He does not want to do anything . . . work around the farm or anything. He has to be told everything several times. I have to ask him to wash every time he comes to the table or goes to school. We expect the boy to forget some-times, but whenever we question him he gets angry and goes to his room and slams the door. Dewey has various ways he persistently uses to aggravate Mr. Dahlen. He noisily stomps up the stairs, coughs and loudly clears his throat when Mr. Dahlen is talk-ing, chews his food with his mouth open at the dinner table, and when he is asked to do any little thing he usually just sits for a period of time before respond-ing. All of these things, while perhaps small in them-selves, are more than exasperating in total.

The final incident for Mr. Dahlen (and for me, too, for that matter) came just a few days ago. Dewey, when he was going to school, forgot to close the fence gate and Goldie, Marvin's beautiful Irish Setter, got out of the yard and began to follow the boy to school. Well, when Goldie got out on the main highway, she was hit by a car and limped home almost dead. Marvin was so mad that when Dewey got home from school he made Dewey go out with a .22 and put the dog out of its misery. Dewey cried that he did not want to do the deed, that he had not meant to let the dog out, but Marvin forced the gun into the boy's hand and made him squeeze the trigger. Dewey cried even harder, claiming that he loved the dog. But the boy needed to be taught a lesson about responsibility. After the crack of the small rifle, I looked out the kitchen window and saw Dewey on his knees, sobbing into his hands. Marvin did what he had to do. He made the boy help him drag Goldie's body back behind the tool shed and bury it. After Marvin came back into the house he said that he wanted nothing more to do with the boy and has not spoken a word to him since. I think that whole incident did it for the both of us!

I hardly imagined that I would have to write you this letter concerning Dewey, Dear Clarissa, but I can't see how I can stand it much longer. We can manage Dewey only until the end of May or the first of June at the latest. We feel that it is too upsetting to all of our routines to have him longer than that. Hopefully this may give you time to work out something.

We like Dewey and feel sorry for him. However, we can no longer have him here in our home. Will you please let me know when we can bring him up to Grand Forks or when you can come and get him. I am so sorry, but I just can't do anything differently. It's too bad his dad isn't man enough to have him.

Your friends in faith,
Marvin and Mabel Dahlen

Miss Clementson had been offering passionate, ongoing prayer for the Lambson children, especially Dewey, from the very beginning of their incursion into the welfare system; but the Dahlens' letter came as a last, crushing blow to her faith. The young social worker gave the Dahlens' letter to Director Daniels, after which she immediately resigned her employment with the Lutheran Welfare Society and left straight away for Minneapolis where she later secured a position as secretary with International Business Machines. Often she thought about Dewey, wishing she had the resources to adopt him. But in the end, though she cried quite often, Clarissa Clementson never regretted her decision to leave the career that had, after all, claimed such a large part of not only her life but of her soul as well.

With great regret Director Daniels accepted her resignation and assigned Mrs. Ethel Olson, from the LWS Fargo Office, to determine and implement the plans needed for once more dealing with Dewey. Mrs. Olson, a no-nonsense person who had been with the agency a number of years, immediately reviewed Dewey's lengthy brown-jacketed case file, after which she recommended to Director Daniels that the miscreant Dewey be transferred back to the Cass County Adolescent Center in Fargo. "He should no longer be coddled but should instead be made to 'sit on his blisters'," she commented sternly to her superior. The director accepted her suggestion without hesitation and made arrangements for the boy to be returned immediately to the Center by bus; Dewey's transfer took place on May 29th, 1946.

Mr. Horace Thydeson, surprised to see Dewey back once more, did the follow-up intake evaluation after the boy had been back at CCAC for a few weeks. He entered the following observation into Dewey's bulging record file:

Dewey Lambson, LWS Transfer: observations since his second committal to Cass County Adolescent Center in May of 1946.

Dewey still appears to be a very troubled, self-centered, almost anti-social child, who has shown little or no improvement since coming to our facility. He is constantly jealous of the other children at the center and has been continually mean and nasty in his relations with them, which has made his stay here even more difficult. When sent to different boarding homes, he has deliberately tried to hurt various animals at the farms and is in continual conflict with the adults at the homes where he has been sent. And all the while he pretends that he has not been aware of his undesirable behavior. Thus it has become extremely difficult to place him with any of the families that are available. But strangely enough, he can be an affable, likeable boy when he really wants to be.

In the short time of Dewey's second stay here at the Center things have not gone so well. He continually tries to make everyone feel sorry for him by complaining about how abused he has been and is. Nothing seems to be good enough for him . . . there isn't anything that seems to satisfy him. The group life is not what he needs, at least not in the group settings as we have them here at the Home. If the boy can do anything to irritate any of the staff, he certainly does it. Unfortunately I am not here all the time and present when he acts out against others. Therefore, I have given my permission to the staff and counselors here to use any measures necessary to take him in hand and make him understand that he must act otherwise. I think that this is what he needs. We know something of the trouble in the private homes where he has been and their failure with him. Here when he sets out as he does to be nasty and wants to hurt others with his mean words and hateful actions, the men of the house have been directed to reach over and collar him and sit him down hard and tell him that he has reached his limit. If that does not work, they have my authorization to slap his mouth, or else use other means of physical punishment in order to make him obey. I think that such physical measures will help greatly in controlling his behavior.

My next course of action is to contact the Lutheran Welfare Society and see if they have a concrete plan of action regarding the boy. My hope is that the child's parents will be able to once again assume responsibility for him as I don't know how much longer he will be able to stay at our facility.

I sometimes wonder what will become of Dewey. When he was here last year, I tried several avenues by which I might get closer to him, but his attitude of defiance kept me from doing anything for him. I was severely disappointed when we parted, for the very reason that I could do nothing for him. I had hoped that I could gain his confidence and respect. But his presence was like a bomb. He destroyed all order and peace and my good intentions went into the wreckage also. This is not a very complimentary summary of his stay this last time, but all I have said is true. I only hope that his stint with us this time will wind up differently. I wish the boy could shake himself loose. He would be so much happier. If I could only reach him, but I don't know how!

> H. Thydeson,
> Chief Administrator, CCAC
> 8/16/1946.

Unfortunately the Chief Administrator's hopes for Dewey's successful turnaround never came about. During the late summer and early fall of 1946, Mr. Thydeson became aware of various reports from the Fargo Juvenile Authorities. Dewey and Arty Johnson, another boy from the Center, had been caught down on Central Street stealing cigarettes and soda pop from the storage area in the rear of Ted's Super Value Market. The two were also suspected of taking bicycles from the bike racks behind Roosevelt Junior High School, located not too far from the Center. Dewey and his friend actually stole four bikes altogether . . . first taking two and wrecking the front wheels and then returning to steal two more. They rode the stolen bikes all afternoon that day and then tried to sell them for $2 each to two skinny elementary students they met during their escapade. In addition, several times over the summer Dewey continued to pick up things when he went into stores and the Fargo Juvenile Authorities twice accused him of shoplifting at the downtown F. W. Woolworth's Five-and-Ten. Whenever confronted with these misdeeds, Dewey would just stick his chin out and say to the accuser, "Yeah? Well, prove it!"

Mr. Thydeson, therefore, became more than relieved when he heard from Mr. Daniels of the Lutheran Welfare Society. Mrs. Cora Lambson, it seems, was attempting to once more regain custody of her children. Director Daniels wrote the following letter to Mr. Thydeson:

9/15/1946
Mr. Horace Thydeson
Cass Country Adolescent Center
Fargo, North Dakota

My Dear Mr. Thydeson–

In reply to your recent correspondence regarding the future of Dewey Lambson, I find that at the present time we have been unable to make a final determination about the Lambson children. I totally agree with your suggestion that Dewey should be returned to his mother. Indeed, at least four of the five Lambson boys should be eventually turned back to her custody. When the Lutheran Welfare Society originally took over responsibility of the Lambson boys from their mother, the impression was left with us at the time that temporary guardianship was given to the agency and that the boys should be eventually returned to their mother. This has always been our position. The return of her children could only take place if and when she reestablished herself, found adequate housing for the lads, and properly supervised and cared for them. We have at all times attempted to keep this thought in mind when making plans for the boys.

Now, in fact, Mrs. Lambson is insisting to have her children returned to her. She has remarried a man by the name of Eddie Cain and now she and her husband have visited our Grand Forks office and requested, even demanded the return of Cora's children. The two belligerently maintained that Mr. Thorstad of Farmington had told them that they could have all of the children back and showed me a letter to that effect. This necessitated my explaining the position of the Lutheran Welfare Society. I stated that when she abandoned her children, the LWS had been awarded custody of them by the State of North Dakota and as such we had the responsibility to determine the advisability of the children's return or not. If we felt it advisable, we would have to make a report to the Court, who would determine whether or not they felt it expedient for our responsibility to be terminated. I said that Mr. Thorstad had not been within his right to make any recommendations and that he was only doing so to absolve the town of Farmington, as well as Neilson County, of any further financial obligations. I also advised Mrs. Cain (Lambson) that the LWS would not at this time make any recommendations to the Court for a termination of our responsibility. Too much has gone on between the mother and her children for us to arbitrarily turn responsibility for them back over to her.

However, I would like to suggest that perhaps we could return the children to her, as their natural mother, one at a time, starting with the oldest, Dewey, to see how she handles their care. Additionally, someone of authority should continue to assist her in the supervision of the children as they are returned to her. These boys have presented many problems to LWS and have been difficult to supervise. Mrs. Lambson herself has not fully demonstrated by her attitude and actions that she is ready to assume full responsibility for the children. She has not always been too cooperative in working with the agency and some of the things that she has said and done have made it difficult for us to help the boys to make a good adjustment in society and to prepare them for their return to her, i.e., the issue of turning over the monthly allotment funds she had committed to give the agency. I doubt very much she even acknowledges the harm her behavior has done to the youngsters and to their ongoing maladjustment. Our interests are ONLY in the children's welfare and she must certainly come to realize that. In fact even now Mrs. Cain (Lambson) has been observed still chasing around to dances and we have heard other negative reports from time to time concerning her conduct. LWS feels that she remains still not a fit person to raise her five boys, at least not all together and not at the present time.

Under these conditions, we cannot recommend that the boys be given back to her. However, because the Cass County Adolescent Center in Fargo will probably not be able to help Dewey Lambson overcome many of his aberrant and self-destructive behaviors, we further recommend that he be returned to his mother to test her willingness to change in order to get all of her children back into her care. If he makes the transition successfully, the other four brothers might also be returned. Should Dewey adjust in his mother's home, LWS would without question consider returning the other boys.

The four other brothers are living in various homes and centers in the region, save for Dewey, who is currently at your facility in Fargo. We cannot stress enough the inadvisability of all of the remaining boys returning to her. Any return would have to be incremental. Also, any return of the children should be done with the exclusion of Darrell. Darrell has been in the same home since he left the Lake Charles Receiving Home in June of 1944. We recommend that he remain in this home and that if his mother wants him to be returned to her, much thought and consideration should be given to this transfer before he is taken from the Goodwin home in Mayville.

Given these circumstances, we at the Lutheran Welfare Society would welcome your expertise and advice regarding Dewey Lambson and the above recommendation.

Respectfully,
Mr. Ethedge Daniels, Director

Mr. Thydeson, as the head of the Adolescent Center, became much relieved by the LWS's disposition of the troublesome boy and agreed wholeheartedly with the plan of operation. The decision essentially meant that he and CCAC would not have to deal with Dewey Lambson any longer. Consequently, Thydeson implemented the transfer of Dewey with great haste, least any of the authorities he had been corresponding with should have a change of mind. In early October, Mrs. Olson, who technically still remained the LWS caseworker advocate for the Lambson children, logically became the one dispatched to retrieve Dewey from the Center and turn him over to his mother, who by then had relocated to a farmhouse just a bit west of Fargo, in the town of Casselton. Dewey showed little emotion when Mrs. Olson came to the Center and curtly introduced herself. The only thing he asked her was, "Where's Miss Clementson? Why ain't she comin' ta get me?"

She ignored his question and told him she had been placed in charge of his case and was taking him home to his mother and stepfather. Dewey sat pensively silent for most of the car ride—not excited or surprised or distressed or trusting—just passively accepting another new, jarring twist in his life. Finally he spoke: "So, my ma's goin' to get us back, huh?"

"No, not all of your brothers, just you," she replied, with a certain rigidness in her voice. After a few minutes had passed, she added, "If all goes well with you and your parents, your brothers Duane, Lloyd, and Leeland will be allowed to return also."

"Yeah, so?!" was his only response and they rode on in silence for the remainder of the trip.

When the car pulled up into the bare yard of the dilapidated farm house, somewhere on the outskirts of Casselton, a rather small agricultural community, the mother stood at the front door threshold, anxiously waiting, shifting her weight from one skinny leg to the other. Her husband, Mr. Cain—tall, overweight, unshaven, and rough looking—stood supportively behind his wife, his clenched fists dug into his hips. Mrs. Olson sized him up as being somewhat doltish . . . as someone who could probably be easily led.

When she saw her son Dewey riding in the passenger seat, Cora clapped her thin hands joyfully before her face and smiled wide. All of her blustery talk and false promises and empty hopes of the past years had finally brought at least one of her children back to her. Watching Dewey emerge from the social worker's car was certainly a victory, however small, for her. She honestly believed that eventually she would have all of her "darlings" returned to her. Dewey got out of the car and just somberly walked past her and her husband into the house.

Mrs. Olson did not linger long for the homecoming. After having officially turned Dewey over to his mother and stepfather, she reminded both of the parents that the return of the other Lambson children remained contingent upon how well Dewey adjusted and how well he was cared for. "The Court will have to order the transfer of any more of your children," she admonished sternly, "and I will continue to monitor your home situation for the LWS in order to inform their decision. Please call me if you have any questions or difficulties." Then she left with an abrupt "Goodbye."

Her pressing caseload, however, kept Mrs. Olson from checking up on Dewey and his home life with any degree of regularity and once more things did not go well for him. Focusing her professional attention and efforts on the many other children she had to deal with, especially those who exhibited real hope, she was unable to visit Dewey and the family. But in late November Mr. and Mrs. Cain came to her office, asking about the possibility of Dewey returning to LWS care and the other children coming back instead. The parents complained they had tried to make Dewey go to school, but he refused. All he needed to do was attend school for one more semester and he could complete the sixth grade so that he could at least maybe get a decent job when he reached the age of sixteen. But he was too lazy to go. Having determined the boy to be destined for failure, they now wanted him returned to CCAC and the other four boys released to them. When Mrs. Olson informed them that was "quite impossible," Mr. and Mrs. Cain threatened her and the agency with legal action. When the angry couple left her office, Mrs. Olson reported to her superiors that obviously there had been very little improvement to the family situation and recommended that no change should be made to the status of all five children. She ended by summarizing that "though Mr. and Mrs. Cain (Lambson) may be actually trying to do well by the children, their limited education and lack of insight and perseverance prevent them from carrying through with many of the needs that are apparent to everyone else concerned." Almost immediately upon finishing the report she moved on to other, more pressing matters.

The next time Mrs. Olson saw Dewey was in the spring of 1947, when he was being held in the Juvenile Detention Center in Fargo. She had been to a LWS professional training session in Bismarck and upon her return she received a telephone call from a Mrs. Matthews, an official from the City Juvenile Justice Court, advising her that Dewey Lambson had been detained by the Fargo Police. When they were contacted by the police, Dewey's parents had given the authorities Mrs. Olson's name. A week prior to Dewey's apprehension, the police had received a confidential report from a young man who worked out at the Northern Automotive Parts Store; Dewey had approached him about stealing a car so they could have a way of getting around the city in order to swipe the headlights and hood ornaments off other cars, and that he had a place to sell the stolen goods. The informant and his parents did not wish Dewey to know that they had given the police the information since they suspected he would seek retribution if he knew it. With these facts in hand, Mrs. Olson called on Dewey at the detention center.

"I guess you know why I'm here," she started out curtly when they brought him into the small interview room. Purposely she tried to wring any sympathy from her voice and she did so quite successfully.

"No. Why don't ya all jus' leave me alone."

"Well, then, do you know what you have done wrong and why you are being held here? The police don't *just* arrest people for no reason."

"I ain't done nothing!"

"Seems like the police suspect you of planning to steal a car and doing other criminal mischief."

"Yeah? Let 'em prove it!"

"Humph! Seems like trouble follows you too closely!"

"I don't know why the cops picked me up and why I gotta stay here at the detention center. They tol' me I would only be here one night and now it's been three. Ain't fair. I ain't done nothing."

Sure that sternness remained the only way to respond to the delinquent boy, she went on somewhat derisively. "Well, now, what do you suppose would cause the police to become suspicious of you? Do you think that they would arrest you if you were innocent? Have you done or said anything that would make them suspicious of you?"

"I guess they just like to pick on me," Dewey said and then he slumped down in the chair, folded his arms across his chest, and stared reflectively at the wall for several minutes before he spoke again. "They been pickin' on me ever since they accused me of stealin' them bikes at the school. Besides . . . I was just given that guy at Northland a long line. He's the one that musta squealed. I tol' him we was goin' to steal the car and the headlights, but I only did it to go him one better since he is such a dang liar himself. He's always blowin' about how tough he is!"

"I see," said Mrs. Olson, not totally convinced of his veracity. His voice had become a bit whiny and defensive and she felt a small surge of triumph.

"Yeah! I ain't dumb! I'm smart enough not to get into any more trouble 'cause the police'll be laying for me."

Without commenting, Mrs. Olson turned and abruptly left the room. Because Dewey had been picked up without charges, she called Mrs. Matthews and demanded that the boy be released; the authorities certainly could not justify detaining him any longer on mere suspicion. Mrs. Matthews reluctantly agreed and notified the police sergeant at the front desk; the sergeant, however, gruffly insisted that Mrs. Olson sign for the boy, even though she assured him she would be returning Dewey immediately to his parents in Casselton.

Dewey, feeling much relief when they were finally out in the free air beyond the Detention Center, sat back casually in the front seat of the agency car. "Has my mom been up to see you . . . in the las' week or two?"

"I haven't seen your mother for some time now. Why?"

"Then she's lyin' again. She's always lyin'. She told me she saw you last week and you said that my brothers were comin' home and because I was so much trouble to her that I was going back to the Adolescent Center. She's such a damn liar!"

They drove on further west in silence, but because some time had passed since her last visit, she had forgotten where the Cain household was. Dewey gave her directions, speaking in a detached sort of manner. "Follow Highway 18 north until ya come to the grain elevator. Then ya turn left at the Town Hall Cafe. Our place is the last one on the right," Dewey instructed her, with little enthusiasm at the thought of being home again. He said little else for the remainder of the short ride.

"Yes, I remember it now," she said when the troubled home at last came into sight.

"Well, are my brothers comin' home or what? When 'er they comin'?"

"Well, I'm not quite sure they will be," she replied hesitantly, not knowing exactly what to say, what to tell him.

After learning of Dewey's run-in with the law, Mrs. Olson had consulted with her supervisor about the status of the Lambson case. She found out that the decision to return the other brothers to their mother and stepfather had still not been made; the agency continued to resist turning Duane, Lloyd, and Leeland back over to Cora. Based upon

Mrs. Olson's on-going observations and recommendations, the final decision would be made at a later date by the LWS. And with his latest involvement with the law, Dewey certainly had not been adjusting very well in the home; apparently Mrs. Olson would need to gather still more relevant information in order for the agency to be able to recommend that any other Lambson children be returned to their natural mother.

Mrs. Olson parked the agency Ford coupe in the unchanged yard of the house. When the two went inside, the welfare worker began making notes to herself regarding the current living conditions within. The house consisted of a small kitchen with a sink full of dishes, a cluttered living room, and one bedroom—conditions which certainly would not permit the return of the other brothers.

"Where do you sleep, Dewey?"

"I sleep right here in the living room. Over on the couch."

"Are you comfortable here?"

"Naw. The couch is lumpy . . . worse than the bed in the jail. My feet hang over the end, too."

He stood silent for a few moments as he stared at the tattered sofa, shifting almost imperceptibly from one foot to the other. "I always hear 'em fightin' in the bedroom. Yellin' and screamin'. Keeps me awake lots." His voice became barely audible as he spoke from deep within his reflections.

The fact that the boys would all have to sleep in the living room, she noted to herself, would seem to be a deterrent to any future custodial arrangements. No one appeared to be at home, with no indication of where the parents were or when they would return. Mrs. Olson poked around the kitchen a bit, looking in the cupboards above and beside the sink. Inside one of the cabinets she found a few shriveled potatoes, some butter, a moldy half loaf of bread, an empty fifth of Pilgrims Gin—the extent of the meager provisions within the household. While she continued inspecting the premises, Dewey drifted out to a lean-to shed in the back-yard, which housed several caged rabbits, and returned after a brief time.

"They won't be back for awhile, I figure . . . probably a week," Dewey observed sarcastically when he came back into the house.

"How do you know?"

"They pulled a whole bunch a grass from out by the fence yonder and put it in the rabbits' pen. They also put a big pan of water in there for 'em, too." He felt cynically confident in his detective work. *He* knew his parents well. Snickering a bit, he added, "Didn't want anything to happen to 'em."

"Your parents really take good care of those rabbits, don't they." Mrs. Olson's voice had softened somewhat and for the first time Dewey looked into her eyes.

"Yeah, I guess they do," he answered, understanding her implication. "They musta gone up to Grand Forks for the weekend. They're lookin' for someplace else to stay."

"Really? Why is that?"

"This here house is maybe gonna be sold, so we might have to move again. But we don't know when or where yet."

"Do you have some place to go until they return?"

"Naw. I'll be okay."

Apparently Dewey had become well adjusted to coming and going as he pleased; his mother and stepfather also were much accustomed to doing likewise, without any due con-cern for the welfare of their young son. Little had changed since Cora had first left her sons years ago. Mrs. Olson gathered more and more support for her ultimate recommendation of denial regarding the return of the remaining brothers.

"Do you keep busy, Dewey?"

"Hell, no! There ain't *nothin'* to do around here. I just hitchhike into town."

"Don't you have a job?"

"I was workin' a job at the hotel. But I was fired after one day. The guy that I worked for said I 'didn't know the ropes'. Cheated me, too! Didn't even pay me for the one day! Said I was in training! Shoot, I shoulda hit him and took it anyway. Damn cheat!"

"You need to have some sort of productive employment, Dewey. Otherwise you're going to get into trouble again."

"Yeah. I s'pose."

"Can't you find work on a nearby farm? There must be many farmers that could use the help of a healthy young man like you."

"I wouldn't work for no farmer . . . they always gyp you."

"Why do you say that? Why would you distrust farmers?"

"I heard about a rich farmer over by Larimore. He hadn't met his obligations to two or three of his workers. Messed around with the young kids that went to work for him, too. I heard it from my stepdad!"

"Dewey, there are many sad instances of dishonesty in every line, but that needn't reflect on the majority who do business honestly." Dewey snorted abruptly at her naiveté and gave a short, mocking laugh as well. She continued on. "Think of farming on the basis of the good physical exercise and good, honest wages. I think, also, that such work might keep you away from the downtown area."

"That's where I *want* to go to work. Downtown. There is always something to do down there. People and money. I got friends down there, too."

The discussion between the two trailed off into several minutes of quiet in which both seemed to be calculating and carefully structuring their next comments.

"Can the agency buy me a new pair of shoes?" Dewey asked finally. He crossed his right leg over his knee and showed her the gaping split in the soul of his scuffed shoe. "The rain keeps getting in and my socks get soaked. Gonna catch a dang cold!"

"The agency is no longer accountable for your clothing, Dewey. Your mother will have to buy them for you. She is responsible for you now."

"Yeah. Okay," he snorted once again. "Then can you loan me $2.00? My mom's birthday is comin' up and I wanna buy her some good smellin' bath water. She likes that stuff."

Mrs. Olson's response to him was measured . . . not unkind, but precisely phrased for full impact. She wanted her tone to indicate the dire nature of his situation and that there would be no turning back. "Dewey, if anything else happens . . . if you get into trouble again, you cannot return to the agency or to the adolescent home . . . you are no longer a child. You will need to stay with you mother and stepfather until you are old enough to leave."

He carefully constructed his response. "I don't like livin' with 'em. Especially my stepdad. He's awful dumb."

"Do you know what is going to happen if you get into trouble before that time . . . before you are old enough to leave?" She waited for his comment, but his silence indicated that he still was listening. "If you get into trouble with the police again, it is out of my hands, or your mother's hands, or the agency's hands, or the center's hands." She paused again, wanting to be sure that he understood the import of her words. "If you do anything wrong . . . anything at all . . . you are going to be sent to the state juvenile facility at Mandan. There you will stay until you are old enough to be on your own. You understand that, don't you?"

"Yeah, I know." He waited for a few more moments before he spoke again. "Can you loan me the two bucks?"

Mrs. Olson did give Dewey the two dollars before she left that day, digging into her own purse and household money to do so. For the first time since she had met the boy, she felt a genuine sorrow and compassion for him. However, her response differed significantly from her predecessor's. She returned to her office in Fargo, where she immediately wrote and filed a report recommending that the four remaining Lambson children *all* stay where they were, indefinitely. The time to do something for Dewey had long since passed; he was too mature and set in his ways to do anything with him. His fate had been sealed long ago. As hard as the agency had tried, the boy seemed doomed to fail. Based on her experiences, Mrs. Olson remained steadfastly certain that of all the boys Dewey would continue to move steadily, unswervingly towards a life of violence and desolation. And in fact her prediction proved to be more than somewhat accurate.

One chilly evening in the fall of 1947, Dewey got into a flailing fistfight with his stepfather regarding a small amount of money that the young man had squirreled away. Seems the father demanded Dewey pay five dollars as a small reimbursement for the expenses involved with keeping him and providing him room and board. Because both had been drinking, the stepfather more so than the stepson, few blows landed and the struggle became more of a wrestling match. The man winded quickly, so Dewey merely shoved him roughly to the wooden floor, kicked him twice and then a third time, gathered up his few belongings, and left the house for good. One of Dewey's newfound friends on the south side of Fargo took him in.

Interestingly enough, in his emerging manhood, Dewey had become as handsomely tall and as wild as his father Iver. In fact, he grew into the mirror image of his father when he was Dewey's age. And more than one of the local girls found their young, pretty selves drawn to him, to his comely aloofness. This attraction made Dewey an asset to his male acquaintances, giving them instant access to numerous romantic and sexual adventures they had heretofore only been vaguely aware of or had only fantasized about. Those few brief months became perhaps Dewey's wildest, freest times. Indeed, his unruliness . . . his numerous romances and drinking with raucous buddies and his short-lived jobs . . . became much more than mere adolescent rowdiness. Instead, his behavior became driven by the angst of deeply embedded, unspoken memories and psychological wounds, which wildly, relentlessly drove the boy-turned-young-man as he lived each day with an ever growing intensity . . . certainly a building audacity and complete disdain for the community around him. Word had it that he had gotten Millie Gaulky in trouble one night when both of them had been drinking quite heavily. "Yeah, so?! Prove it!" was his only response when Mr. and Mrs. Gaulky angrily confronted him. The parents went away with no resolution to their daughter's situation. Dewey, to get even with them and their accusations, began seeing Millie's younger sister Audry quite regularly until she too became "with child." Dewey left her just as abruptly, paying little or no attention to his responsibility towards her or her sister, or their parents, or to the mores of the broader community, for that matter. He had found a new power in his ability to use other people.

However, his newfound spirit of uncontrolled and uncontrollable youth could not keep him free of society's inevitable censure. Six months after leaving his mother and stepfather's house, Dewey found himself confined to the Mandan State Reform School, charged with and convicted of armed robbery and stealing a car down on Center Street for the purpose of "joyriding." Because his crimes had not only been audacious but numerous as well, Dewey's sentence was open-ended: he would remain at the reformatory for "an indeterminate time, lasting no longer than his twenty-first birthday."

The transition to his new residence came abruptly and with great certitude. He arrived on a chilly October day with several other new juvenile delinquents from around the state, all of whom were quickly processed into the institution. After being deloused, getting closely shorn, and having their naked bodies fire-hose cleaned with disinfectant, they were issued their uniforms of blue denim pants and shirts and assigned to a dormitory with forty other boys.

The several unpainted, brick, barracks-like buildings of the reform school, which formed a square around the open dirt parade ground, quickly became his home. The arrangement of the reformatory facilities could almost be a symbol for order and organization . . . an element that Dewey deeply needed. The institutionalized regularity of his new life, though strictly disciplined, provided the boy with a consistency he never had . . . but a constancy he greatly needed. The time at which he arose in the morning, at which he ate his meals, at which he went to bed all were tightly controlled and never varied. "Three hots, a cot, and a roof above" became unfailing entities in his life . . . a steadiness he had never before experienced for any prolonged period in his short life. He came to actually appreciate this security and certainty.

The rigorous daily schedule he followed kept him tired. He, like all the other inmates, spent a good part of the day working in the fields beyond the chain link fence, or in vocational and trades training, such as animal husbandry, welding, and carpentry. Dewey enjoyed working in the carpentry shop and even thought that one day he might like to become a carpenter. The remainder of his and of the other juveniles' time was devoted to compulsory schooling, which held little interest or relevance for Dewey. Various other activities such as sports, calisthenics, military drills, and sometimes even movies and recreation, interspersed the set events of their daily life. The only thing required of him was to remain tough and to show no fear or concern for anything or anybody. And not to take any guff from anyone. Once he had caught Rodger Kidd stealing contraband cigarettes from his locker. He worked Kidd over pretty good, punching him in the gut and then kneeing him in the face when he doubled over, bloodying and almost breaking the boy's nose and loosening several of his teeth. Because Kidd had always been one of the toughest characters at the facility, word of Dewey's fearlessness and quickness with his "mitts" spread rapidly; after that, everyone else pretty much left him alone.

The regimen of his daily life had been good for him physically, but anger and resentment still constantly dominated his thoughts and seethed within him. And he remained desperately alone. No one had come to visit him, unlike some of the other guys at the reformatory. One time he received a letter from someone at LWS, which stated that his father had been severely wounded in Europe, but had survived the war and was receiving on-going care at a Veterans Hospital some place on the East Coast. The old man, though, had never visited him, had not even written or called. His mother stopped in the Bismarck-Mandan area once and telephoned the facility. However, she did not come to visit, even though she said she would, and he stayed up very late into the night waiting for her. As in the past, disappointment stabbed deeply into his soul, but also as in the past he just said nothing. When she called again the next day, though, he told her in a cold voice he was done talking and hung up the receiver. Dewey supposed she had probably been visiting her old friend from the Mobility Tractor Company and didn't have time for her son. She apparently had left her second husband, Mr. Cain, and was living with a man in an apartment in Fargo. She never did get her children back, although she continued fighting the LWS for their custody. Cora, in spite of everything that had happened, never stopped wanting to be a good mother—an impossibility under the terms and conditions that she always dictated, Dewey decided. After that day, he never spoke to his mother Cora again.

And on that March afternoon in 1949, a year and a half after his arrival, and only a month until his eighteenth birthday, a time for decision and change was at hand. Dewey sat silently in the open bay area of the dormitory, rocking back and forth on his bunk. Not knowing whether his mood resulted from anger or mere restlessness, the young inmates residing in the immediate area pretty much left him alone, avoiding his darting eyes. Everyone knew that Dewey would fight at a moment's notice and thus remained diffident in his presence. Reaching into his pocket, Dewey drew out his silver pocketknife, opened the blade, and began flipping it at the square wooden support beam a few yards from his bed. Over the past year he had stuck the dark brown support so many times that the wood looked as rough hewn as the timber of Christ's cross. Though the activity involved two major institutional infractions—possessing a weapon and maliciously defacing state property—nobody ever said anything to him, not even his warders.

In the lingering dusk, he stopped suddenly and again looked out the window that provided him with the merest glimpse into the vastness of the world that lay outside of his own narrow existence. Across the way the dirt parade ground stood still and empty . . . as barren and desolate as the juvenile lives subjugated within the almost prison-like institution. A bit further past the field, a lone cottonwood grew large and green, marking the bank of Christopher Creek; the tree served as the centerpiece for the recreation area where, with good behavior, the boys were allowed to go on Sundays and holidays. A twenty foot ring of rocks surrounded the tree and small clumps of marigolds and blue bonnets and wild grass grew under the tree's shade during the summer months. There was even a picnic table, a fire ring, and a pair of horseshoe pits within the common grounds. This had become his favorite spot in the whole place.

After a few moments he stared back down blankly at the black-and-white photo on the small stand beside his bunk; the picture, taken by some unknown "uncle" long ago, showed a faded vision of himself and his brothers, with his mother in a plain, dark gray summer dress, kneeling happily in the middle of her young children. He smiled slightly as he reflected on that time together as one . . . as a family . . . as a brotherhood. But since then he and his brothers remained ever on the move; they had become as scattered as flaxen straw in the wind, blown across the prairieland of the Dakotas. Imagining now what they must look like proved difficult for him; he could only remember their young faces . . . which must have changed greatly. Someday they would all be together once again, he supposed. The next month, when he became free, he perhaps would try to find them all. He began to once again methodically stab his knife into the post, balancing the blade tip between his right thumb and finger and throwing with ever-growing intensity, getting up, wrenching it from the wood each time, then throwing it over and over, harder and harder, until the weapon missed and went skipping and spinning down the center aisle, narrowly missing Hank Evans, who only looked in fearful disbelief at Dewey and said nothing. Dewey, in turn, gave Hank the fixed, tough, contentious, "Yeah, so what! Whadda ya gonna do about it?" glare.

Earlier that day the monitor of the dormitory accompanied him to the school superintendent's large office. The tall, skinny man began the session with a long sermon about the institution's mission of teaching its attendees "sobriety, thrift, industry, and prudence." The time, he knew, had been hard on the boy due to the discipline required to keep order in the school. He had always been reluctant to use harsh punishment to achieve obedience of the inmates, but did so only when necessary and only as a last resort. Now the superintendent was pleased to inform Dewey that he did not have to serve out the remaining three years of his sentence, if he chose not to. Because his term was indeterminate, the young man could gain early release from the institution by merely joining the military in April, when he reached the age of eighteen. Otherwise, the superintendent sternly reminded him, he would remain at the institution until he was twenty-one. Now the time had come for the boy-turned-man to move on, no matter how comfortable institutional life had become for him. His escape was now so very near. Dewey nodded his consent and loosely shook the superintendent's soft, outstretched hand to seal the deal.

In May of 1949, the superintendent of the Mandan facility sent Mrs. Olson and Director Daniels a letter indicating that Dewey no longer could be considered a ward of the state of North Dakota. In a short report, he indicated that Dewey had been getting along all right at the reform school, but that he remained aimless and still had crazy ideas. He had, however, totally stopped wetting his bed. On the day of his release—April 30th, his eighteenth birthday—a corrections officer from the Mandan State Reform School had accompanied Dewey to the recruitment office where the young man became a member of the United States Army. With the closing and sealing of his case, custody of Dewey Lambson had been formally vacated, thus terminating unceremoniously the agency's and the agents' social responsibility. After reading the letter, with a great sigh, either of relief or consternation, Director Daniels wrote a last, terse entry on Dewey's voluminous cumulative file: "May of 1949—Dewey Lambson discharged to his own responsibility, having joined the military."

Epilogue

People marveled at his ability to "see straight to the heart of the matter." His uncanny perception allowed him to lay aside all emotion and to approach each and every issue before him in a very pragmatic, uninvolved way. In fact, some would even call him completely dispassionate in his judicial decisions. His political supporters said that his astuteness and clear sightedness were probably the primary reasons why he had become the youngest State Attorney General in North Dakota's history—the same qualities that would, no doubt, someday enable him to become the governor of that fine state. Even his political adversaries commented on, no, highly respected, his doggedness, his thoroughness . . . his compulsiveness with the rule of law . . . with what was "right." Indeed, a clear sense of responsibility and commitment had become and still remained his driving force.

But the litigation before him proved vastly different . . . extremely troubling; the case reached out to him, touching him at an emotional level, tugging at him in an affective rather than a rational way, leaving him almost immobilized in his ability to understand completely and then to act decisively, based on the knowledge at hand.

In the seeming disorder of his law office, Duane Lambson sat behind his oversized mahogany desk, upon which were several piles, of different heights, composed of file folders containing testaments of varying importance.

Hunched over in perplexity, he pondered deeply the matter at hand. Much time had passed since he had experienced such uncertainty, such bewilderment in knowing what to do . . . such intellectual, and even emotional, paralysis were reactions unfamiliar to him. For the most part everything in years past had seemed unambiguous and clearly straightforward. Since his time in college he had prided himself on his ability to "detach and decide." But the letter paper-clipped to a thick manila file folder—the only remaining tangible aspects of Ivel Naranjo' short life—proved to be to the contrary. The file and letter eluded the certainty of those two words . . . made them sound almost trivial and cliché. As Duane reread the text a number of times, wave after wave of bitter memories welled up in his mind, blurring his logic and reason and almost overwhelming his sense of self control.

The letter, typed neatly beneath an official letterhead, was from his good friend Joseph "Joe" Archer, the Chief Prosecuting Attorney of Rolette County, who had sent the entire packet by official state courier to Duane's law office in Bismarck two days earlier. After giving a synopsis of the pending indictment, Prosecutor Archer went on to ask Duane—as a detached third party—to please evaluate the merits of the case. Joseph, deeply concerned, sought his friend's expertise concerning the feasibility of prosecuting the case and if prosecution was possible how it could best be accomplished. Duane's initial response bordered on harsh resentment; why should he become involved in the case, especially when Archer certainly possessed enough competence not to have to seek advice and help from anyone. The matter became progressively more disconcerting to Duane.

He emptied the entire file onto the desk pad before him and again began carefully sorting the materials, hoping to gain some small element of enlightenment and perhaps resolution, yet knowing beforehand what he would find. Almost immediately a small photo of the boy fell to the top of the heap of memoranda. With a good deal of trepidation, he picked up the smudged photo—obviously a school picture of a youngster, probably taken just at the start of second grade. The boy's straight black hair had been shortened into a crew cut; wearing a pullover sweater, the youngster showed a wide, big-toothed smile to the camera. "You see, I really am happy," the photo seemed to be saying. Duane could only see himself as the boy and the vision continued to reopen and expose and pick at the raw memories that had only scabbed over, and never really scarred up with the passage of time . . . the scars that so often harden and deaden the soul.

Setting the photo back down on the desk, he looked up from the file and began gazing absently out his window to the first hints of the spring thaw. *The Farmer's Almanac* said that 1977 would have a hard winter but an early spring, and the old book always foretold the weather correctly. The time was early April, his own birth month, and the daytime temperature outside had risen just a bit past freezing for the seventh day in a row. Water dripped steadily from the tips of the icicles hanging off the eaves of the office building across the way; snow in the streets had turned to a black, mucky slush that scrunched under the tires of passing cars and people's plodding, rubber overshoes. The bright sun hung back, dampened by fog-like clouds that rose from the thawing earth. The past winter had been particularly hard. Several blizzards had pressed down from the north, dumping massive amounts of snow on the surrounding plains. When continually configured and reconfigured by the driving winds, the fallen snow formed drifts that seemed to go on forever and ever, on into the infinity of the ethereal horizons. Fine sheets of snow mist blew off the crested edge of those barren, dune-like drifts, often hanging still in the air like a frozen spray. When the storms pressed eastward, and the temperature dropped to twenty or even thirty or more degrees below zero, brilliant sundogs flanked the yellow-red sun on both sides as it crossed the deep blue, frigid sky. For most of those hard winter months, ice fog and the white of the snow-covered land blended into the stormy gray of the sky, forming a uniformly bleak world—a frozen world in which all of the varying forms and sizes of life were forced to ultimately band together for survival. Yet each year, with a growing, pulsating heartbeat of life force renewal, spring grudgingly came, resurrecting the dead earth. The morrow would always be better.

With great hesitancy State Attorney Lambson forced himself to return to the situation at hand, though the spread out papers only evoked in him more and more disquieting, disturbing visions from the past. The school photo was of the boy Ivel Naranjo, a youngster who had just a few months before died a violent, tragic death up on the Turtle Mountain Reservation of the Chippewa Nation, near the town of Belcourt. Reading further into the file, the lawyer became even more deeply saddened. According to the police reports, Ivel lived on the Meadow Ridge section of the reservation, with his aunt, Nina Naranjo, and his grandmother, Carla Naranjo, both of whom had been raising Ivel and his two younger brothers since early in 1975, when the boys' mother had

simply disappeared. And because they had no legal or identifiable father who would claim them, the brothers were put
into the custody of their aunt and grandmother, who grudgingly took them in. Acquaintances and neighbors alike related
to local tribal authorities that Ivel and his brothers had been
pretty much happy, normal youngsters up until early 1976;
at that time the bruises and welts began appearing and Ivel
started withdrawing more into himself . . . becoming silent
and taciturn. Also about that same time Rylan Ahote, Nina's
fiancé, had moved in with her and her mother Carla, into the
small, dilapidated, already overcrowded singlewide trailer
just on the outskirts of Belcourt. The North Dakota Child
Protective Services became aware of Ivel and his brothers
shortly thereafter, when Rylan and Nina up and left for two
weeks, leaving the old grandmother in charge of the boys. In
her frustration Carla had turned to both the tribal authorities
and the State Child Protective Services for assistance. However, both agencies claimed that the other was responsible
and nothing of any consequence ever happened.

The further Duane Lambson read, the less able he was to
suppress his emotions and bring his professional expertise
to bear. He had seen many things in his career as a lawyer
and prosecutor . . . and had thought himself inured to most
crimes and hardened to most criminals. But this particular
travesty worked on him at a gut level. Sore memories that
he had suppressed for more than three decades continued
to force themselves into his consciousness in a relentless
stream . . . a turbulent, opaque torrent. The rundown farm
and its large, spreading cottonwood tree; Cora and Iver and
the violent night the father had slapped Dewey to the ground
and left the family forever; the young and pretty Miss

Clementson; Lake Charles Children's Home; his own time in the welfare system; his seldom hearing from his real mother and never from his father; his total estrangement from his brothers.

With the passage of time, Duane had, probably purposefully, not thought much about his brothers—about Darrell and Leeland, about Lloyd and Dewey; over the years their separation from each other had been very nearly complete. After their time at Lake Charles, the five had become almost total strangers. For his part, ever since his teenage years, Duane had committed himself to not looking back . . . to forgetting the past and getting on with the business of life and living. In so doing, he became obsessed with success. His fear of failure drove him in his relentless pursuit of his own promising law career; his almost gnawing sense of responsibility engendered in him a lasting passion for his growing family—for being intensely responsible to and for the ones he loved . . . his wife and son and daughter. As a consequence he had neither seen nor heard much from his brothers . . . after all, they had their own consequences to face, just as he had his own demons to deal with.

The last Duane heard, his youngest brother Darrell had grown up to become a successful doctor. After marrying Cheryl Brossart, the "princess of Mayville"—indeed, one of the most beautiful girls the town had seen in generations—the couple moved east and used the extended families' wealth to put him through Harvard Medical School. Having established his own successful pediatrics practice in Boston, he divorced his now "evil princess" wife and went in rather rapid succession through three more marriages. Strangely enough, all four relationships had produced a total of five children—three boys and two girls—none of whom he had custodial care of. In a brief telephone conversation once with Duane, Darrell jokingly told him that his only vices had become smoking too many fine cigars, drinking too much good whiskey, and falling for pretty women who sapped his wealth through alimony and child support. When Duane asked him when he would return to visit with the Goodwins, Darrell replied coolly "Probably never." He maintained that he had pretty much "shaken the dust from his sandals" when he left Mayville . . . "Hickville" he had called it. Ensconced in his own social environs, never again did he return to his place of birth and upbringing or have anything more to do with it or its people. On that point Darrell remained forever adamant.

Duane's second-youngest brother, Leeland, remained in Jamestown, still living permanently at the Brimington Vocational Rehabilitation Center, still working in the shoe repair shop . . . repairing more shoes with one arm than many of his fellow employees could with two . . . earning a small subsistence wage. Duane had once gone to see him; feeling guilty about Leeland's meager, almost monastic existence and circumstances, he had offered his brother a chance at a new start. He had decided that, whatever the cost, he would bring slow Leeland to Mandan and make him a part of his own family . . . set him up with his own shoe repair shop. But Leeland declined with a simple "Nope," giving no elaboration or explanation . . . he was content where he was . . . with his "lot in life," as he succinctly put it. Duane realized that his younger brother had reduced life to a very simple philosophy and with that realization Duane somewhat came to terms with his own existence. The two brothers sat in Leeland's tiny quarters, quiet for almost the entire visit, having really nothing to say to each other . . . having nothing in common. Duane left him a new charcoal colored sweater and two cartons of Camel cigarettes, as well as a brand new Zippo lighter and a can of lighter fluid. Both brothers promised to write and call each other, which they seldom, if ever, did.

The phone rang on Duane Lambson's desk, jarring him sharply from his thoughts. His friend Joe Archer was calling to ask if Duane had gotten the Naranjo file.

"Yes, I received it yesterday . . . and I've been going over it. The case is a tragic one."

"Where do we stand on this one, Duane? I want to move on this guy quickly . . . but I'm not sure how. That kid must have gone through hell before he died. I don't want this Ahote guy getting away with it . . . I don't want 'em running!"

"I know. I know," Duane agreed slowly. "Look, I can't talk now, Joe. I've just begun to go over the file again. I promise I'll give you a call back as soon as I've had enough time to think it through."

The two talked on for a few more moments about nothing of consequence. Then Duane hung the phone up and began to review the spread of materials again . . . the sheaf of yellowing, coarse bond paper that now represented a young boy's tragic life and death. Ivel's second grade teacher first noticed the boy's bruises when the grimacing youngster had great difficulty taking off his sweater at the beginning of class one morning. On May 5th, 1976, she reported her suspicions to the school principal who in the privacy of his inner office examined Ivel's small back, where he found several prominent grayish brown welts. He called the Turtle Mountain Sheriff's Department and reported the abuse, but those officials did nothing. The principal subsequently called the county office of the North Dakota Child Protective Services; in their investigation, officials from the NDCPS office also found bruises on Ivel's back and leg, as well as a blackened eye. Ivel offered various explanations for his injuries: Ahote had been rough housing with him on the living room floor and had pushed him a little too hard; he had stumbled over a tree root while running in the front yard; a friend had accidentally hit him in the eye with a stick. County authorities closed the case on May 19th with the following conclusions clearly written on the bottom of the complaint form: "Child abuse not verifiable."

Then in January of 1977 the Turtle Mountain authorities once again became aware of Ivel when he was taken to the Angeles Emergency Clinic in Belcourt. His right-side jaw was red and his cheekbone was so swollen that his eye had become a mere slit. His young body had numerous bruises, in various stages of healing. Ivel explained softly that he had fallen off of a high fence in the backyard. Nina Naranjo described in detail to the attending doctor how her nephew always had been just a clumsy kid who was continually tripping or falling or running into things. The local child protective officials, having been called by the hospital and doctor and asked to investigate the suspicions of maltreatment, however, couldn't find or do anything. The Ivel Naranjo case was again closed on January 20th with the following conclusion: "No verifiable evidence of child abuse could be found."

Oddly enough, though, according to the records, Ivel's two brothers had been removed from their aunt and grand-mother's home and put into foster care, probably due to Grandma Carla's unrelenting complaints to the agency about having to care for all three of the children. Conversely, their removal meant that Ivel was left totally defenseless . . . fur-ther abandoned and condemned to be the ongoing victim of his "guardians." The defenseless youngster, left by himself to face the monsters that held him captive, must have felt abandoned . . . totally alone. Duane knew exactly what the child must have experienced . . . the isolation . . . the loneli-ness . . . the fear . . . the desperation.

Duane's early separation from his brothers had, in the same way, affected him deeply. He had missed Lloyd and Dewey greatly during those difficult times, probably because he had the closest affinity with them . . . the three together had shared the most tribulations and meager joys of their young years.

Lloyd had been and remained very much like a phan-tom. After escaping from Fargo, he had gravitated to the West Coast. Then one time in the mid-1960s he showed up in Bismarck in the midst of his wanderings, stopping to see Duane because Lloyd had gotten word that his older brother had made something of himself . . . had served a tour of duty in the navy . . . had graduated from law school . . . had met and married a nice young woman, Caroline, and they together nurtured both a family and a fledgling law practice. Lloyd spent an entire day with his brother, talking well into the night, long after Caroline and the kids had gone to bed, telling Duane of his disparate history. In the years since they had seen each other, Lloyd had been to almost every western state, where he had held a variety of jobs, living off the fruits of his labors; for varying lengths of time he'd been a used car salesman, body shop detailer, blackjack dealer, petty criminal, house painter, and a real estate salesman. The city of Sacramento had even employed him as a fireman for a short period of time in the summer of 1957, but summarily fired him when suspicion arouse that he had intentionally set several fires around the city. They could never prove it, though, Lloyd adamantly maintained. Up until the time he left California and traveled to see Duane in Bismarck, his primary occupation had been a field worker, or more specifically a day laborer. At the time of his visit to his brother, he belonged to a custom combining crew harvesting crops along the Midwestern farm belt; they had begun in early summer in Texas and were grinding their way through the territory, working northward until they would eventually wind up in the vast wheat fields beyond Winnipeg, Canada.

In addition to losing two more of his front teeth, Lloyd had, over the years, gained and lost numerous close relationships, both male and female. Somehow these liaisons never matured into any long term, deep commitments. This perhaps could best be attributed to the fact that, as Lloyd maintained, "I never had anyone or anything that I couldn't walk away from. Don't want the bother!" And as Lloyd went on to reveal to Duane that night, in somewhat of a whisper, his not wanting to have close relationships was also due to the fact that all of his associates, women and men alike, drank heavily, even more than him, and so they could not be trusted. For example, during his most recent employment as an agricultural worker in Coachella Valley, he had met some "pretty tough fellas." Picking avocados and artichokes in the desert heat had left the skin of his arms and face leather brown and his voice had acquired a distinctly California accent. His tan made the two long, white scars etched on his face distinct. While the two talked slowly back and forth, late in the evening, probably sometime after two a.m., Lloyd slowly pointed to the two thin lines and described in detail how his head had punched through an automobile windshield one rainy, drunken night in El Centro. He and some of his Mexican "amigos" had acquired a glass jar of raw alcohol and filtered it through slices of bread so that the impurities wouldn't kill them when they drank it. They then hotwired an almost-new, racing-red Chevy Camero and went partying and joyriding on the south side of Chula Vista until they ran a stop light on Chavez Street, broadsiding a Helms Bakery truck. Upon being released from the hospital and then from his six-month prison sentence in the Chochilla County Jail, he wanted desperately to head back to the Midwest. His close brush with death made him anxious to once more see the vast prairies of his birthplace. As they sat together, Duane thought about how life must have never really been a true learning experience for his younger brother, but instead merely a series of disjointed encounters with reality, from which nothing ever was gleaned.

Early the next morning, after staying up almost all night reminiscing with his older brother, Lloyd rejoined his combine crew and disappeared as quickly as he came. He simply vanished, just like his mother had done years ago. Duane later received several postcards from his vagabond brother, but had gotten nothing in the past four years. Duane wondered if perhaps Lloyd was dead, just like their oldest brother Dewey.

Dewey had actually been the first of the five brothers to die. Now, just as with the dead child Ivel, all that remained of Dewey were a few pieces of official paper and some scraps of memorabilia that came to represent and substantiate his brief, turbulent existence on this earth . . . a sad tribute to life's longing for itself. Duane kept all of his brother's medals and records and military death certificate in a square, gray metal box, tucked away in a drawer in his home office. For some reason Dewey had named Duane as his only living relative and therefore Duane had received the death notice from the military, as well as his brother's records and personal belongings.

The military file that Duane had long ago received contained a glossy photograph as well, a head-and-shoulders military shot that revealed an unsmiling young warrior/man, his face and jaw set and his eyes intense, dressed in his Class A uniform, with the American flag as a backdrop. On the back of the photo, in his almost undecipherable handwriting, Dewey had scribbled a brief poetic phrase that perhaps best summarized his philosophy of life and living: "Fightin' and fuckin' and livin' with danger/I'm gonna be an Airborne Ranger!/D. Lambson, 6Jun1951." Duane supposed that with the first clip of .30 caliber ball ammunition Dewey had fed into and fired from his heavy M-1 rifle, with the first hand grenade he hurled, with the first bayonet that he plunged into a straw enemy on the obstacle course, his brother had found his true calling . . . his salvation. He must have been a lover of war . . . of conflict . . . of violence . . . of pain-enforced discipline and intense physical endurance. He had lived violently and had died just as violently.

According to the records, after joining the U.S. Army in 1949, Dewey shipped out to Japan and from there he fully participated in the Korean War, where he emerged as a much decorated veteran and hero. The file detailed how he had been an infantryman with the First Cavalry Division. During his combat tour the warrior brother had been a part of the amphibious landing at Pohangdong and the back and forth see-saw campaigns along the Korean Peninsula, earning several battlefield decorations, including the Bronze Star and a Purple Heart. Following eighteen months of almost continuous, certainly courageous fighting, as well as several battlefield promotions, Staff Sergeant Dewey Lambson rotated back to Hokkaido, Japan, and then to Fort Bragg, North Carolina, where he served as a machine gun training NCO. Later, in the mid-1960s, he rejoined the First Cavalry Division and completed three tours of duty in Vietnam; he was awarded two more Purple Heart medals and the Medal of Valor. According to an accompanying commendation letter, during the Battle of La Drang Valley, the fearless soldier earned the prestigious award for "rescuing three of his comrades from a burning Huey helicopter, all while under withering enemy fire from a nearby thicket. While accomplishing the rescue, Sgt. Lambson continued to return fire with an M-60 machine gun that he held with his free arm. Sgt. Lambson showed incredible bravery and little concern for his own safety, which inspired his fellow soldiers to continue pressing the attack." Duane could well picture what must have been the intense expression on Dewey's face that hot jungle afternoon as he unselfishly risked himself to save his brothers-in-arms . . . probably much like the half-crazed look he had when he hung farmer Wolfe's Duroc pig.

His manila record jacket told much about Dewey's life and death. Even though he had an exemplary war record, the soldier had "no respect for authority" and tended to "fight whenever the opportunity presented itself, whether it be with fellow soldiers or with superior officers." Copies of several Article Fifteens and two Court Martial summaries indicated that the decorated combat veteran exhibited few viable coping skills in non-battlefield situations; he had risen and fallen in the ranks quite a number of times in his career; whenever awarded with a position of authority, Dewey would at some point in time disobey a direct order from a superior or perhaps mistreat a soldier under his command. One of the court martial proceedings involved an incident at Fort Bragg when he had kicked and grabbed a young recruit by the hair, then pulled him all the way up along a sandbagged bunker during a live fire exercise, all the while calling the boy a "dirty, sniveling coward." The record spoke volumes about Dewey's life and times.

Duane found one particular document in the file to be especially insightful—the Security and Intelligence Division's investigation report on Dewey's death. He had died in June of 1968 of multiple stab wounds to the back and neck, as well as numerous severe concussions to the head, all of which resulted from a bar fight in Raeford, North Carolina, a small town just southwest of Fort Bragg. Though no one had been identified as the perpetrator, the general SID summary of the incident found that Dewey, who had been drinking heavily, tried to pick up a girl at a local tavern, which provoked her boyfriend. The next day the owner of the establishment . . . the Outpost Bar . . . found Dewey's dead body, bloodied and posed in the fetal position, lying in the far corner of the bar's rear parking lot. Military authorities suspected that the soldier had been attacked by several locals when the bar closed and he left the establishment by himself. But because there were no witnesses, and none of the civilians in the town would provide any helpful information, no one was ever prosecuted for the murder and his brother's death went unpunished.

Duane could only imagine what had occurred that night. His tall, handsome, brazen brother walking up and making time with a young, pretty, flirtatious girl . . . maybe putting a strong arm around her waist and pulling her closely to him . . . doing so right in front of her redneck boyfriend . . . probably scorning and making little of him; the boyfriend and probably several of his friends waiting outside the bar for the soldier, gripping their baseball bats and knives tightly in anticipation of the soldier's appearance; the violence of the scene when the combat veteran staggered from the bar and the pack fell ruthlessly upon him. Dewey, no doubt, fought like hell before going down, but succumbed to that which would inevitably overpower and kill him. Duane would never know the actual specifics of the tragic story . . . indeed, would never see his brother again. He was now gone and Duane could never fully comprehend the violence that permeated and defined his brother's life . . . just as the violence that had been so prevalent in Ivel's young life.

The memory of his brother and his untimely, brutal death, forced Duane to once again focus on the file before him. A little over three weeks after his initial treatment at Belcourt's Angeles Emergency Clinic, Ivel had once again been taken to the hospital, but this time the boy lay in a deep coma. The NDCPS investigative reports indicated that family members said they heard a noise and found Ivel lying on the floor of the family home, twitching. They explained that the boy had always been accident-prone and had acted strangely since his fall from a ladder in the front yard earlier that week. Ivel Naranjo died on March 1ˢᵗ, 1977, having never awakened from the deep, lifeless sleep of his coma. The copy of the coroner's autopsy concluded sterilely that the malnourished boy died not from starvation, but more so from "multiple traumatic injuries," including a blow to the head. He had "numerous bruises with some so deep they reached the muscle." His jaw appeared dislocated and several of his small fingers had been broken, according to the report. The little child had suffered for a long, long time before he finally escaped his keepers and left this terrible world.

Yet after reviewing all of the scattered materials, Duane sadly concluded that Nina Naranjo and her mother Carla Naranjo, as well as Nina's boyfriend Rylan Ahote, could only be held on charges of child abuse. Because no witnesses to the abuse could or would testify, none of the three could legally be charged with the higher crime of second degree murder. He would have to deliver the opinion/decision to his friend Joseph Archer. The eager, able prosecutor would not be able to charge anyone with Ivel's death. Duane knew his friend didn't have the evidence to charge any of the three perpetrators—probably the real culprit being Rylan Ahote—with Ivel's death. No one would ever know what happened to the child on the night of his death . . . or the many hours or days or months or years leading up to it. No one would talk about it. Not the sheriff's office or the hospital or the three suspects or their families or their neighbors or the North Dakota Child Protective Services.

No one. And, of course, Ivel could no longer speak for himself. But if he could, Duane wondered what he would say about the people that had killed him. And about those who ultimately remained responsible to and for him . . . not only the perpetrators, but about *all* those who stood silently by and let it happen. The net of blame could certainly be widely cast. When and where does child abuse start and when and where does it end? And with whom? How can all of the terrible terms and definitions even begin to articulate such a human travesty? On the bottom margin of Archer's letter he wrote, "The spectrum of child abuse is wide and terrible . . . an appalling, severe indictment of the community in which such tragedies occur and exist."

Duane slowly closed the file and left the office in mid-afternoon. He would call his friend later . . . perhaps in the morning. Time was not relevant now . . . certainly not for Ivel. Maybe he would call his brothers, too . . . those that he could find. Darrell and Leeland . . . maybe he could even locate Lloyd. The state prosecutor went home early to his family so that he might spend extra time talking to them . . . time to be with his wife and son and daughter. He very much ached to tell Caroline the story of Ivel Naranjo, of Dewey Lambson, as well as all of the thoughts and memories he had encountered that day. But he could not. Perhaps some other time. Instead, he only talked to his family about the small stuff of their lives that day and then he told them, without reservation, how deeply he loved them. In the next few weeks . . . when the sun had warmed the land and the frozen ground had become a little softer, a bit drier . . . he would take them to the nursery down in Mandan and buy a tree. A grandchild tree. And plant it in the backyard.

A cottonwood, maybe. One that would grow strong and straight and sturdy and enduring. One that would spread its staunch limbs and thick, shady branches for future generations of young lives. One that would dig its roots solidly, tenaciously into the ground and always stand resolutely.

Later that night, in bed, in the silent darkness, while his wife slept quietly next to him and his two children lay sprawled comfortably in their bedrooms, safely across their beds, he wept softly into his hands, crying for himself and his brothers, and for Ivel and his siblings, and for the children of the world—those destined to be the brothers and those doomed to become the keepers.